“ISSUES”

SHARON ST. JOHN

"Issues"

For information about this title or to order other books and/or electronic media, contact the publisher:
Sharon St. John
San Pedro, California
SharonStJohnAuthor.com
sshotsie@gmail.com

Library of Congress Control Number: 2019914536

ISBN: 978-1-7333030-3-3 (Hardcover)
978-1-7333030-4-0 (Paperback)
978-1-7333030-5-7 (eBook)

Printed in the United States of America

Cover and Interior design: 1106 Design

You can also contact Sharon at her social networking accounts:
Facebook—https://www.facebook.com/Sharon-St-John-Author
Twitter—https://twitter.com/sshotsie
Instagram—https://www.instagram.com/sshotsie/

In loving memory of
my favorite little guy, Nipsy

04-28-2008 to 10-02-2009

Contents

CHAPTER 1

Life Sucks

It's Monday morning; Lord, how I hate Mondays. It's the beginning of the week, and I have nothing to look forward to by the end of the week, Jessica pondered as she sat at her desk, staring out the floor-to-ceiling window of her office. The voice of her secretary broke her long gaze out the window.

"Jessica, here are the quarterly reports for you to review."

"Thank you, Charmaine. Hey, Charmaine, let me ask you a question: Is it me, or do I have less work now that I have made head accountant of this firm?"

"That's part of the perks," Charmaine answered. "This is why we fight so hard to climb the corporate ladder. It is all about making more money and doing less work for it. Tell the truth, Jessica: it has to feel good seeing "Ms. Jessica Tyler" plastered on the door of the largest accounting firm in Nassau County."

"Girl, I can't front; it feels damn good. It feels like I'm in my own little glass house in the sky."

"You know what, Jessica? One day, I hope not to be working as someone's secretary," Charmaine admitted, while fantasizing about her future in her head. "I hope — by the time I'm twenty-five years old — to have accomplished what you have accomplished in your professional life."

Jessica took a deep breath and replied, "It has been a blessing to have accomplished all of this at such a young age and knowing that I didn't have to get my knees dirty to do it. Charmaine, would you like to have lunch with me later?"

"Who will take the calls if I am at lunch with you?" Charmaine asked.

"That's why we have voicemail," Jessica replied, sarcastically.

"Speaking of voicemail," Charmaine replied, "your sister Renee called, and I will have to pass on lunch today. I need to check on my friend who is being evicted today."

"Oh, wow — sorry to hear about your friend, Charmaine. Alright, I'll give my sister a call now, and please hold all other calls because I need to prepare before I go to this meeting." As she dialed her sister's work number, she couldn't stop thinking about her boyfriend, James. *I hope James comes over tonight. I could really use a little sexual pick-me-up.* Her intimate thoughts were interrupted when her sister answered the phone. "Oh, hey, Renee. What's up? Charmaine said you'd called."

"Yes, I did, and why can't you answer your own damn phone?" Renee asked with attitude. "You do absolutely nothing all day long. You can answer the damn phone."

"Girl, state your business," Jessica snapped back. "I have meetings that I have to attend — and why am I explaining myself to you, Renee? What do you want?" Jessica asked.

"I just wanted to know if your mother called you today," Renee said.

"She is your mother, too, and no, she did not call. Now, get to the point. I have a meeting in fifteen minutes," said Jessica.

Renee replied, "Yeah, right. All y'all do is sit around, sipping coffee, and planning your next whack-ass office party. Anyway, Tawana called, complaining about that all-girl school her father put her in."

Jessica cut her off in mid-sentence, saying, "Her daddy put her there — that's not our problem," with a lack of compassion in her voice.

"Well, mommy said Tawana wants to come and live with us," Renee said.

"Did mommy say, 'Yes'? More than that, where will she sleep?" Jessica asked with real concern in her tone.

"I don't know, because you know how hard it is to talk to your mother and get a straight answer," Renee replied. "At first, she said that she didn't want any teenagers in her house. Then, like always, she made it about her. She started with the 'That's-my-first-daughter's-only-child' speech, which led to her finally saying, 'I have to take care of her.'"

Jessica listened impatiently, and, with disgust in her voice, she said, "We all need to talk about this when I get home."

Renee responded, "I won't be home until eleven-thirty tonight."

"Whatever, Renee. If I'm asleep, just wake me up."

Renee was done with that topic as well and decided to change the subject by asking Jessica, "Are you cooking when you get home?"

"I'm not sure. I have to see what James wants for dinner," Jessica said.

"But I thought he was doing some party in the city tonight," Renee said.

Jessica replied, sounding confused, "I don't think so — it's Monday."

"You really need to get out more. The best parties are on Mondays, Tuesdays, and Wednesdays. I'll see you at home. Besides, one of the damn kids is at the door," Renee said, sounding agitated.

Renee slammed the phone down and turned to face the little boy standing in the doorway of the office. He said, "Ms. Renee, can we go into the playroom?"

Renee stood up and walked toward the living room to see if the door to the playroom, which was a small room right off the living room, was open and said, "No, the playroom does not open until six o'clock. Did you do your homework?" she asked.

"Not yet. We were waiting to see if one of the volunteer tutors was going to come and help us with our homework," he said.

"Go do your homework, and then worry about the playroom," retorted Renee.

As she began to walk toward the staircase, she heard her name being bellowed from the office: "Renee! Renee! We should be getting one new family in tonight around seven o'clock," yelled Ms. Beryl, her boss.

"Okay, boss lady," Renee yelled back.

Ms. Beryl yelled in reply, "Renee, I told you not to call me that. It's a mother with three kids. Put them in the Rosa Parks room. Millie is upstairs cleaning it now."

"Are you getting ready to leave now, boss lady?" Renee asked, still yelling in the hall.

"Yes, I have to pick up the boys from school today," her boss replied.

Renee called out to Ms. Beryl again. "Get home safely, and I'll see you tomorrow." Then Renee yelled from the bottom of the stairs up to Millie, a co-worker, "Millie, do you need any help up there?"

"No, I'm almost done. I'll be down in a minute," Millie said.

"I think the new intake just arrived; I'll do it," Renee told Millie.

Renee opened the door and greeted the lady and her three boys standing on the front porch. "Hello, my name is Ms. Renee Tyler, and I am one of the evening supervisors here."

The woman entered the house with a look of uncertainty on her face as she stated, "My name is Desire Williams, and these are my three sons: Jamal, Jamel, and Jacob."

Renee responded, trying to sound comforting and uplifting to the boys, "Hey, guys. Would you like to go into the playroom while I talk to your mommy alone for a minute?"

The boys screamed out in unison, "Yeah! Mommy, can we go, please?"

Desire, trying to sound reassuring, said, "Sure, and be careful not to break anything."

As soon as the children had left the office, Renee became all about routine business. "Okay, Ms. Williams, I need to ask a few questions and give you the rules and regulations of the house. After that, I will take you on a tour of the house and show you to your room."

With the boys out of view, Desire was able to reflect on what had led her to be in a shelter, and tears began to stream down her face. She cleared her voice just enough to ask for tissue. She whispered the words, "I can't believe I'm here. He promised he would — never mind."

As Renee handed her the tissue, she continued in her matter-of-fact way. "What brings you to Angel Guardian Inn?"

Desire shifted in her seat as she began to explain. "My kids' father just stopped taking care of us. He just would not pay for anything. Not food, not clothes, and definitely not rent."

Renee reacted as if this were no big deal, just an ordinary story that she heard every day. She moved right onto the next question without even a pause. "Do you or any of the children have AIDS or HIV?"

This question angered Desire to the point where she snapped. "My *children,* bitch? Don't ever ask me a question like that about my children! It is all about the job with you, huh, bitch? People come in here and pour their heart out to you, and you just go down your list of questions to make room for the next poor homeless family."

"Lady, I don't know you, and you don't know me, but I strongly suggest that you calm down and don't make the mistake of calling me 'a bitch' ever again," Renee replied, trying to be as professional as she could. "I'm doing my job, and if I sit here and listen to your whole life story, I am eventually going to have to ask that and many other questions you may feel are too personal. Now, I take it the answer to my question is 'No,'" she said.

Desire calmed herself down and humbled herself enough to answer the question. "I was just tested, but I haven't received the results yet. I'm sorry for calling you a bitch — but I'm just really stressed out. If a man can just up and leave his own kids, there must have been a woman involved, so I know he was cheating on me, and that's why I got tested."

Renee decided to check her tone while asking questions, because she realized that this woman was really going through something. She thought to herself, *I wouldn't know what to do if I was put in this woman's shoes.* She decided to ask one last question before letting her go tend to her children. "Are you currently employed?"

Desire answered with shame in her voice. "No, he made me quit my job." Desire thought to herself after she answered the question, *I had a good job in one of the most prestigious law firms in Nassau County as a paralegal. I was making $75,000 a year, and now I don't know where my next seventy-five cents will come from. I believed him when he said a good mother stays at home and raises her children.* She remembered when he told her to let a man be a man. He said a man was supposed to take care of his family. She remembered her mother's words when she warned her about not being dependent upon a man.

As Desire sat in the corner chair of the office, still wiping tears from her face, she whispered under her breath, "I was so stupid to listen to him. I thought he would do the right thing for his family. My mother taught me better than that." Desire regretted her words when she'd told her mother, "Not *my* man — he would never hurt his family." Her tears began to flow again as she sobbed, holding her hands to her head in shame.

Renee tried to comfort her by reminding her that she needed to calm down before her children saw her upset. "I'll take you to your room now. You'll meet the coordinator in the morning, and she will further explain all programs and options available to you while you are living in the shelter," she explained.

As they exited the office, the boys came running back toward them, yelling, "Mommy, this place is big. Is Daddy coming to stay in our new house?"

It broke Desire's heart to lie to her children, but she had no choice, so she answered, "No, sweetheart. Daddy is staying with his friend." She hugged her son and followed Renee toward the staircase.

Renee showed them to their room, all the while thinking about leaving work earlier so that she could go home to have the conversation with her sister and mother. "Millie, all of the chores are done, and the intake has been completed. I told her about the 10 p.m. curfew; no spending the night out, no visitors in or on the premises, and she knows about the chore board. So, with that said, do you mind if I leave now?"

Millie answered, sounding annoyed by the question. "Renee, stop asking me stupid questions, and just leave. It's only one hour."

Renee was relieved to get off early, so she grabbed her bag and yelled, "Bye, Millie — see you tomorrow." She called Jessica to inform her that she'd gotten off early and that she was prepared to have the conversation about their niece, Tawana.

Jessica told her that she was cooking dinner for James, so that it would be waiting for him when he got home.

Renee took offense to the fact that Jessica referred to their house as "James's home." She repeated the word "home," inflecting her voice to ensure there was an exclamation point behind it.

Jessica tried to clear up the reference to it being James's home by saying, "You know what I mean."

Renee brushed off the comment and said, "See you when I get home. My song is on." As she sang along with the music, she was hoping Sam and the fellas would be at the house, because she was looking forward to having a drink.

Back at the house, in the kitchen preparing the lasagna, Jessica was frustrated with the fact she couldn't reach James on the phone. "Hello, James. It's me. I'm making your favorite — lasagna. Call me when you get this message."

When she disconnected from the call, she began talking out loud to herself. "That shit really gets on my damn nerves. Why do I always have to leave a message and wait for him to return my calls? Just answer the damn phone! I wonder if he is cheating on me. No, not *my* man. What am I thinking?"

"Jessica, who are you talking to in there?" her mother asked.

She ignored her mother's question and changed the subject by asking, "Mother, where is the oregano? I just bought some, and I can't find it. I am sick of everybody using my things."

Her mother responded rudely, "Well, look for it!" bothered by the fact that Jessica had ignored her question.

Renee entered the house just in time to interrupt the tension in the kitchen, screaming, "Hey, everybody! The cutest of all the Tyler women has arrived home."

"Renee, don't come in here with all that noise. I have a headache," her mother told her.

Renee replied with a slick comment. "Oh, Mother, please. Something is always wrong with you."

"You two — please don't start," Jessica interjected. "Let's just talk about Tawana. Renee said you told her that she wants to move here because she hates her school, but I think she just wants to stay here because of Renee."

"Jessica, why do you always do that? Why does it have to be because of me?"

"Because she talks to you all the time — that's why, Renee."

As Renee started to respond, Jessica cut her off, growing weary of that banter and saying, "I don't have time for this. Are you going to let her stay here, or what?"

Their mother said, "There's more to it than her just not liking the school anymore. Her father won't pay for it because of her grades, and he says she can't stay with him."

Renee said, "It was her father's new wife that led to the decision not to let his own daughter live with him."

Jessica interjected, "Again, I ask: Is she going to stay here? Better yet, when is she coming, and where will she sleep? Because it sounds like you have made up your mind, Mother."

"She is my firstborn grandchild, and I will not leave her out in the cold," their mother said.

"Oh, lord, Mother — please don't start with that long speech again," Renee said and suggested that Tawana stay in Jessica's room because it was the bigger room.

Jessica raised her voice, saying, "Oh, *hell,* no" to Renee's suggestion.

"Jessica, please! It's only for a little while, I promise. I'll make sure of it," their mother pleaded.

"What about when James comes over?" Jessica questioned.

"Jessica, you care more about some man than you do your own family. Don't talk to me about some stranger when a family member is in need. James don't pay no bills up in here, so he doesn't count," their mother said in anger.

Renee cheered her mother on for setting Jessica straight. "Say it again, Mother. You tell her like it is."

Jessica replied, "Mind your own business, because if it were Sam, you would be saying the same thing."

The bickering between the two sisters commenced, and their mother shut it down just as she'd done in the past when they were children. "Both of you girls shut up and listen. I plan eventually to convert the porch into a bedroom/living room combination for Renee and give her room to Tawana."

Renee displayed her approval of the idea and wanted to know how soon this would take place.

"I have to speak to a few people to see if they know someone who can do the job cheaper than it would cost me if I had to hire a contractor," their mother explained.

"So, it's been settled. She's coming to stay. I'll call her tomorrow to tell her the good news," Renee said.

Jessica questioned in her mind, *Good news for who? I am twenty-five years old and have to share my room with a sixteen-year-old.* "I'm going to bed," she said. She left the kitchen, forgetting that she was cooking dinner. She was so upset that she didn't even realize that James had never returned her call.

Renee said, "Forget her. I need a drink. Have the fellas come by?" she asked her mother.

"I don't know. Ask Jacob. He's been downstairs all day."

"I'm sorry, Mother. I know that he's your nephew, but he needs a job."

Her mother said, "He is your cousin, and he has been trying to find a job."

Renee rolled her eyes as she said, "Whatever, Mother. You make excuses for everyone when you're not the one working to support their lazy asses. Good night, Mother."

Renee left her mother standing in the kitchen and retreated to her room. She was still thinking about having a drink, so she called her best friend, Kit, to go to the local lounge, called Nipsy's. Kit agreed to have drinks because she was going through some personal drama of her own. Renee hung up and told Kit she would pick her up in fifteen minutes. But before she could leave the house, her mother was at her door, asking if Sam was coming over tonight.

"I don't know, Mother. Seriously, what is it you like about him so much?"

"Well, for one, I know him. He has been coming around here for years and has always been very respectful. I just like him, and I think he's a good man."

"Anyway, Mother, I won't be gone long. If he stops by, let him in."

As Renee pulled up to Kit's house, she could hear the sound of two women in a heated argument. She blew the horn to get Kit's attention to come outside.

"What's up, Kit? I hope Nipsy's is not too crowded tonight."

"Girl, let me tell you. My aunt is getting on my nerves. She flipped out last night because Eric came over."

"Was that the reason you guys were arguing just now? Because I could hear you from the car."

"Yeah, she's still bugging out," Kit said.

"Did y'all get caught doing the nasty in her house or something?" Renee asked, jokingly.

"No, we were just standing in front of the house when she came outside all drunk and acting stupid. She started talking about how I looked like a slut standing out there like that. Girl, it took all I had not to slap the shit out of her."

With a bewildered look on her face, Renee said, "Kit, you know you sound crazy, talking about how you would slap your aunt. What did you do?"

"I told Eric to just leave, I called her a drunken bitch, and then I went back into the house."

Renee started laughing out loud. "How you gonna call her a drunken bitch and then go into her house? You got a lot of nerve. Where is that bartender with my apple martini? I'll pay for yours cause you're gonna need your money when your aunt sobers up, realizes that you called her a bitch, and throws your ass out." Renee enjoyed a gut-busting laugh at her friend's expense.

"That ain't funny, Renee. You don't know how bad I wanted to punch her in the eye."

"Well, Kit, let's raise our glasses and toast to the day we'll be able to afford our own place."

Kit was over that topic and wanted to take the spotlight off of her and put it on Renee. She asked, "What's going on with you and Sam Perry?" with a smirk on her face.

A smile came over Renee's face as she answered, "It's going, and I didn't think that, after being friends for so long, things would work out the way they have. It's really OK so far. My mother seems to like him more now, for some reason. Sometimes when I come home, he's sitting in the kitchen talking to her."

Kit took this moment to poke fun at Renee. "That's why she likes him. Anybody who sits and talks to your mother — she likes them."

"What you trying to say about my mother?" Renee asked, rhetorically.

"Stop acting like you don't know what I'm talking about, and let's get ready to go. I have to get up early in the morning," Kit said.

Renee replied, "Yeah, I'm ready to go. Kit, did I tell you that my niece is coming to live with us?" On the drive back to Kit's house, she told her about the conversation with her sister and mother. She explained that they thought Tawana wanted to live with them just because of her. She told Kit about Jessica's only concern being James and when he comes over. She further added that she thought James was cheating on Jessica.

Kit had her own opinion upon hearing that piece of information. "That is some real disrespectful shit. I hope you didn't tell that to your sister."

"No, of course not, but if I had proof, I would tell her in a heartbeat. Anyway, see you later, and I'll call you once I get home, if Sam isn't there. Goodnight, Kit, and thanks for coming out with me."

When Renee got home from Nipsy's Lounge, Sam was waiting in her room. Renee wanted to know how long he'd been waiting there and why he hadn't called.

Sam said, "I got here right after you left, and your mother let me in. She also told me about your niece, Tawana, moving in."

Renee didn't want to have the conversation about Tawana moving in again, so she just brushed it off with a quickly response. "Yeah, it should be cool." She also changed the subject really quick by asking, "Are you planning on spending the night?"

Sam didn't hesitate with his answer. "Nah, because I need a clean uniform for work in the morning."

Renee giggled and said, "You need a clean uniform every day."

"Hell, no — my uniform ain't considered dirty until I wear it for two days. Sometimes I'll go three days, if I don't spill anything on it."

"You are so nasty," she said, while smiling really hard. "Anyway, what's in the bag?" she asked.

"Oh, I stopped by the video store and got *Why Did I Get Married?*"

"Alright, put it in, and I'll be right back with some popcorn — and you'd better not fall asleep, either, Sam, or I will throw your butt out."

Sam replied with disbelief in his tone. "You won't do anything. The best thing you could do would be to let me sleep because you want me to spend the night." Sam proved her right — he fell asleep before the couples in the movie made it to the cabin.

She set Sam straight and sent him home to his own bed. After he left, Renee went to bed, hoping to have sweet dreams of one day marrying Sam. Her dreams were interrupted early in the morning, when she woke up feeling sick.

The sound of Jessica screaming, "Renee, get out of the bathroom" didn't help the situation. She kept repeating, "You don't have to be at work until three o'clock — get out."

"Shut up!" Renee yelled back. "I feel sick. I think all that butter on that popcorn last night made me sick."

"Just get the hell out of the bathroom!" Jessica screamed at the top of her lungs. She started talking loud at her mother. "You need to put another bathroom in this house!" Jessica stood in front of the bathroom door, taunting Renee. "You should have taken your ass to bed instead of eating popcorn with Sam all night!"

"Don't take it out on me because James didn't come over last night," Renee said, wiping her mouth after throwing up.

"Just get the hell out of the bathroom, so I can go to work!"

Renee finally opened the bathroom door with a smirk on her face as she walked past Jessica.

By the time Jessica got to work, she was mad at the world and ready to take it out on everyone. She snapped at Charmaine as she asked, "Did I get any calls?"

Charmaine responded with a sassy tone, "Good morning to you, too, and no, there have been no phone calls as yet."

Jessica didn't pay any attention to how Charmaine responded because she was in deep in thought about James. *What the hell happened to him last night? Why wasn't he answering his phone? I hope he's all right.*

Charmaine interrupted her thoughts to let her know that she had a call on her private line coming through. She also took that time to ask if she could take lunch a little earlier. Charmaine explained, "My girlfriend and her kids that I was telling you about yesterday are living in a shelter in Hempstead, and she needs a ride to pick up some of her things from storage."

Jessica offered for her to take the rest of the day off, but Charmaine said, "No, maybe an extended lunch will do the trick."

As Charmaine walked out of the office, closing the door behind her, Jessica answered her private line in hopes that it would be James. When she heard his voice say, "Hello," she couldn't help but pepper him with questions of concern.

"James, what happened to you? Why weren't you answering your phone? Why didn't you call me? Are you all right?"

"Slow down, woman. I was out with my friends, and I left my cell phone in Tony's car," he said.

She questioned him about the party she heard about him deejaying at from Renee.

"Did I tell you about that?" he asked. "Never mind. It really doesn't matter, but yes, I did do that party. After that, Tony and some of my boys went out to this after-hours spot in Brooklyn."

Jessica was just happy to know that he was safe. She wanted to see him, so she asked, "Are you coming over tonight? I need to talk to you about something."

He responded nonchalantly, "We'll see what happens."

Jessica was taken aback by this response and said, "What does that mean?"

"Just what I said — I'll call you later and let you know."

Jessica, still showing concern, said, "Okay, sweetie, you must be tired. Go and get some rest."

Charmaine knocked on the door and peeked her head in to remind Jessica that she had a meeting that started in ten minutes.

James heard Charmaine in the background and suggested he should let Jessica get back to work.

Jessica wanted a definite time that she should expect his call, but James offered nothing. He just said, "I don't know. I'll call you later. Bye," and hung up the phone abruptly.

Jessica sat staring in disbelief at the phone in her hand, thinking, *He must really be tired because he didn't even let me say goodbye.* She started calling for Charmaine to come back into the office but remembered that Charmaine had left early for lunch. She sat at her desk, holding her head in her hands, trying to pull herself together before going to the meeting.

Meanwhile, Desire was trying to get used to living in one room with her boys, in the shelter. "Kids, get ready. Aunt Charmaine will be here soon. We're going to drop you off at school, and I'm going to the storage unit. I will pick up two toys apiece for you guys."

Her eldest son questioned, "Is Daddy coming to pick us up from school today?"

With a disappointed tone, she answered, "I don't think so, baby. Let's get downstairs before we miss breakfast."

As she sat at the dining-room table, feeding her boys a bowl of Frosted Flakes cereal, with all the other women and children living in the shelter, she fought back the tears from rolling down her face. The sound of Charmaine blowing the horn was a welcome distraction from her private thoughts. She rushed her boys out of the house with haste.

"Charmaine, girl, thank you so much for everything. I don't know what I would do without you."

Charmaine responded, very sympathetically, "It's no problem. That's what friends are for."

Desire, still feeling sorry for herself, said, "I feel so stupid all the time. I should have listened to so many people, including you, when it came to Jay."

Ever the supportive friend, Charmaine added, "We live, and we learn. Nobody wants to listen to someone who is not in the relationship tell them about their relationship. It all just sounds like hate in the end."

"I never felt you were hating on me, but I do feel you need a man, Charmaine."

Trying not to sound defensive, Charmaine replied, "I'm not looking, but if someone comes along, then great. If not, my world won't come to an end."

Desire started to reminisce about the good old days, when they would have a ladies' night to discuss their men.

Charmaine agreed, saying, "Ladies' night is not a bad idea. We should do it this weekend."

Desire reluctantly explained, "I can't spend the night out, or they'll think I have a place to stay. It's bad enough that now I have this young girl in there at night telling me what time I have to be in the house and what time to go to my room. And all of this because I chose a man over good, common sense."

"I'm sorry that you have to go through that, but one night out does not mean you have permanent housing. You and the kids can stay with me," Charmaine offered.

Desire made an attempt at being funny and said, "I think you're drunk in anticipation of ladies' night because there is no way that we can all stay in your studio apartment."

Charmaine, trying to sound optimistic, stated, "We can make do."

"I love you for what you're trying to do, but I need my own. I'll be on top again, and no man will ever bring me down again. I can promise you that, Charmaine."

Charmaine switched gears in the conversation and asked, "Have you spoken to Jay at all?"

"No, he won't answer his phone or return my calls. I don't even know where he's staying."

Charmaine gave her a stern look. She questioned, "What did you do with his things? I know you're not paying to store his shit, too."

Desire looked her straight in the eye and gave her that "Bitch, *please*" look as she said, "*Hell*, no. I was stupid, but I wasn't in a coma. That sorry sack of shit was slowly moving his stuff out. When they came to put us out and I started packing, I noticed he didn't have anything there."

Charmaine said, "I wish you would have stayed in touch with me. Maybe I could have helped you see things more clearly before it was too late."

"Charmaine, I don't think there was anything you could have done. He knew what he was doing. He slowly but surely manipulated my mind, body, and soul. He made me think I didn't need anyone but him. Friends and family came second to him and his needs. He was my world."

"See, Desire, this is why I will always try to remain true to the saying, 'No man above God and myself.' I threw the "myself" part in there because I learned to never love anyone more than you love yourself. Do you remember that guy Brian I was with?"

"Yeah, girl — whatever happened to him?" Desire asked.

Charmaine explained as she mentally went down memory lane. "I loved that man so much, and he just loved himself. Every week, this man was coming up with all sorts of things he needed or wanted to make his life better. My stupid ass thought it was my job to make his life easier and better. I was spending all of my financial-aid money on this fool. I was buying stereo systems, paying for car repair, and buying a new pair of sneakers every week. I thought the more I gave him, the more he would love me. Then I got pregnant, and he didn't even want to have the baby. But he didn't want to pay for the abortion, either. That's when I knew it was time to say goodbye. He didn't want to share the most precious gift on Earth, like creating a life and watching it grow with me. And for that, I hated him."

Desire questioned with concern in her voice, "What happened to the baby?"

Charmaine hung her head down, feeling sorry for her situation but relieved at the same time. She responded, "God must have said it wasn't my time. Then he changed his mind, and he took the baby back."

Desire reacted with shock and sympathy at hearing of her friend's personal struggle. "I'm sorry you had to go through that by yourself. I feel like the worst friend on Earth."

Trying to make her friend feel better about not being around during her time of grief, Charmaine said, "Don't worry about it. At that time, there was nothing anyone could have said to make me feel better anyway."

Looking back, Desire had to admit to herself that she had seen the signs that something was wrong with her relationship with Jay. She explained to her friend, "I saw signs, but I kept telling myself, 'Not *my* man. He wouldn't do that to me. I have been good to him. I have given him three beautiful sons.' I guess in the end, none of that made any difference. A man will do what he wants to despite who gets hurt in the process. Charmaine, you're my girl, and I don't want you to let yourself become bitter over what happened with Brian. Not all men are bad. There is someone out there for everyone. Jay, on the other hand, just has not met his match."

Charmaine tried to lighten the mood when she said, "How are you, of all people, gonna tell me not to become bitter when we are standing in a storage facility surrounded by your things because of a man?" She giggled and said, "Girl, let's get this stuff and go because I have to get back to work soon."

"Once again, Charmaine, thank you so much."

"No problem. Now, let's go, because Ms. Jessica keeps a tight schedule, and I only asked for an extended lunch."

Back at Jessica and Renee's house, their niece Tawana finally arrived.

"Hey, grandma, thank you so much for letting me live here with you guys. I thought I was gonna go crazy at that school."

"Tawana, you are my grandchild, and you are as beautiful as your mother. God bless her, wherever she may be."

In a somber tone, Tawana asked her grandmother if she thought her mother was dead.

Momma Tyler was doing her best to sound as optimistic as possible when she answered, "I don't know. I pray that she is somewhere getting her life together and that she will come home soon. You and your sister will need her. You young ladies will be going through a lot of changes in your young lives as you enter into womanhood."

Tawana interrupted her grandmother in mid-sentence, saying, "I think she's dead."

Momma Tyler was not accepting of this type of energy being put out into the world, and she committed to shutting it down immediately. "Don't you ever let me hear you say that again! Until there is proof, she will always be alive."

Tawana, feeling overwhelmingly guilty, quickly and sincerely apologized to her grandmother, letting her know that she did not mean to upset her, and changed the topic with an entire list of questions: "When is Renee coming home? Is Jessica mad that I am sharing her room? Did you tell my sister that I was going to be living here? Because she is going to be mad."

"Listen, one question at a time. I am getting old. I can't keep up with you youngsters anymore. Now, one, Renee will be home soon; two, Jessica will get over it; three, no — I have not spoken to your sister."

Just then the doorbell rang, and Momma Tyler was relieved because she did not want to engage in the conversation any longer. Tawana ran to see who was at the door and became ecstatic to see who it was.

"Oh, my God! Hey, Sam, and what's up, Eric? What's going on, guys?"

Both Sam and Eric were shocked at how much she had grown. Sam said, "Wow, I know that's not little Tawana that used to steal money out of Jessica's Bible to buy penny candy at the store. You got so big. How old are you now?"

"I am sixteen now. I just had my birthday July 25."

Eric joined in on the questioning and asked, "Did you finish school yet? Are you going to college?"

Tawana replied, with uncertainty in her tone, "I doubt it. School and me just don't get along anymore. Eric, what's up with you? You seem very different."

Eric, standing there feeling very mellow, said, "Naw, I'm good. I just smoked a bud — that's all."

Tawana's entire face lit up at hearing that piece of information. She shouted, "Oh, yeah? Where's it at?"

Sam was shocked to see her become so excited. His voice went up an octave when he said, "Tawana, don't tell me you smoke!"

She matched his octave when she replied, "Hell, yeah. I can roll a blunt with one hand!"

"Damn, girl! What the hell was going on up at that school?" Sam said.

"I'll tell you if Eric sparks some trees."

Eric was having no part of that, and he told her, "Yo, Tawana — you bugging out. I can't smoke no bud with you."

She acted as if this were an inconceivable notion and asked, "Why not?"

"You're like my little cousin. I can't do that — plus Ms. Tyler is right upstairs," Eric said.

"So, let's go to the park," Tawana said, being persistent.

"We can go to the park, but I'm still not smoking with you. If someone else wants to smoke with you, then I can't stop them, but it ain't happening with me," Eric said, making himself very clear.

"Eric, why you acting like that? I am sixteen. Please stop treating me like I am ten years old or something. Sam, would you tell him? I am almost grown."

"What you want me to say? I don't smoke, but if I did, I wouldn't smoke with you, either," Sam told her.

Tawana began to pout, saying, "I can't wait for Renee to get home."

At that exact moment, Renee walked into the house loud and full of herself. "Speak of an angel, and in she walks. Tawana! I am so glad to see you. Look at you. Where did you get all that ass and hips from? Let's go get something to eat and go to the movies or something. Eric, call Kit, and see if she wants to come."

"I ain't calling her house because her aunt be bugging out," Eric replied.

Renee started laughing at Eric as she said, "Oh, yeah. I heard about the other night. Let me go call her and get my big pocketbook so I can put the bottle in it. By the way, we have to stop at the liquor store so I can get my Hennessy."

Tawana yelled out with glee, "I'm with that!"

Renee shut that right down. "You are not drinking anything. Your grandmother won't be cursing me out tomorrow," she said.

"Oh, here we go again. People, I am sixteen years old. Would you stop treating me like I am a kid? I hope this is not how it's going to be the whole time I am living here," Tawana retorted.

Renee asked a semi-rhetorical question, "Can you buy your own bottle?"

Tawana answered, "No," under her breath.

Renee abruptly said, "Then you are a kid, and you can't drink with me. Now I am done with that topic. Sam, did that popcorn make you sick the other night?"

"No, why?" Sam questioned.

"I was sick as hell the next morning. I don't want any popcorn when we get there. I think the butter may have been too much for my stomach," Renee answered.

Tawana decided to interrupt their private conversation and take the time to thank her Aunt Renee for making her first night there so nice.

Once they returned home from dinner and a movie, Tawana thanked Renee again by calling her "Aunt Renee" as a sign of respect. Renee did not receive it as such when she responded, "You are welcome — and cut the shit with that 'aunt' stuff."

Tawana smiled at Renee and went into her new room.

"Tawana, turn off the lights! I am trying to sleep," Jessica yelled.

"Hi, Jessica. I just wanted to say 'Hi,'" Tawana said.

"Well, say 'Hi' in the morning. Now, turn off the lights," Jessica scowled.

Tawana turned the lights off and stormed out of the room, headed straight for her grandmother's room. "Grandma, Jessica is a grouch. I don't know how we are going to survive in that room together."

"Well, you girls are gonna have to work that out among yourselves because I am not getting involved."

She left her grandmother's room and stomped over to Renee's room. "Renee, can I sleep in your room tonight?" Tawana asked.

"As a matter of fact, you cannot, because Sam is spending the night tonight," Renee said.

"What! Grandma let him spend the night and sleep in here with you?" Tawana responded, sounding shocked.

"Yes, and don't get any ideas," Renee answered. "You will not have the same privilege because you don't pay any bills around here yet. Emphasis on the 'yet.' Now get out of my room, and goodnight."

The entire house was woken up by the sound of the doorbell in the early-morning hours. Momma Tyler, totally frustrated, asked, "Jessica, what damn floral shop delivers flowers at seven o'clock in the damn morning?"

"I don't know, and I don't care. They are beautiful," Jessica said. She inhaled deeply as she read the card, "Dear Jessica, I am sorry for the other night. Please accept my apology. All my love, James."

"These are the reasons why I love him," she added after reading the card aloud.

Renee was at the top of the stairs, looking down at Jessica standing in the living room admiring her flowers. She said, "I am glad that you love them and him, but do it quietly. Some of us are still asleep."

Jessica looked up toward the steps, showing all 32 of her teeth and shouting, "Renee, look at these roses!"

Renee, showing complete disinterest, told her that she would see them later, went back to her room, and slammed the door.

Behind closed doors, Renee was brainstorming out of control. *Why do I feel sick again? I didn't have popcorn last night. I know I didn't drink that much. Lord, oh, please, Lord, don't let me be pregnant. Sam and I just started dating. I don't want to mess things up with a baby. It can't be. We always use condoms. There was that one time when it came off inside of me. Renee, you are going to make yourself crazy. Stop it. Go get ready for work.*

Jessica arrived at her office feeling like she was on cloud nine and blissfully in love. "Good morning, Charmaine," she said, excessively cheerful.

Charmaine, a little taken aback by her cheerfulness, asked, "Aren't *we* in a good mood?"

Jessica couldn't help but brag about the two-dozen peach-colored roses she'd received that morning.

Charmaine responded with a totally pessimistic attitude. She said, "That is so sweet. What was he feeling guilty about?"

"Charmaine, stop being like that. There was no guilt — he did it just because he loves me."

"My bad. James must be special. Most men buy roses only when they are guilty of something," Charmaine added.

Jessica responded proudly, "Not *my* man."

"Anyway, Jess, I was thinking about having a ladies' night out. Nothing too big, maybe play Pokeno at my place, and then go to Club Shotsy's on Saturday."

"That sounds like fun. Do you mind if I call my sister and ask her if she wants to come? She may want to bring her friend."

Charmaine thought about it for a moment and said, "She can bring a couple of people — not too many. My place is not that big."

"Cool. I will call my sister at work and ask her now."

Over at the shelter, Renee had just walked in the door when she was greeted by Desire. "Good morning, Renee. I thought you worked evening shift."

"Good morning, Ms. Williams. I switched shifts today. I have an appointment later this evening. How is everything with you and the apartment search going?" Renee asked.

"I haven't received my letter from Golden Rule yet. Most realtors want to see it before they will help you," Desire answered.

"That's true. I forgot about that. Well, what about the job search?" Renee asked.

"I haven't worked in some time now," Desire said, "and most places want to start me as if I'd just gotten out of college. I have three kids to support. I can't afford entry-level pay."

"I hear that. Something will come through for you. Maybe I can ask my sister if her legal department is looking for someone."

"That would be great. Can you, please?" Desire asked, sounding very intrigued.

"I will let you know what she says."

Just then the sound of her boss's voice carried through the hallway. "Renee, telephone. It is your sister!"

"Okay, boss lady, I'm coming. Speak of the devil. I will ask her now." As Renee was walking back toward the office, she was thinking to herself, *I hope there is no family drama because I just can't deal with it right now.*

"Hey, Jess. What's up?" Renee asked as she picked up the receiver.

"My secretary, Charmaine, wants to have a ladies' night out on Saturday. Do you want to go?"

Renee didn't hesitate to answer. "Yeah, sure. Why not? Can I ask Kit if she wants to come? While I have you on the phone, can you see if your legal department is in need of a paralegal?"

Jessica was overwhelmed with all of Renee's questions — all asked in less than one minute and without waiting for an answer to any of them.

"I figured you would ask if Kit could come, so I already asked Charmaine for you, and the answer is 'Yes,' but as for the job, who is it for?"

"This lady who lives here at the shelter."

"Not one of those ghetto people!" Jessica yelled into the phone.

"She is very nice; you would like her. Her man left her with three young boys," Renee explained.

Jessica, feeling sorry for the words she'd just used, said, "God bless her. Some men need to be castrated before they have a chance to reproduce," she added.

Renee burst out in laughter. "That's a bit harsh, but I know how you feel. Anyway, just ask around for me, and I will speak to you later."

Renee went through the rest of the day in anticipation of her appointment later on that evening. As she pulled up to the building, she sat in the car to gather her thoughts before going in. She stepped out of the car fully focused and prepared for whatever was about to come her way.

"Hello, Dr. Carl. How are you?"

"I am great. I haven't seen you in a while. What brings you here?"

She took a deep breath before she answered, "I just haven't been feeling myself lately. I have experienced frequent headaches and nausea, and sometimes I get lightheaded."

The doctor asked, "When was your last period?"

Renee tried to head the doctor off at the pass. She could tell that he was headed toward a diagnosis of pregnancy. "I am not pregnant, Dr. Carl. I have been careful."

"Let's be sure. I want to take a blood sample."

"Okay, doc — but I know I am not."

"Well, Renee, everything else seems fine. Your blood pressure is good. I will call you with the result tomorrow."

She left the doctor's office feeling semi-confident. She called her friend to fill her in on the doctor visit.

"Hey, Kit. What's up? I just left the doctor's office, and he said that everything seems fine. But on another note, my sister's secretary, Charmaine, wants to have a ladies' night out on Saturday. Do you want to go?"

Kit responded, sounding down and unsure of her future, but she was still in need of some fun. "Yeah, I'll go. I hope it's a sleepover, because my aunt said I have to leave by Friday."

Renee was shocked to hear that because Friday was tomorrow. She asked, "How much money have you saved for your apartment so far?"

"Not much, because I was paying my car note and giving her money. Girl, you know I don't make that much money anyway."

"We have to get you a better job, first and foremost. I will ask my mom if you can stay with us for a while. You can stay in my room with me. It'll be tight, but we will make it work."

"Renee, come on — seriously? What about Sam?"

"Sam will have to stay at home. I can always go to his place, and you can have the room to yourself some nights. I will call you tomorrow, and we can set up a time to help you move your things. Also, call Eric so he can help, too. By the way, why didn't he let you stay with him?"

"He said that Mike, one of his boys, had just moved in with him," Kit replied.

"Okay. Well, I'll speak to you later. I'm going to call Sam now."

When Sam answered his phone, Renee just began to speak: "Sam, are you coming over tonight?"

"Yeah, I'll be there. Renee, why don't you ever say 'Hello' when you get on the phone?"

She replied, with attitude, "Why? You can see that it's me calling from the caller ID."

Sam just left it alone. Instead of arguing with her, he just said, "I'll see you when I get there."

As Renee hung up the phone, she thought about her attitude and how rude she may have come off on the phone. She started thinking to herself, *I hope — as a matter of fact, I know — I am not pregnant because I am not sure if I want to be a mother. But Sam would be such a good father. Maybe it could work out if I am.*

Renee snapped herself out of deep thought and called out, "Ms. Tyler, I need to talk to you."

"Renee, how many times do I have to tell you that I am your mother and that you will respect me? You can call me 'Mother,' 'Mommy,' or 'Mom.' I don't care. It's your choice, but you will respect me when you address me."

Sarcastically, Renee said, "Alright, already. Now, how do you feel about Kit?"

"What about her?" Momma Tyler asked.

"She is having a problem with her aunt, and she needs a place to stay temporarily."

"Renee, why would I want to take on her aunt's problems?"

"Mother, her aunt *is* the problem. She is drunk all the time, and she takes all of Kit's money. She has no other family to turn to."

"Well, how long is 'temporarily'?"

"She is already looking for an affordable apartment, so it shouldn't be long. She is willing to sleep on the floor in my room because, at the very least, she will have peace of mind."

Momma Tyler agreed to let Kit stay for $200 per month toward food and utilities.

Jessica walked in on the tail end of the conversation. "What are you guys talking about in here?"

"Our mother just agreed to let Kit stay here for a little while," Renee answered.

Jessica was trying to be funny when she said, "This house is becoming like the North Shore Animal League — we are taking in all sorts of strays."

Renee took offense to Jessica's comment and told her she was not funny.

Jessica felt the need to defend her point of view by stating, "All your friends always seem to need help. Let's see, what happened to your friend Vanessa, and your friend Patty, the teenage mom? Where are those friends now?"

Renee fired back, "Jessica, at least I *have* friends. Name one person that you can call a friend."

Momma Tyler became disgusted with both of them for their behavior and yelled, "Cut the shit! You girls are going to make me lose my religion. The girl is staying here, and that is that!"

Jessica, still wanting to have the last word, said, "We have only one bathroom in this house, for five women. That's a problem in itself."

Renee was finished talking to Jessica and wanted to know where Tawana was.

Momma Tyler said, "When Sam came by, Tawana asked for a ride to the mall, and he took her because you weren't home yet."

Renee, trying to be funny said, "Okay, Mommy. I am going to call Kit and give her the good news. Then I am going to lie down. I am tired. Thanks again."

As Renee walked away, Jessica looked out the window and saw James pull up. She ran outside like a toddler being picked up from school by her mother or father.

"Hi, baby. I missed you. Your flowers were beautiful. Come upstairs, and let me show you how much I appreciate what you did. More than that, I just want to show you that I love having you in my life. Nobody has ever made me feel the way you do. I will never cheat or lie to you. You have all that I need and want in a man. You are honest and faithful, and you are not afraid to show your love."

James sat on the bed, looked her in the eye, and told her, "Jessica, you are my world, and I never want to do anything to hurt you."

Jessica felt this was the perfect opportunity to see where the relationship was going, and she asked, "James, how do you feel about children?"

The energy shifted in the room when James started to ask the question: "Are you . . ."

Jessica changed the mood back before he could finish the sentence. "No, I am not. I was just thinking it would be a wonderful way for us to express our love for each other."

James seemed relieved for the moment but flattered at the same time. He asked, "Are you sure about this?"

"I am very sure. You have no kids, and I would love to — in fact, it would be my honor to carry and give birth to your firstborn."

"Oh, wow, Jess. 'My firstborn.' That has a nice ring to it. I still think we should wait until I get my name out there as one of the top deejays around."

Jessica offered some reassurance. "You don't have to be Funk Master Flex to have a baby," she said.

"Come on, Jess, you know what I mean. I just want to be able to take care of my family. It is a beautiful thought, and I love you for considering me as the father of your firstborn. God will let us know when the time is right for us to have a baby. A baby is really a gift from the Big Man Above anyway."

A commotion downstairs distracted him briefly. He heard Sam's voice. "Let me go say 'What's up?' to Sam," James said.

Tawana ran up the stairs past James as he was going down, straight to Renee's room.

"Hey, Tawana. Did you and Sam just get back? Renee asked as Tawana burst into her room.

"Yes — come see what I bought. Let's go into Jessica's room."

As she burst open Jessica's door and a weird stench drifted past their noses, she uttered, "What the hell is that smell in here? Did you guys just have sex? It smells like rubber and sweaty butt cheeks in here," Tawana said.

Jessica's face turned Kool-Aid red with embarrassment, and she yelled, "Shut up, and get out."

Tawana was laughing at her as she said, "No, open the window, and look at what I bought at the mall."

Renee said, "Girl, I can't take the smell in here. Come show me later."

Jessica picked up on something with her sister that was off, and she made a comment. "Your nose is super sensitive. Renee, are you pregnant?"

"Hell, no! Sam acts like he has stock in the makers of Midnight Black condoms. Where is he anyway, Tawana?" Renee asked.

"He is downstairs talking to James. By the way, Jess, he is fine. Good catch, girl," Tawana said while smiling at Jessica.

Renee yelled downstairs, "Sam, when you finish talking to James, I need to speak with you!"

As Sam entered the room, Renee blurted out, "Sam, I think I may be pregnant."

Sam was annoyed with her delivery. "Renee, you can't just blurt it out like that."

"Sam, I love you, and what better way to show it than by giving you a baby?"

"Renee, please. That sounds like something from a soap opera. Just play it by ear. You may not even be pregnant."

Sam could tell something else was going on with Renee, so he pleaded with her to tell him what else was going on.

Renee said, "Well, as far as the pregnancy goes, you are right. I am waiting for the doctor to let me know for sure. But the other thing is that Kit will be moving in with us."

"Oh, yeah? Where is she going to stay — in the living room?" Sam asked.

"Sam, that's where it gets a little tricky," Renee answered. "She will be staying in here with me."

She tried to smile and give him puppy-dog eyes, but he wasn't falling for it.

"I have nothing against Kit, but why can't she stay someplace else?"

"You know she doesn't have family like that. And one more thing: I volunteered you to help her move her things."

She puckered her lips to give him a kiss, and he backed away as he said, "Oh, Renee — come on. That's what she has a man for. Why can't Eric help her?" Sam questioned.

"The both of you together will be so much faster. Just think about it. I will get to spend much more time at your place now. Isn't that what you've always wanted?"

Sam had been contemplating how he was going to tell her some news of his own, and he figured this was as good a time as any.

"Yes, but I have to tell you something. My sister is moving in with me until she finds an apartment of her own. I am giving her my bedroom, and I will be sleeping in the living room."

Renee was trying to put a positive spin on both situations by saying they'd work themselves out. "I just want to enjoy the rest of the night together and be alone. Who knows when we'll be able to be alone again?"

"That is exactly what I mean . . . when? Just one more thing: When did you volunteer me? Because I have to help my sister, Lisa, move in," Sam said.

"Tomorrow after work," Renee told him.

"Renee, didn't you think that I might be tired after work? Plus, I have to help my sister on Saturday."

"All the more reason we should go to sleep," Renee said. "Come over here, and let me put you to sleep. Goodnight, babe."

Momma Tyler was the first of the ladies in the house to wake up and was greeted by James and Sam in the kitchen.

"Good morning, Ms. Tyler," they both said.

"Both of you guys stayed in my house last night. I am going to start collecting rent after a while."

James offered her a slick comment. "I will pay rent if you have breakfast ready every morning."

"James, get the hell out of my house," Momma Tyler said.

Both Sam and James said "Goodbye" to Momma Tyler, and, before they could shut the door behind them, Momma Tyler was yelling upstairs for Jessica and Renee: "Get downstairs — right now!"

Jessica yelled back downstairs that Renee was in the bathroom forever again. Renee finally got out of the bathroom and heard her mother fussing downstairs. So, she rushed downstairs to find out what was going on.

"Let me tell you two something. Those boys are very nice, but they don't pay no bills around here, and I don't want them spending the night every day. I know you girls are grown, but this is still my house. And Jessica, I don't want to hear that same old song about 'you getting your own place.' I'll believe it when I see it. I hope you understand that I am very serious."

Renee was upset that she was making such a big deal about nothing, and she walked out before her mother could finish her speech. She went back into her room, knelt down by the side of her bed, and said a silent prayer before calling the doctor's office. *Oh, God! Dr. Carl—please be in the office. I can't wait another minute to hear the results.*

"Hello. Is Dr. Carl in?"

"No, ma'am. This is his service. The office will be open today at 10:00 a.m. Would you like to leave a message? Or, if this is an emergency, you can go to the emergency room at your local hospital."

"No, thank you. I will call back later." Renee sighed with disappointment as she thought to herself, *Renee, just go to work, and don't think about it.*

Jessica, on the other hand, was still happy from her day with James. She called Charmaine to go over the agenda for the day before going into the office. She also took that time to find out if they were still on for ladies' night Saturday.

Charmaine reassured her that it was still on and that the guest list would consist of only five girls.

Jessica inquired about her friend who was living in the shelter. Just as she was about to tell her that her sister, Renee, actually worked in a shelter, her other line beeped in. She rushed off the phone and told Charmaine that she would see her at the office.

Jessica and Renee were both heading out the door for work when Jessica asked when Kit was moving in. Renee informed her that she should be moving in that day and that she was about to call Kit to verify the details of the move.

"Hey, Kit. Sam is on-board for today after work. Did you speak with Eric to make sure he will be there?"

"Yeah, he will be there. My aunt may act the fool when we show up."

"That's alright, because we shouldn't be there long if you are only taking clothes, right?"

"Well, I do have my television and my computer, and I don't want to leave anything behind," Kit said.

"That shouldn't be a problem. We can put most of it in the basement. What about your mail?" Renee asked.

"I applied for a PO Box, because I don't want your mom to think this was a permanent move. I've already put my name on the list for an apartment on Terrace Avenue in Hempstead."

Renee was both shocked and disappointed with hearing that she'd applied for an apartment on Terrace.

"Kit! No, you did not!" Why would you apply for an apartment on a drug-infested street like Terrace Avenue? I am sure there was some other low-income housing that you could have found."

"What, girl? That is all that I can afford right now. I have no other choice," Kit responded.

"What about Eric? Aren't you guys serious?" Renee asked, still a little shocked.

Kit, still feeling the pressure of losing the support of her family, namely, her aunt, answered, "I love Eric, but he wants to take things slow. I know he loves me, too, and I don't want to rush him and mess things up. I have enough going on with my family — I don't want to lose my boyfriend, too."

"I will pray that you get a better job so you don't have to live over there," Renee said. "One time, I went over there with this girl to pick up some money from her baby father, and, while I was waiting in the car, this girl started yelling that she was going to jump out of the window! She was hanging halfway out of the window, and the people on the street were yelling, 'Jump, bitch, jump!" It was absolutely crazy. Then some guy in the crowd started shooting in the air, in broad daylight, and nobody ran or ducked for cover. I was sitting in the car, having a mild heart attack. I thought to myself, *This must be the norm over here, because there are kids everywhere — like roaches in the night — and they're not even crying, screaming, or anything.*"

Kit listened intently to the story, but it didn't change the fact that that was all she could afford right now.

"Anyway, we just have to see what happens. I have to make another call, and I will see you later," Renee said before she hung up. She decided to call the doctor's office again before going into work.

"Hello. Is Dr. Carl available?"

"No, Dr. Carl won't be in the office today. He was called to an emergency at the hospital. He will return to the office on Monday."

"Did he leave the results for a Renee Tyler?"

"Ma'am, Dr. Carl never came into the office today, and he is the only person who can give results over the phone."

Renee, feeling deflated after hearing that, went inside the shelter and was greeted by Desire.

"Good morning, Ms. Renee. I had a job interview at this actuarial firm as a file clerk today. I think it went well."

"Well, I am glad that you are having a good job search. By the way, do you have a current resume? Because my sister said you will need it if there is a position available."

"I was just working on that. It should be ready by Monday. The file-clerk job was entry level and required only a basic application, but if I get that job, it will be some money coming in."

When Desire mentioned "Monday," that's when it hit Renee that it was going to be an entire weekend before she would know for sure what her pregnancy status was.

"Oh, wow. I didn't realize the weekend was here already. Have you heard from your son's father?" Renee asked.

Desire answered, "Yes, sort of. He called my father and told him that he'd moved in with one of his friends; he left a cell-phone number for me to call him on — he wants to see his sons."

Renee let the question slip from her lips without thinking that it might sound insensitive or rude: "Are you going to let him see them?"

"No. I thought it was very funny that he would even *think* that I would," Desire responded.

"When I did your intake, you didn't mention your father. Why didn't you and the boys go and stay with him?"

"My dad stays in a one-bedroom in a senior-citizen apartment complex. He barely has room to turn around in there. Besides that, my dad didn't want to have anything to do with me because of Jay. He never approved of my relationship with Jay. He felt any man who could not look a father in his eyes when speaking about his daughter was not an honorable man. I just thought my dad was a little old fashioned. I guess, looking back, there was something to his theory after all. That is why I found it so funny that Jay called my father, of all people. I just happened to call my father to let him know where I was, because he is the only family I have left."

Renee thought about Desire's statement regarding her father and had to admit that her mother was not very far off the mark when it came to judging someone's character, either.

"Well, I need to use the bathroom, and I am sure you need to go work on your resume."

While sitting on the toilet, Renee decided to run a hypothetical situation past her co-worker when she got out of the bathroom.

"Hey, Ms. Millie. I need to ask you a question. My sister thinks she may be pregnant, but she is not sure if her boyfriend will be happy. Should she not tell him and have an abortion or tell him and see what he says? If he doesn't want it, should she keep it anyway?"

Millie asked, "What did you tell her to do, Renee?"

"Well, you know me. My attitude is 'If a man does not want my baby, then he does not want me, and he has to go.'"

"Renee, that may be good advice, but what about the baby?" Millie asked.

"I would personally give the gift back to God," Renee said.

Millie simply asked, "Why would you not accept the gift for what it is — a baby?"

Renee came back with a simple answer: "Not every woman is built to be a single mom. I know that much about myself. I couldn't do it, and I don't think my sister could do it, either."

Millie felt compelled to tell Renee her personal experience with her pregnancy.

"When I told my husband I was pregnant, he left. He came to my first doctor's appointment and heard the baby's heartbeat and just walked out of the room. I did not see or hear from him for two months after that."

Renee interrupted her story. "See — that's what I am talking about. I would have made the appointment to terminate before I could even get up from the table."

Millie didn't address Renee's comment; she just kept telling her story. "I didn't even think about it. Once I heard my son's heartbeat, that was it for me. I knew it was me and my baby against the world. When he came back, I never asked what happened or why. I saw something in his eyes that had changed. He was a different man. He was not ready to take on that responsibility, but wherever he went or whatever he did had changed him. He came back to me a father, not a baby's daddy. With that said, don't be so quick to return the gift of life because some boy is not ready to be a man. God gives women only a few chances to turn away his gift before he makes it permanent. Then you will regret having made the decision you made."

"Millie, you are a stronger woman than I would ever be. I know it seems that, for the past few weeks, I have been leaving early, but do you mind? I am helping a friend move today."

"It's not a problem. I hope all goes well with your sister," Millie said.

"Thank you, Millie, for letting me leave and for listening to me."

Renee jetted off to her car to call Kit to let her know that she was leaving work early and that she would meet her at her aunt's house.

Kit advised her that she was already at her aunt's house and that her aunt was passed out on the couch, drunk.

"Oh, good. That should make things easier. Do you need anything, like garbage bags or boxes?" Renee asked.

"No, I am good. I have been putting some bags in my car, and she hasn't even noticed. I hope she stays drunk and asleep until we move all my things."

Renee asked again, "What's up with you and Eric?"

Kit was very frustrated at this point, and she responded in anger. "Why do you keep asking me that?

"What do you mean?" Renee, sounding like a supportive friend, said, "I still feel like you should be moving in with him. Damn his homeboy. What is his homeboy doing for him? When I see him, I am going to tell him about himself."

Kit calmed down and realized that Renee was just being a concerned friend.

"Look, he may not be ready to live with a woman yet. You, of all people, should know you can't make a man do something he is not ready to do. I love Eric, and I believe that he loves me. I am willing to take it slowly. I hope this is the last time I have to tell you that, Renee."

"Not my girl, hardcore Kit, sounding like some lovesick soap-opera star."

"I am about to make some major changes in my life. The fact that I am moving out tells me I have to grow up, basically overnight. So, if things don't work out for Eric and me, then I know I have to take that love that I was giving to him and keep it for myself. But I know I will have to keep pushing."

"Kit, you are killing me right now, but it is good to hear the change in you. I thought you were going to live there forever and that your biggest responsibility would be which shoes to buy with an outfit."

"Renee, you should be the last person to talk. You live with your momma and your sister!"

"Yes, but we pay the bills. What do you know about that — trying to be smart?" Renee said, smiling.

"Nothing, but I hope to soon find out. I hope the guys hurry up because I want to get out of here."

Renee let her know that she was pulling up to her aunt's house, and Kit ran down to let her in. The sound of Kit running down the steps alerted her aunt, and she began to yell.

"Kit! Kit! Kit! Is that you?" her Aunt Ruby screamed from the couch.

"Yes, Aunt Ruby, it's me. Renee is coming over."

Kit, flashing her hand at Renee to come in and be quiet, ushered her in the door.

"Hush — maybe she will go back to sleep," Kit warned.

Her aunt Ruby, not realizing that Renee was already in the house, yelled out, "I thought I told you I didn't want that skinny black bitch in my house."

"Ignore her, Renee. Go upstairs," Kit requested.

Her aunt sat up in time to see Renee trying to sneak past her going toward the stairs.

"Hey, you, darkness, fudge princess — get the hell out of my house, and take my no-good niece with you."

"That is just what I am going to do. You drunken . . ."

Kit stopped Renee mid-sentence before things really got out of hand.

"Oh, Lord, Renee! Go upstairs!" Kit urged.

Her aunt, still not very coherent, asked, "What did she say?"

Trying to calm things down, Kit replied, "Nothing. Go back to sleep. I will be leaving shortly."

She pushed Renee up the rest of the steps, and once they were in the room, she said, "Why did you do that? Things could have gotten really ugly. Let me handle my aunt."

"Okay, but I will not be disrespected by anyone. Let's get the rest of your things and leave. Who the hell is she calling 'black'? She is one shade away from a power outage her damn self. You know what? I think I better go outside now," Renee said.

"Yes, please do — before you make a bad situation worse. Eric just texted me; he is coming down the block."

"Is Sam with him?" Renee asked.

"He didn't say, but my aunt is up now, damn it!"

"Kit, what the hell is going on here? Why are all your so-called 'friends' at my damn door?" her Aunt Ruby questioned.

"Eric, wait upstairs for me, please," Kit said. Aunt Ruby, I am moving out. I am going to stay with Renee until I find my own place."

Her aunt stumbled to her feet, trying to walk toward Kit, saying, "You're moving? You're too stupid to move out on your own. You will be back. You saw what happened to your mother when she tried that mess. You gonna be just like her. Get the hell out of my house then, you ungrateful bitch. You ain't nothing but a wasted fuck. You're ugly, and you look like the aborted baby you should have been. Go, bitch, go. Get out!"

Kit, feeling empowered, stood strong as she said, "Your words can't hurt me anymore. As for my mother, she was shot running away from you and your husband, the pedophile. Yeah, you thought no one knew about that. I am positive she is happier in death than living here with you. I am sure there is a reason why your sorry excuse of a husband started messing with little girls. Were you not woman enough for him? Hell, even his sorry ass left you. You came into this world alone, and you will surely go out the same way."

Kit looked toward the top of the steps and called up, "Eric and Renee, please hurry up, so I can get the hell out of here."

Renee and Eric rushed out the door with bags of Kit's clothes and placed them into Sam's car as soon as he pulled up. Once everything was loaded up, Kit turned to Renee and hugged her tightly.

"Renee, you are my very best friend, and I want to say thank you again for helping me make this move. I will never forget this. You can always depend on me. I love you, girl."

"I love you, too. Now, put the past behind you, and drive off into the future," Renee said.

Everyone burst out in laughter at the corny statement, and Kit suggested they go have a drink after they unpack.

Eric said, "*Hell*, yeah. After dealing with your aunt, I need two or maybe even three drinks to calm my nerves."

As they arrived back at Renee's house to unload, Sam got the full picture of everything Kit had.

"Yo, E — your girl got a lot of shit."

Eric replied, "That's why she couldn't move in with me. Her stuff would have been all over my place."

Renee did not appreciate that comment, and she tried to make Eric feel bad by saying, "But you will let your friend move in with you, though."

"Yeah, my man Mike. He finally left his girl because she was one of those crazy chicks. I never met her, but he said she was getting to be too much for him to deal with. First of all, Renee, he moved in before Kit decided that she wanted to move out of her aunt's house, so don't come at me like that," Eric said.

Kit pleaded with Renee not to start anything with Eric, so Renee left the situation alone.

Sam suggested they all go to Friday's so they could get some food along with drinks.

"My man said happy hour is popping over there," Sam said.

Sam pulled Eric to the side to ask if he'd heard that the girls were going out this weekend.

"Yeah, Kit mentioned it to me," Eric responded. "We should roll out, too. Let's go to Club Shotsy's. They're playing Pokeno at some girl's place who works with Jessica. I'm gonna call my man to see if he wants to roll."

Sam wondered if he knew Eric's boy.

Eric said, "Naw, we met at this club in Brooklyn. I got into some beef, and he stepped up. I didn't even know him, but we have been cool ever since. He's a truck driver, and he deejays on the side."

Sam said, "You know, Jessica's man, James, is a deejay. I'm going to ask him if he knows him."

Eric explained, "He's just starting out. He hasn't even played at any clubs yet. So far, he's only made mix CDs for people."

"Then James probably wouldn't know him," Sam said.

They finished up and headed out to Friday's.

"Why is it every time we come in here, they put us in the back?" Kit questioned.

"Because they know you are going to get drunk and loud," Renee said. "Be for real, Kit. You know you can't hold your liquor."

"I am not loud, but you may be right about the liquor part," Kit said.

Renee didn't entertain the rest of that conversation because she was intent on re-addressing Eric and the living situation.

"Hey, Eric, why is it that your boy . . ."

Kit cut her off immediately, before she could finish her thought.

"Renee, please don't start. Not now!"

"Eric, you are so lucky my girl asked me not to."

Eric snapped back because he was tired of her side-eye and judgement. "Not to what? I don't have to explain myself to you, Renee. We have our relationship, and you have yours."

Renee realized that she was friends with both Kit and Eric. She wanted to lighten the mood before things got too serious.

"You got a pass tonight. Now let me get one of your chicken fingers, punk."

They all laughed together when Eric changed the topic to the upcoming ladies' night planned for the next day.

Renee questioned why he was asking about ladies' night.

Eric insisted he was just asking a question, just making general conversation. "Renee, you are too suspicious," Eric said.

Renee added, "I know men a little better than you think, and I don't trust them as far as I can throw them. I have learned that men don't just ask a question. Men ask questions for several different reasons. Some are making sure that you won't be anywhere they may be so you won't catch them doing things they shouldn't be doing. Some are hoping to catch you doing things they feel you shouldn't be doing so they will have an excuse for what they have been doing. Some are trying to score brownie points by acting like they care or are truly concerned. Very few actually do care. Most are making plans before you start to answer the question. Knowing you two, I would say you are making plans. So, my question to you is, 'Where are you going?'"

Sam interjected, "So, you don't trust me?"

"I trust you more than most," Renee answered.

Eric wanted to dig a little deeper with Renee's theory on men.

"What is it, exactly, that you think you know about men?" Eric asked.

Renee responded, "I know men are never satisfied. They are constantly pushing their luck. A man would have a good woman in his corner, a real ride-or-die chick, and they will fuck it all up for fifteen minutes with new pussy. A big butt and a smile go a long way for most men."

"You said 'most,' which means we are not all like that," Eric said.

"Yeah, the rest are gay or on the down-low, swinging the peter both ways. I can't forget about the ones who are in jail," Renee said.

Kit wanted in on the conversation, and this was her opportunity.

"That is some nasty shit right there. Can you imagine finding out that your man was cheating on you with another dude? Most women can forgive a man for cheating with another woman, but I think there is no apology for sleeping with a man."

Renee wanted to be real about the situation, so she said, "It's not that easy for a man to say he is gay. Women come out saying they are lesbians, and it is no big deal. Men see a lesbian as a challenge, and most women just don't care about it if they are not into it. Men are seen as disgusting human beings that should be banished from the face of the earth. I don't condone it, but I understand why some brothers would keep it a secret."

Sam felt it was his turn to jump in on the convo when he added, "There is no excuse for that down-low shit. If you are gay, then be gay. Life is too short to live unhappily because of what someone else may feel about who you are and who you choose as your partner in life. And on that note, let's drink — and the second round is on Kit. That is my payment for today's move. I have to go soon because I need some sleep before tomorrow, when I have to help my sister move in with me."

Before they left the parking lot of Friday's, Renee asked Sam if he needed help with moving his sister in.

Sam declined and told her to help her friend settle in and that he would call her later.

As the ladies arrived back at the Tyler residence, Kit was rethinking the sleeping arrangements.

"Renee, I understand if you want your room to yourself. I could sleep in the room in the basement."

"Girl, please. Ain't no way I am letting my girl sleep in the basement next to my crazy cousin, Jacob. He came upstairs the other day talking about how he has to go to work because the hospital called saying he had emergency surgery this morning. I fell out laughing. That fool actually thought he was a doctor. He does need to find a job, though, because he's not that crazy. I don't know why my mother won't have him committed."

"Because she is just like you — always looking out for other people. I can't say it enough: I really appreciate this. Let's go to sleep and prepare for a good time tomorrow," Kit said.

CHAPTER 2
Ladies' Night

"Jessica, can I go with you guys today?" Tawana asked.

"Sure — do you have any money? We play for quarters."

"Play what?" she asked innocently.

"Pokeno."

"I thought you guys were going to a club or something," Tawana asked, sounding puzzled.

"No, we are just going to play cards, drink, watch a movie, and talk shit. You can still come if you want to," Jessica offered.

"I'll come, but you guys should go out."

"Even if we did, you are not old enough to go."

With a smirk on her face, Tawana replied, "I have my ways."

Jessica shook her head in disbelief. "I don't even want to know, but if they catch you at the door, you're on your own. Let me ask Charmaine, before I go inviting more people over to her house," Jessica said.

Jessica went upstairs to call Charmaine, but her phone line was busy.

Charmaine was calling Desire at the same time Jessica was calling her phone, and the call to Desire went through first.

"Hey, Des. What's up? How is everything going for you and the boys? I am so sorry you won't be able to come over tonight."

Desire answered, "It's okay. I don't want to mess up my chances here, but everything else is moving right along. I had a job interview, which I think went well. And as far as the apartment search goes, I am waiting for this program that helps people living in the shelter."

"Still no word from Jay?" Charmaine inquired.

"I don't want to hear from him. I thought the boys would have been affected by not seeing their father, but it has been just the opposite — the kids stopped asking for him. In fact, Jamal said we don't need a daddy because he will take care of me."

Sounding very concerned about that statement, Charmaine said, "Desi, that statement alone says they need or think about him. He is just trying to be strong for you. That is a lot for a six-year-old to handle. You should see if they have a therapist who volunteers there."

"It couldn't hurt, I guess. Maybe I should ask to see a therapist for me as well."

"You should, Des. I am just here, straightened up for ladies' night tonight. I know I originally said that it was just going to be cards, drinks, and a movie, but I think I want to go out. I just want to hear loud music and have some extremely ugly brother push up on me."

The laughter was deep and heartfelt, and Desire told Charmaine, "Girl, you are crazy!"

Charmaine said, "You know that's all I attract when I go out. The dude with gold teeth talking about shorty red bone — 'You got room for one more in those jeans?'"

"I wish I could go. Those were the days. Everything just reminds me of how much I have sacrificed to be with Jay," Desire said as she reminisced.

"Girl, you have to put that life behind you. That is all a thing of the past. Life goes on, with or without you. You might as well move right along with it."

"You are so right, Charmaine. Well, I have to go cook. It is my turn to cook for the whole house. I will speak to you soon. Love you, girl."

Charmaine disconnected the line from Desire and realized she'd missed a call from Jessica. The two ended up playing phone tag, because, when she called Jessica, she was on the other line trying to call her boyfriend, James.

Jessica never got through to James because he was on the phone with Sam.

"Yo. What's up, Sam?" James said. "Yo, you know the girls are going out tonight, so I thought this would be a perfect opportunity for the fellas to chill."

"Yeah, my boy E, who is dating Renee's friend Kit, had the same idea. He said he is going to ask his boy Mike to come through. It will just be us. He said he wanted to check out Club Shotsy's."

James replied, "Bet, I'm with that. I heard that spot is jumping on Saturday. I was trying to get a guest-deejay appearance in there. They want you to pay them to let you mix. That's some bullshit, but I'll meet you guys there at eleven o'clock. Well, let me go, because Jess is calling on the other line now."

He clicked over to the other line. Jessica was so happy to hear his voice that she got all choked up and stumbled over her words because she wasn't expecting him to answer the phone.

James said, "Hey, baby. I was just getting ready to call you because I have this show tonight, and I need to borrow the car. I know you girls are going out, so maybe your sister can drive if you let me use the car."

"Of course, you can. What's mine is yours, sweetheart," Jessica said.

James told her he would be there shortly to pick up the car, and he quickly hung up the phone before she could finish saying, "I love you."

Just then Renee walked into the room to ask if they should take one car, since they were all going to the same place.

Jessica had to reply, "Yes, because James is using my car tonight."

Renee dropped her head and sighed. "Why does he always have your car?"

Jessica, not wanting to be bothered, just looked at her sister standing in the doorway and said, "Renee, please don't start," and then yelled, "Kit, do you mind driving?"

"No, I don't mind driving, but I don't want any of this sisterly bullshit in my car," Kit yelled back.

Renee couldn't guarantee that, so she said, "You know what? I will take my own car because I don't want no problem."

Jessica said, "Well, good, then. Charmaine called and asked if you guys wanted to go out after the Pokeno game to some club."

Both Kit and Renee said, "I'm with that."

"So then bring your get-busy clothes with you, and we can change over there. We are going to start the Pokeno game earlier because we want to get to the club before the line gets crazy, Jessica said. I want to get to the club about 10:30 p.m., because the radio said somebody named Swizz Beats is supposed to be there."

Tawana started laughing and said, "Damn, that is really early. I can tell you girls don't get out much."

"Well, I got to make a run before we go," Renee added.

Kit questioned where she was going, and Renee answered with a slick, sarcastic remark.

"Somewhere that will give you enough time to clean my room before I get back."

Kit raised her eyebrows and asked, "What are you trying to say?"

"You are my girl, but you are sloppy as hell," Renee said as she walked out the door.

Renee entered the door of Walgreen's Pharmacy, looking up and reading the signs above every aisle, until she came to the aisle with the pregnancy tests. Her mind started racing, *Oh, God, Renee. Which one do you choose? First Response, Clear Blue Easy, or EPT? Buy them all, because you never know. Maybe you should just wait for Dr. Carl.*

She stopped and asked a stranger in the aisle, "Excuse me, ma'am. Which one of these is more accurate?"

The lady was offended and responded with a slight attitude. "I don't work here, but you can go to the pharmacy desk and ask one of them."

This lady made her feel stupid and self-conscious, so she thought, *Renee, take your ass home and enjoy what might be your last night of drinking and freedom.*

She got back in her car and turned up the radio to drown out the thoughts in her head.

Back at the house, Tawana was still trying to get a definite approval for her to go out with them to the club tonight.

"Hey, Kit. Can you talk to my aunts and see if they will let me come with you guys to the club tonight? Tawana asked.

Kit responded, "You can't go to the club. You are too young."

"Oh, my God — not you, too! I am going to be bored in here all by myself," Tawana said.

"Then call a friend or go to the mall," Kit suggested.

"With what money? Grandma always says she doesn't have any money."

"Try to ask her when we leave. She may feel sorry for you and give you the money," Kit suggested.

As Tawana was about to walk away, Renee entered the house.

"Oh, good, Renee, you're back. Can I please go with you guys tonight?" Tawana asked.

Renee answered Tawana without thinking about the question.

"Yeah, sure. I don't care. Kit, please give me a few minutes in the room alone."

Tawana, feeling elated that she'd been granted permission to go out with them wanted to double-check that she'd heard what she'd heard correctly.

"Kit, you heard her say I can go, right?"

"Yeah, I did, and something must be wrong with her."

Tawana went skipping down the hall to inform Jessica that Renee said she could go that night.

Renee went into her room still in deep conversation with herself. *Oh, Lord, there are so many women in the world who would welcome this gift! Why did you give it to me? I need a drink. Shit, I can't drink. Already, this "maybe baby" has changed my life.*

Kit, knowing that something was truly wrong with her friend, banged on the door.

"Renee, are you OK?" Kit asked.

"Yes, come in," Renee answered.

"Renee, do you realize you just told your niece she can go to the club tonight?" Kit questioned.

"Yeah, I know. If she gets in, then good for her, but if not, then she is on her own."

"Okay. Well, apart from that, is everything OK with you?"

"Yes, I am fine."

She was answering her friend's question, but her mind was saying, *Why can't I tell my best friend?*

Instead, she asked, "Are we ready to go?"

Kit responded, "We've been ready. We were waiting on you."

All the ladies arrived at Charmaine's house, and Jessica made the introductions.

"Charmaine, this is my sister Renee, her friend Kit, and my niece, Tawana."

"Nice to meet you all," Charmaine said. The food is in the kitchen and drinks on the counter. Please feel free to help yourself. I will set up the table for the game."

Kit admired Charmaine's apartment and wondered if they had any vacancies.

Charmaine told her that she'd opted for the studio apartment to save money, because it cost $1,250 versus the one-bedroom for $1,500. She laughed as she said, "The one-bedrooms all come with a balcony, but if I want fresh air, I will open a damn window and save 250 bucks per month."

Kit laughed and said, "I hear you, girl. I hope they have another studio. But, on another note, I've never played this game, so walk me through it."

"It is very simple, and I plan on taking all of your drinking money."

"That's OK, because I don't plan on buying any of my own drinks," Kit added.

Charmaine inquired about Tawana's age, and Renee let her know that Tawana had already been told what the deal was.

A cell phone started ringing in the room, and everyone turned to Kit to alert her that it was her phone that was ringing.

Kit refused to get up and check her phone, stating, "That ain't nobody but Eric. He is trying to find out what club we are going to tonight. I won't tell him because I don't want him popping up on me."

Renee chimed in, "I told you they had something planned."

"Please don't start with your man-bashing," Kit said.

"All I am saying is that men always have an agenda with a backup plan. We, as women, put all our eggs in one basket all the time. We should keep a spare tire also," Renee added.

Jessica wanted to make it clear to her sister that it was her eggs and her basket, and, if she chose to put all her eggs in her basket, then that was her business. Jessica said, "I don't have to play those games, because James is not like that."

Charmaine, thinking about her past with men, said, "They are all like that."

"Well, not *my* man," Jessica added, feeling very confident.

"Famous last words of every woman who put all *her* eggs in *her* basket," Renee said sarcastically.

Jessica, disgusted by her sister's negative attitude, wanted to put her in her place gently when she said, "Women like you who can't trust anyone drive yourselves crazy. You think everything is a game even when you find a good man. Women like you run the good ones away and end up with shit. Women like you think you have to control a man in order to love a man."

"Oh, please, Jessica. Do you think that, because you have been with one person for two years, it means he won't cheat and that he should be trusted? It doesn't mean he loves you any more. All that means is that you guys are in a comfort zone, and that does not mean love. Think about it — two years, and where are you? Has he proposed marriage? Has he ever suggested that you two move in together? How does he feel about children? When you think about it, all you have is two years. For all you know, James could be with someone else right now."

Kit tried to stop the bitter word exchange between Jessica and Renee by asking, "Why can't you two get along for more than five minutes? It is tiring having to listen to you two all the time, with the same thing."

Renee answered, "We are just talking."

"Well, if that's *talking*, I'd hate to be around when you are *fighting*. With all that hate, you guys are going to corrupt the young one," Charmaine told them.

Tawana smiled and said, "I am taking mental notes, but I do have my own theory about men."

Renee, being the skeptic that she was, said, "Let me hear the inexperienced take on men."

Tawana said, "Okay, Auntie. I would simply say: judge every man on an individual basis. You ladies have made blanket statements about men all night long. When two people get together, it is always good in the beginning. You should enjoy those times and wait to see how he handles himself in the bad times. I think most men will show you who they are without you even having to guess or ask questions. The problem is we, as women, block out those signs, or we make excuses for them. We seem to think we have superpowers. We all think our love is all that it will take to turn a bad man good. The only person who can change a human being is God. I believe if you show them who you are and how you love, then they will either reciprocate that love or disrespect it. If they give it back twofold, then keep him, but if they take advantage of that love, then, by all means, let it go."

Charmaine nodded her head in agreement and said, "I believe you ladies have just been schooled by your own niece."

Jessica was sitting at the table, just staring at her niece in awe.

"My jaw is still on the ground. I am so impressed with how much you have grown up. A child after my own heart. I must admit that was deep for a sixteen-year-old."

Tawana, patting herself on the shoulders, said, "At sixteen, I have gone through some thangs," as she smiled a childlike grin.

Kit jumped up from the table and did a little happy dance because she had taken the win of almost $80 in quarters from the ladies.

Kit said, "Now that I have taken your money, I am going to get ready to party. The first round of drinks is on me, or I should say, 'on you guys.'"

Renee stood to her feet and twirled on her heel, saying, "Okay, you got that, but I will be the showstopper tonight."

Jessica wanted to cut her down a notch by saying, "I hope you know that a showstopper is not always the best dressed — it could be the worst dressed."

Renee laughed and said, "Whatever, hater! I am going to look good."

"We will see about that. The dress I am wearing makes my ass look like it glows in the dark. There won't be a man in the place that won't want this."

"The only person you care about seeing you in that dress is James," Renee said.

"That's right, so don't hate on me because I have a real man," Jessica said.

Renee dove back into her own mind. *I feel so guilty partying and thinking about drinking while I might be pregnant. Maybe I should just act as if I am pregnant. That way, I won't feel so bad if I really am.*

Kit interrupted her thoughts.

"Renee, what are you deep in thought about?" Kit asked.

"Nothing. I can't wait to get my groove on," Renee responded. "Tawana, if they let you in, do not embarrass me."

Tawana winked her eye at Renee and said, "This is not my first time."

All the ladies shouted in unison, "What!"

"I'm just playing, but I know how to act."

"Jessica, please stick to the two-step, because you know you can't dance," Renee warned while laughing.

Jessica said, "I am going to act the fool tonight, and Charmaine, don't say anything on Monday."

Charmaine said, "I hope I find me a man tonight so I don't have to witness that."

As they pulled up to the club, for once, Jessica and Renee were on the same page, questioning Tawana about how she was going to get home just in case she couldn't get in.

Tawana, feeling very confident in her ability to get into the club as they stood in line, told them, "I am getting in, so I don't need cab fare. Ladies, watch me work the door."

"Hey, mister. My birthday is officially tomorrow, and that's when I'll be twenty-one, so can you grant me an early birthday present and let me in?" Tawana asked while stroking his hand.

The bouncer locked his eyes on Jessica and said, "Because you are so cute and honest, I will think about it. On the other hand, if you get your girl in the dress to save me a dance, I will let you all in at no charge."

"No problem," Tawana said, as she turned to Jessica and explained the deal she'd made with the bouncer.

Jessica responded, "I can't dance with him. What if James's friends are in here?"

Renee, growing impatient with her sister acting as if she were married to James, said, "Girl, it's just a dance. Stop acting like that. Say 'Yes,' and then just dodge his ass all night if you have to. Just get us in the damn door."

Jessica stepped up to the front of the line to address the bouncer.

"Hi, my name is Jessica, and I would be honored to dance with you later."

The bouncer introduced himself as Drake and told her he would be looking forward to dancing with her later as the ladies were escorted past the velvet rope. Once they'd made it inside the club, Jessica turned to Tawana with a smile and said, "Little girl, you are a mess."

"I know, but we are in, and I am going to get my freak on," Tawana said.

"Yeah, well — don't get too freaky. I am still your aunt, and I will . . ."

Tawana cut her off as she was walking away and said, "Jess, will you go have a good time for once in your life?"

Raising her voice above the music, Jessica said to Tawana, "If we get separated, meet at the bar upstairs at 2:00 a.m."

Renee said, "First round is on Kit, so let's go to the bar. Tawana, once again, you will not drink with me, and my friends will not be buying you drinks, either."

"Could you stop acting like that? Just let me get one drink — dang," Tawana pouted.

Renee said, "Buy it yourself," thinking that Tawana didn't have any money.

Tawana showed her when she asked the bartender for a Hennessy and ginger ale.

"Where did you get the money from, Tawana?"

"I have my ways," Tawana replied.

"Alright. Well, do you, little girl?"

"Auntie, will you please stop calling me that in here?"

"I will, if you stop calling me 'auntie' in here."

"Renee, what are you drinking?" Kit asked.

"I don't know what I want to start with, so I will let you off the hook this time. I will have water for now, but get Jessica a Long Island Iced Tea. She will think it's a nonalcoholic drink."

Kit started laughing. "You are stupid. That is not nice, but I am going to get it anyway."

Once everyone had their drinks, the ladies made their way over to the dance floor.

Tawana said, "I have schooled you ladies on men. Now watch me work it on the dance floor."

Renee looked Tawana up and down, handed Kit her water, and said, "Little girl, please. I ain't that old, and I still got moves. Watch this."

Tawana was so fascinated with her aunt's ability to move her body to capture the stares of everyone in the room.

Tawana said, "Oh, shit! Look at the men in here, lusting after her. How the hell did she get control of her booty muscle like that?"

Kit smiled and said, "Practice popping one cheek at a time in the mirror — but her damn knees are going to pay for that move right there."

Renee left the dance floor feeling satisfied that she'd let her niece know that she still had moves. She asked Kit for her water as she stepped off proudly.

Renee thought, *Oh, Lord! What kind of mother am I going to be? Out here dropping it like it's hot? Forget about that for one night, and have fun. Renee, you have got to stop talking to yourself before someone notices.*

With the sound of the bass from the music, she was brought back to the present when she asked, "Where is Jessica?"

Kit answered, "She went into the bathroom, hiding from the bouncer. He is cute. She should keep him as a spare tire."

"Kit, please. Jessica acts like she is forty-five years old and married for twenty. I think James is a dog, but I can't say anything?"

"Renee, you're my girl, but why are you so bitter? You have a good man now, but you keep holding on to what those other idiots did to you. If you keep that up, you are sure to lose the one God has sent you."

"Please don't start preaching to me in here, Kit. Men are not to be trusted. Sam is a good guy, but he is still a man. You really think Eric did not ask you to move in because of a homeboy? He knew you needed to get away from your aunt long before his homeboy came into the picture. He is still hiding something."

"Look, Renee. At the end of the day, Eric is my business, and when I decide I don't want to deal with his shit, I know how to walk away. How do you know that it's not *me* who doesn't want to move in with *him*? It was my decision, because I didn't want to jump from the frying pan into the fire. I don't know what it will be like living with a man, and if I made that move and it turned out badly, then I would be right back where I am now. I am done talking to you about this. I'm going to do me."

Renee thought, *Well, now that I've pissed my friend off, and I can't drink, and I can't think of anything else except the fact that I might be pregnant, coupled with the fact that everybody else is on the dance floor except me, I think I should just go home.*

While walking toward the door of the club, Renee bumped right into Sam.

"Sam, what are you guys doing here? I knew you were asking those questions for a reason," she said.

Sam threw the question back at her, "What are you doing here? I thought y'all was having some card game."

"We did, but we decided to come here afterward," Renee answered.

Sam, noticing that she was headed for the door, asked, "Well, where are you going?"

"I don't feel well, so when you see the girls, let them know I went home. Have fun, but not too much."

Renee gave Sam a kiss on the cheek and told him she would text him when she got into the house.

Sam went straight to find Eric to tell him the girls were there in the club.

"Yo, E. I just ran into Renee on her way out, and she said all the girls are here. Hopefully — because this place is packed — we might not see the girls."

Eric said, "Damn. I was trying not to see them at all tonight. I need a break."

Sam said, "I hear you, man. Sometimes Renee can be a bit too much."

The guys were trying to stay low key in the small corner of the club so they wouldn't be seen, but it didn't work.

"Hey, guys. What are y'all doing here?" Tawana said as she walked up behind them.

The guys both whispered, "Damn!" under their breath.

Eric spoke up first. "We should be asking you the same thing."

"Relax, guys. They know I'm here. I came with them," she said.

Tawana said, "Sam, come on. Let's go dance."

Sam responded, "Let me get a drink first. What are y'all drinking?" he asked.

"Oh, snap, Sam. Are you really going to buy me a drink?" Tawana questioned, sounding excited.

"One can't hurt you, right?"

Eric said, "Get me a Corona, and I'll be here when you get back. Tawana, don't hurt the brother."

As Eric was standing in the corner, a random guy came over and sparked a conversation.

"Yo — what's up, man? This place is packed tonight. Are you here alone, or are you on the prowl? I'm sorry; let me introduce myself. My name is Tank. I saw you before at The Lounge."

"Nice to meet you. My name is Eric, and please excuse me. I see my homeboy over there. I'll see you around."

Eric walked away from the weird dude and headed toward his friend across the club.

"Mike, what up? How you been? I noticed you moved some of your things in, but I haven't seen you."

"I have been working a lot, but I'll be there tonight. I'll be back in a minute. I want to speak to the manager about letting me deejay here one night," Mike said.

"Cool. When you come back, we need to talk about some things," Eric told him.

While Eric was walking back to the small corner of the club, he accidently brushed up against Charmaine. Not knowing who she was, he simply apologized and kept moving.

Charmaine thought to herself, *I must be losing my touch. Not even one ugly brother asked me to dance. Thank God Kit paid for that first drink, or I would have paid for all of my own drinks tonight.*

Just then this guy walked up beside her, asked the bartender for a B52, and told her to light it up.

Charmaine thought to herself, *Good God, he is gorgeous, and what the hell is a B52?* She figured, *What the hell? It can't hurt to say "Hello."*

"Hi. My name is Charmaine. Can you tell me what that drink was that you ordered?"

"It is a layered drink. The top layer is 151-proof alcohol, and that's why it ignites. My name is Mike, by the way. Would you like to try it?"

"Sure, why not? I have to blow out the flame first, right?" Charmaine questioned.

"Of course — wouldn't want you to burn that pretty face."

"Thank you. Your face is not bad, either," she said as she gave him a sexy wink.

Charmaine thought about what she had just said and felt embarrassed. *What the hell am I thinking? He's prettier than me.*

Instead of making her feel awkward about her comment, he said, "Look, Ms. Charmaine, I have to get up early, but I would love to tell you more about that drink and others. If you are interested, we can leave and go to a smaller, less-noisy place."

Charmaine knew that girl code dictates that, when you come together, you leave together, so she said, "Let me find my girls and let them know I am leaving."

Mike said, "Let's sneak out the back door, and you can send them a text message that you left with your future husband."

Charmaine blushed as she said, "You are very sure of yourself — and I don't even know my new last name yet."

Mike winked his eye, grabbed her hand, and led her toward the back door as he said, "All in due time."

During this time, Jessica finally surfaced from her hiding place in the bathroom and was searching the club for her girls, when she bumped right into the bouncer, Drake.

"Hello, Ms. Jessica. Were you trying to dodge me?" Drake asked.

Jessica replied quickly, "No, not at all. I have been trying to find my friends and sister."

"Well, the birthday girl has been on the dance floor downstairs all night; the brown-skinned girl left two hours ago, and the light-skinned girl with the mole above her lip left with some guy out the back door about an hour ago, so can I have this dance now?" Drake asked.

"Yes, but I must warn you, I really cannot dance," Jessica said as she gave him an innocent smile.

"Okay. So then, before you embarrass us both, let's just have a drink and talk for a minute."

"In that case, let me start by telling you that I have a man," Jessica said.

Drake, wanting her to relax a little, said, "It's just a conversation, not a proposal. And, I like the way you said your 'man' and not 'boyfriend.' So, what do you do for a living, Ms. Jessica?"

"I am the executive accountant of the largest accounting firm in Nassau County," Jessica responded proudly.

"Well, that sounds special. I am just a cop, but I do this on the side. I have my own house in Freeport."

"I live in Roosevelt, but I know a lot about Freeport. What street do you live on?" she asked.

"I live on Independence Avenue," he answered.

"Oh, wow. That's not that far from me. Freeport and Roosevelt are neighboring towns. How long have you lived there?"

"I recently moved there from Brooklyn, so I don't know a lot of people," he said.

She tried to be coy with her next question. "You and your girlfriend, or you and your mother?"

"That is cute, but I am a bachelor. My mother passed away two years ago, and I was what some would call a momma's boy. She worked hard for that house in Brooklyn, and everything in it reminded me of her. I decided to sell her house and allow myself time to heal without all the reminders. And before you ask your next question, the answer is 'No.' I do not have any children. I am twenty-six years old, with no girlfriend and no kids."

Jessica said, "I can feel your mother smiling down on you. I don't know you at all, but I would say you made her proud."

"Well, Ms. Jessica. Tell me a little about yourself."

"Well, I am twenty-five years old, and, like you, I have no children. I told you about my job already, so that leaves the answer to my living situation. I do not own my own home, but my sister and I split all the bills on the house my mother owns."

Drake chuckled as he said, "That is a nice way to say you live with your mother."

"I want to move out, but my sister doesn't make that much, and between her and my mom, they couldn't afford to maintain that house."

"So, you plan on letting that hold you back forever?" Drake asked.

"That is rude, considering I just met you, Mr. Drake."

"I wasn't trying to be rude, but it sounds like you are sacrificing your happiness and what you really want for someone else."

"I have been trying to convince my mother to get a smaller house, one that they can afford, but she just keeps dragging more and more people up in that house. I think she likes having all the company. I personally hate it. There are days when I come home from work and I don't want to see anyone."

Drake listened intently and offered, "You think you want that until you have it. There are days I wish I had someone to come home to. When a man or a woman achieves more in life, the harder it becomes to find a partner to share it with."

Jessica gave his words some thought before she replied. "I thank God every day that I have James in my life. He fulfills every emotional as well as physical need that I have. He makes me want for nothing."

Drake caught the hint with the reference to James, so he concluded with, "I hope he truly deserves and appreciates you for the beautiful woman that you are. It has been a pleasure talking to you, but my break is over."

"It was nice to meet you, Drake."

"Hey, you actually remembered my name! Should I take that as a sign of something?" He smiled, eagerly anticipating her answer.

"Yes, a sign that I truly enjoyed our conversation, and before you go, I want to apologize because I *was* dodging you earlier. I am guilty of judging a book by the cover."

Drake tilted his head and shrugged his shoulder as he said, "No problem. I get that a lot. Maybe I will see you here again someday. Goodnight, Ms. Jessica."

Jessica walked off in search of the girls once again.

Eric finally caught up with Sam and let him know that he'd noticed Tawana had him on the dance floor all night.

Sam replied, "I know, man. She wouldn't let me leave the dance floor because she didn't want any of these dudes trying to push up on her. Where were you all night?"

Eric dropped his head in disappointment, "Kit found me at the bar. Let's just say my night did not go well. Are you ready to go?"

"Yeah, but we got to wait for the girls. They all went to the bathroom."

"Let's leave before they come back!" Eric shouted over the music.

Sam couldn't do that in clear conscience, so he said, "Let's at least make sure they get back to their car safe."

Eric gave him a disapproving look and said, "Do you have to always be the perfect gentlemen?"

"Whatever, man. Right is right."

CHAPTER 3

Facing Facts

Another stupid Monday at the office, Jessica thought, as she called Charmaine to come into her office.

"Please close the door, and tell me what happened to you on Saturday," Jessica questioned Charmaine.

"Well, ma'am, I met this guy named Mike at the club, and he was so nice. We went for a walk along the Belt Parkway, and everything was perfect — the weather, the company, and the conversation."

"I bet it was. I got your text message; your 'future husband,' huh?"

Charmaine smiled from ear to ear and said, "I was just playing then, but he definitely has potential."

"Well, I hope it works out. You deserve to be happy. I thought James would have been calling me all night, but he didn't. He texted me early this morning to tell me he loves me and that he didn't want to crowd my space. I love the fact that he trusts me so completely. I thought that was special."

"It's good that you have a man like that in your life. It makes the relationship less stressful. I know you don't go out much, but did you have a good time on Saturday, Jess?"

"I had a very nice time. That bouncer dude turned out to be a very nice guy," Jessica said.

Charmaine looked up as if she couldn't believe what she was hearing.

"Oh, wait. Does James have competition, or what?"

"Of course not," Jessica answered quickly. "I just said he was a nice guy. Let's get back to work. We'll talk later."

"Okay, but Mike and I are going to see *The Color Purple* on Broadway this Saturday. Do you think James would like to see *The Color Purple*?"

"If I say I want to see it, he would go," Jessica explained.

"Please ask him because I'm nervous about this date. I don't want to give it up on the official first date, but this guy makes me want to do things."

Jessica laughed at Charmaine and told her she would let her know what James said.

Charmaine left the office still smiling, thinking about her date, when the phone began to ring at her desk.

"Hey, Charmaine — it's Desire. How are you?"

"Hey, girl. I was just thinking about you. Did you find a place yet?"

"No, not yet, but that's not what I was calling about. I wanted to know how your ladies' night went."

"It was really good. I still wish you could have been there. I lost the Pokeno game, but I think I won a man."

Desire, completely caught off guard by Charmaine's comment, managed to muster up only the word, "What!"

"Yes, girl. We went to Club Shotsy's afterward, and I met this guy. He is beautiful. We talked all night, and I don't know how I found the strength to keep my panties on. I thought I was losing it for a minute, because not even the ugly brothers in the club approached me. When I think about it, Mike didn't even approach me — I approached him."

Desire let out a chuckle type of laugh and said, "Girl, you are crazy. You did *what* now?"

"I walked up to him and asked him about his drink, and that started the conversation."

Desire, wanting to know more details about this 'Mike' person, asked, "How old is he, and where does he work?"

The moment Desire asked those questions, Charmaine thought about their conversation, and she realized she didn't have an answer for Desire.

Charmaine said, "You know, we talked about everything that night but that."

Desire said, "Well, before you drop your drawers, ask to see the last two pay stubs and a lease agreement."

"Well, damn! You make it sound like he is applying for a loan," Charmaine replied.

Desire retorted, "He is — a loan on the coochie."

"It is so sad that those are the questions you have to ask nowadays. I am glad I spoke to you, because I was so caught up in his pretty face, I forgot all about the basics."

"I am here for you, girl, because I would hate to see you end up in my predicament. On another note, I have good news because I actually start my job tomorrow. I was once a paralegal, and now I have been reduced to a file clerk. Child, I never took public transportation in my life, and now, I am taking two buses with a ten-minute walk for a job that pays $25,000 a year."

In true supportive-friend mode, Charmaine offered, "It is all a step in the right direction. The things you had before, you took for granted; now, because of what you went through, you will appreciate everything that life has to offer, including that $25,000-a-year job."

"Charmaine girl, you have become my conscience. I know everything you said is true, but it gets hard to see the good in anything for me nowadays."

"Well, girl, I have to get some work done, so congratulations again on finding a job, and I will speak to you soon."

Desire disconnected the line with Charmaine just as Renee walked in the door of the shelter.

"Hello, Ms. Renee. Are you OK?" Desire asked.

"Yes, I'm fine. I just have a lot on my mind, but I hear congratulations are in order. I heard you found a job."

"Yes, God is smiling on me. The boys made me an early Mother's Day card. They are my world and all that I live for."

"Have you heard anything from their dad?" Renee asked.

"Not yet. Jay is nothing and nobody to me at this point in my life. I just spoke to a friend, and she set me straight. Jay leaving me was a blessing, so my future is bright."

Millie's voice echoed through the hall as she called Renee to the telephone.

Before Renee ended her conversation with Desire, she told her that she hopes the Lord keeps smiling on her.

When Renee answered the phone in the office, it was the receptionist at Dr. Carl's office.

"This is Dr. Carl's office. Please hold for Dr. Carl."

Renee felt a sinking feeling in the pit of her stomach as he asked how she had been feeling.

"I am fine, Doc. I have been really anxious about my results."

"Well, I have them for you now. Are you ready for them?"

"Dr. Carl, would you please just tell me?"

"You are very pregnant, and you should see your ob-gyn as soon as possible," Dr. Carl told her.

Renee received the information but was hoping the doctor was just playing a trick on her.

"Doc, are you serious? Because I know how much you like to joke around."

"Not this time, Renee. I am serious, and I can't wait to meet the newest member of the Tyler family."

"Thank you, Dr. Carl," Renee said.

Feeling the weight of learning that she was actually pregnant, her mind began to wonder. *Lord, what am I gonna do with a baby? How do I tell Sam and my family? They are going to be disappointed with me. I barely have enough money to support myself. Jessica will never leave and have her own life if she feels she has to take care of my baby. Lord, how do I accept this gift when I can't do right by it? Just tell Sam he's the father, and let him weigh in on what happens next?*

Millie interrupted her thoughts to tell her that line 2 was for her, also.

"Hey, Renee. It's Sam. I was calling to tell you I can't go out to dinner tonight. I have to take care of something."

"But Sam, I need to talk to you," she said.

Sam rushed her off the phone and told her, "I will call you or come by if it is not too late. Talk to you later. I have to go."

Renee disconnected the line and immediately dialed Kit's number.

"Hello, Kit. When you get this message, call me."

Renee thought to herself, *Okay, well, Kit didn't answer. Maybe I should try Jessica.*

Renee noticed that her left hand was rubbing her belly as she dialed Jessica's number with her right hand. She decided not to leave Jessica a message when she didn't answer her phone, either.

What the hell is going on? I just found out my life is about to change forever, and no one has time to talk to me.

Millie yelled from the adjoining office, "Renee, we have three new coming in tonight."

It's true what they say: Life doesn't stop for you and your problems, Renee thought to herself.

Renee walked out of the office, yelling back toward the adjoining office, "I'll go make sure the rooms are ready upstairs."

Jessica was back in her office, staring out the window, wondering why she hadn't heard from James. She picked up the phone to call and leave another message, but he answered the phone on the first ring, which startled her.

"James, baby. What's wrong? You have been so distant and down lately."

"Jess, I have so much going on right now. I think about what you said about us getting our own place and possibly having a baby. I want to make our dreams come true. I need to find a way to make more money so I can take care of you."

"James, I don't need to be taken care of. I make really good money, and I can take care of both of us."

James was uncomfortable with what he was hearing, and he wanted to make it clear to her that it was unacceptable.

"I am not that kind of man. I have to wear the pants in my relationship, so to speak."

"I know that, but that's what loving someone and being in a relationship is all about. When you are down, I will have your back and vice versa," Jessica said.

"Jess, I love you for saying that, but I have to go and make a few phone calls. I want to call Sam and apologize for standing them up the other night, among other calls. I am trying to make some money moves. I will see you later."

James called Sam, but he was on the phone with his homeboy Eric, so he told him that he would call him back.

"Yo, Eric. That was James on the other line. He just wanted to apologize for flaking the other night. What you got going on tonight?" Sam asked.

Eric was silent for a second before he answered. Then he said, "Yo, let me call you back. I think Mike just came into the house, and I need to holla at him real quick."

"Make sure you hit me back, man," Sam said before he hung up.

Eric was more focused on speaking to Mike, and, so, he never heard it when Sam asked him to call back, because he had already hung up the phone.

"Mike, why is it every time I walk into the room, you are rushing out?" Eric questioned.

"Man, please do not start with me today," Mike said, sounding very aggravated.

Eric replied, sounding just as frustrated, "We need to talk about the other night."

"No, we do not!" Mike yelled.

Eric yelled back, "We had sex! That *is* something to talk about."

The shouting match began, and Mike screamed, "I have a girl, and I am not gay!"

Eric shouted, "I have a girl, too, and what we did was *gay*! We have been friends since the day we met, and I will admit I had an attraction toward you then."

Mike didn't want to hear this, so he said, "Man, don't start the shit. I was drunk, and so were you."

"Liquid courage, that's what they call it — right, Mike? Drinking is not an excuse, and I realize that. I used the alcohol to give in to what I was feeling for you. I think I loved you the first time we met at the club. I dreamt that you would be my first experience, and my dream came true. It was everything I imagined it would be. You were so gentle with me. When you entered me, I felt my body explode from the inside out. Your kisses were light, sweet, and tender. Your touch sent minor shock waves down my spine, which caused little goose pimples to form all over my body. Your warm touch melted it all away. You loved the way I gently caressed and kissed your manhood. You can't say you didn't feel that. You were into the whole thing, Mike. Admit it."

"Man, would you listen to yourself? I don't remember that at all! What the hell is wrong with you?"

"Mike, think about it. We'd just met, and, within a week, I let you move in. Why do you think I was even at that club? You knew who I was and how I got down."

Mike was still denying Eric's recollection of the events.

"I was only at that club trying to get a deejaying gig. I felt bad when I saw what was happening to you, so I helped you fight back. None of that makes me gay. I never asked why you were there, because it was none of my business. You said you had a girl, and that was good enough for me. If this living arrangement is going to be a problem for you, I will move out," Mike told Eric.

"Mike, I don't want you to go, but we can't pretend that it didn't happen."

"As far as I am concerned, it didn't happen. I don't even remember it."

"You keep telling yourself that, Mike. You keep thinking that it was the alcohol. Keep convincing yourself that you did not like it as much as I loved it. Michael, you were the one who initiated it," Eric reminded him.

Mike jumped up from edge of the bed, saying, "Now you are just lying!"

"Mike, you wanted to videotape it and sell it on the Internet to make some extra money. Do you remember that?"

"What do you want from me, E?"

"I want you to admit that it happened!"

"It happened — OK? Now what? I don't want to think about it, remember it, or anything else about it. I am not gay, bisexual, or on the down-low!"

"Alright, Mike, I get it. Please calm down. I want you to stay. Don't worry — I won't make any moves on you."

Mike sat back down on the bed and, in a calmer tone, asked, "I thought you said you had a girl."

Eric replied, "I do, and she is a sweetheart, but sometimes, I have this urge and need to dibble and dabble."

Mike questioned, "I thought you said I was your first."

"You were my first sexual-intercourse experience. I have kissed and performed oral pleasures for handsome men such as yourself."

Just hearing that became too much for Mike to listen to, so he said, "I don't want to ever speak about this again. I am leaving, and I will see you later."

Eric lay back on the bed, and tears formed in his right eye and rolled down his cheek from the left eye. He sat up, grabbed the phone, and called Kit.

"Hello. Kit. This is Eric. Can we meet at the park? I want to talk to you about something."

Kit was worried because she wasn't familiar with the tone in his voice.

"Sure. Baby, is everything alright?"

"Yes, everything is fine. I just need a friend right now," Eric said.

Kit rushed over to the park, leaving Renee a message letting her know she was meeting Eric in the park.

As she walked into the park, she spotted Eric sitting on a swing.

"Hey, Kit. Thank you for meeting me on such short notice."

"I am always here for you. Friends first — always remember that."

"Kit, I hope you mean that because that's what I need you to be right now. Here we go."

Kit interrupted him to ask, "Are you sure you don't want to go someplace else to talk? Maybe we can go back to your place or get a room."

"No, I chose the park for a reason."

"Eric, you are making me nervous."

Eric decided to ease into what he was about to reveal by asking general questions.

"Let me ask you a question: When was the last time we were intimate?"

Kit answered, "It has been about a month or so. Why? Is that what this is about, Eric? I have been busy, and so have you."

"Kit, we were never that busy, or *I* was never that busy. I just couldn't do it anymore."

Kit was still puzzled about what was going on, and she asked innocently, "Are you telling me there is something wrong with your manhood?"

"No, everything works just fine. Just let me speak for a moment, totally uninterrupted."

"OK, but try to get to the point fairly quickly. I feel my blood pressure risin', Eric."

"For as long as I can remember, I have had certain impulses. I have tried to put it behind me, but I can't fight it anymore. Sex for me is not the same anymore. I find myself wanting to explore new things. I go out, and I meet people who have the same affliction as I do. I have tried therapy to help me deal with this burden. In my first session, I was told to confront my feelings and give in to the very first instinct I feel when the urge arrives. I went out one night alone, and the impulse hit me, so I went with the feeling, and I kissed another man."

Kit jumped down from the swing, took two steps, got in his face, and yelled, "You did *what*? How could you? Why would you? How dare you?"

Eric tried to reach for her hand to calm her down, but she pulled away and started pacing.

Eric pleaded with her.

"Please hear me out, and listen as a friend. I have been dealing with this for a long time now. I am telling you this because I care about you. I never had sex with a man until recently, and that is why I can't deny it anymore. I love you, and you are a good woman, but I am not the man for you. I am in love with someone else. My feelings for him cannot be denied any longer."

She wasn't listening to anything he was saying. She just kept pacing, talking out loud.

"I need to get checked. Fuck 'being your friend first.' My *health* comes first. You may have given me some disease."

He tried to put her mind at ease by saying, "I was never with a man sexually until a couple of weeks ago. You and I weren't having sex at that time."

"You were sucking dick and kissing other men. How disgusting are you? You make me sick to my stomach. Does Sam know you are gay?"

"I did not know I was gay, so how could I tell anyone?" Eric said. "I will ask you to do me one last favor and let me tell my friend myself."

Kit was walking away as she was talking loudly but then turned back toward him, still talking loudly.

"I don't care what you do. You put me at risk and have the nerve to say that you love me? You are lucky we met in the park, or I would have tried to kill your gay ass. Tell me something: was that your lover who moved in with you?"

"He wasn't my lover when he moved in, but yes, he was the first man I had intercourse with and is the man I love."

She grabbed her head and started running toward her car, yelling, "Oh, God. I don't want to hear any more of this sick shit. I am leaving — and don't ever speak to me again."

Eric stood up to give chase but suddenly stopped as he said, "Kit, I am truly sorry. I never meant to hurt you. I just didn't know who I was, and now I've found myself. I just want to live my life, from this point on, free to be the real me."

Before she slammed her car door, she yelled back, "Go to hell, dick licker!"

Kit drove back to the Tyler house without turning on her lights or stopping for any stop signs. She was hoping that Renee would be at Sam's house so she could have the room to herself, but no such luck. As she opened the room door, Renee was sitting on the bed, staring at her.

"Kit, I am so glad you are home. I need to talk to you — it's important," Renee said before she noticed that Kit was crying. "Kit, what's wrong? Why are you crying?"

Kit was so distraught she started babbling. "Renee, I don't understand. Why me? I give someone my all, and they give me shit. I tell someone I love him and that I will be there for him always, and he tells me he's gay."

Renee was trying her best to slow the conversation down so she could grasp what was being told to her.

"Who told you that? What are you talking about?"

Kit stopped crying for a brief moment to look Renee in the eye and said, "Eric Wright, or should I say 'Eric Wrong'!"

Renee gave her the Gary Coleman "What-you-talking-'bout-Willis?" look and asked, "What the hell are you talking about? Eric is not gay."

Kit's tears started to flow again as she replied, "Yes, he is. He told me himself. That's what he wanted to talk about."

"He said he is gay?" Renee repeated.

Kit answered, "He said he had sex with a man, and he has been going to gay bars kissing and sucking dick. If that's not gay enough for you, then I don't know what to tell you."

Renee switched gears from shock and disbelief to concerned friend.

"Are you OK? What made him tell you now? Please, Kit, do not tell me he caught something and gave it to you."

"He said he's telling me because he loves me. What kind of love makes a man stay with a woman for a whole year while having an affair with another man?"

Renee was confused again by Kit's last statement, so she repeated what she thought she heard in the form of a question.

"He was with this guy for your entire relationship?"

"He said 'No,' but what am I to believe? It doesn't matter anyway. The most important thing is to go to the doctor and make sure I don't have anything. Thank God for the last month, because we weren't having sex. After I left the park on my way back here, I kept thinking, *What did I do wrong?* Maybe if I was freakier in bed, things would be different."

"Girl, now you are just talking crazy. If his sick and twisted ass wasn't sure about his sexuality, then he shouldn't have been in a relationship. If you know you have those feelings or thoughts going through your mind, then you need to make a decision before subjecting other people to your personal issues. That has nothing to do with you. You could have been swinging from a shower rod, and that would not have changed who he is."

"Well, he definitely has issues," Kit said.

"There is nothing we can do about his problem, but we need to get you checked out to make sure you're OK. You can go to Dr. Carl. He is very good. Do you want me to make an appointment for you?" Renee offered.

"Just give me the number, and I'll take care of it. What the hell do I say? 'Hello, I need to be checked for any and all diseases because my boyfriend of a year has been sleeping with men behind my back,'" Kit said in a sarcastic manner.

"Kit, I know you are trying to be funny, but that is exactly what you should say. Listen, no one is judging you in this situation. You are the victim here. Dr. Carl is very discreet and professional. If he finds anything, he will call you himself."

"Thank you, girl. I just want to go to sleep," Kit said.

"Everything will be OK. You just get some rest."

Renee stepped out of the room to give Kit some privacy, and then her mind started wondering. *Her issues topped my dilemma by a mile. I would have felt like such a fool if I was complaining about a baby and she may have some disease. God, bless my friend, and keep her safe. Now back to me, Lord, for one second. Why can't I find someone to confide in about this baby? Maybe I should tell Sam before I tell anyone else.*

Renee decided to pull the trigger and tell Sam about the baby.

"Hello, Lisa. Is Sam home yet?" Renee asked when she called his house.

"Sam went to some comedy club with my other brother and his girlfriend," Lisa told her,

Renee didn't really get along with Sam's sister, Lisa, so she didn't want to give her the satisfaction of knowing that her brother had lied to her about his plans that night.

"Oh, yeah — I forgot all about that," Renee said. "Maybe that's why he's not answering his cell phone. Thank you, anyway. Bye, Lisa."

She hung up the phone thinking, *I really hate that bitch.* Renee sat on the stairs holding her phone in her hand as she thought, *What part of the game is this? Sam never mentioned anything about a comedy club. If the brother went with his girl, then who the hell did Sam go with? Lord, I know my man is not cheating on me already. Here I am, pregnant with his baby, and he is out doing God knows what with God knows who. Renee, just like you would tell your friends — give him the benefit of the doubt, and see what he has to say. Lord, I am going to bed now, but for his sake, he'd better be the third wheel in that equation, or Lord, one of your children is coming home to meet you face to face. Renee, go to sleep and get ready for work in the morning before you talk yourself into a murder charge.*

CHAPTER 4

Suspicious

"Good morning, Ms. Millie. Is Ms. Renee coming in to work today?" Desire asked.

"She should be in a little later. Where are the boys?" Millie asked.

"They were playing in the back yard," Desire answered.

The kids were chasing the ball to the front of the house when a car pulled up and Jay stepped out.

The boys ran screaming, "Daddy, Daddy! Are you coming to stay with us?"

"How are you guys? I have missed you so much," Jay said. "Jamal, what's wrong? You don't want to give Daddy a hug?"

Jamal just stood there, looking at him with a disappointed look on his face.

"I just wanted to see you and maybe take you to school, if your mother doesn't mind," Jay said.

Before Jamal could respond, Desire was at the door telling the boys to come into the house and get ready to go.

As the boys ran past her, she hesitated before she walked toward Jay, standing there leaning against the driver's side door.

"Jay, what are you doing here, and how did you find us?"

"It's a small world, and people hear things. I just wanted to see my boys."

"Well, you have seen them. Now, please leave before they come back," she snapped back.

"What is your problem? I didn't come here to fight with you," Jay said.

"Then why did you come? I know you didn't think I would welcome you with open arms. You left me and your boys broke and homeless. Did you come here to give us some money so we can move out of the shelter?"

Jay just stood there and let her speak, and she did not let up.

"I doubt that very seriously, so do me and your sons a favor, and do not come back here again. Forget about us — the same way you did when you moved out," Desire advised Jay.

"Desire, I didn't mean for things to turn out that way, but I did try to make it work," was all Jay had to offer her as an explanation.

"Get the hell out of my face, and go back to the woman who is stupid enough to be your next victim."

"Desire, stop acting like that. If you really want me to leave, then I will leave, but you can't say that I didn't try to make an effort to be a part of my kids' life."

She gave him a stern look of death, and she said, "Do you realize I was living from hotel to hotel, dragging these boys around like luggage, and you were nowhere to be found? I called everyone I knew who knew you, and no one had seen or heard from you. You didn't even leave a forwarding phone number. Go to hell, and leave us alone. We will be just fine without you. I've started a new job, and I don't want to be late, so goodbye. I will tell the boys you had to leave."

Jay got into the car thinking to himself, *What is wrong with a man trying to see his kids? Why can't she see that I did what I did to help her make a better life for her and the boys? I was only going to bring further heartache if I stayed in the situation. I did a good thing, and maybe one day, she will see that. I just don't want my boys to completely forget about me.*

Meanwhile, over at the Tyler house, Jessica was pacing back and forth, looking out the window every two minutes.

Renee stood there and watched her for a brief moment before asking her what the hell she was doing.

"James still has my car, and I haven't heard from him all night," Jessica said.

"He will show up. He always does," Renee told her.

"I know, but today, I have a major meeting, and I wanted to get to work early. I tried calling his phone several times, but he didn't answer."

"Do you want a ride or what?"

"No, I will give him a few more minutes," Jessica said.

Renee called to Tawana from the bottom of the stairs.

"Tawana, let's go. I will take you to school on my way to work."

Hearing Tawana's name being called reminded Jessica about the night before.

"Tawana, by the way, you are not grown. The next time you come strolling up in here after two in the morning, I will tell Mommy. Do you hear me?" Jessica warned her.

Tawana gave her the *whatever* look as she said, "Yes, I hear you. Stop hating on me because I have a life."

Renee decided to add her two cents to the conversation by asking, "Where the hell were you until two in the morning?"

Tawana answered, "Out with some friends. Do you mind?"

Renee had enough on her mind, so she decided to let it go at that.

"I don't have time for this. Let's go. Kit, I will call you later. Are you going to work today?"

"Not if I get an appointment with Dr. Carl today," Kit answered.

"Let me know what happens, either way. Tawana, let's go, and you'd better not get in my car talking that slick shit you were talking to Jessica," Renee told her.

Tawana had been dealing with some drama of her own, and she decided to pick Renee's brain on the way to school.

"Renee, have you ever found yourself liking one of your best friends' boyfriend more than you should?" she asked.

"No, that would be breaking all the rules of friendship. If I ever found myself in that situation, I would remove myself from the equation. Meaning, we would never all go out together anymore, and I would just stay away from him completely. Is this a problem you are having or someone you know?"

"Yes, a little bit, but he says he has been developing feelings for me as well."

"Let me ask you this: Is your friend truly in love with him, or is this a semi-new relationship? Not that it really matters because you're still breaking girl code."

Tawana looked down and started playing with her fingers as she answered, "Semi-new, but she seems to be into him. On second thought, I really can't tell what she feels for him, but he says she takes him for granted."

Renee questioned, "How can someone be taken for granted in the beginning of a relationship? That's the honeymoon phase — everything is good at that time."

Tawana answered, "Simple things like when she calls, she won't say 'Hello' or ask how you're doing. He says it is the small things that count, and she doesn't do the small things."

"Well, let me ask you this, Tawana: When are you and her boyfriend doing all this talking?"

"We speak on the phone every now and then, but last night, I violated all the rules, and we went out on a date."

"So that's who you were with last night that had Jessica about to snitch on you," Renee said as she laughed.

Tawana smiled and said, "Yes, and I had a great time."

"You need to put a stop to it before someone gets hurt. I will see you at home later. There is nothing worth violating a true friendship over."

Tawana got out of the car, still feeling confused and conflicted over her feelings, saying, "Thanks for listening. See you later."

Renee drove straight to work, singing loudly in the car, trying to drown out her inner thoughts.

Because the shelter was located on a one-way street, across from an auto-body shop, where you can see the front of the house from the two-way traffic, you had to drive around the block in order to pull up to the front of the house. As Renee was getting closer to the shelter, before going around the block, she looked across the yard of the auto-body shop and thought she recognized the car pulling away from the shelter.

"Hello, boss lady," Renee yelled as she walked through the door. "Was that car leaving from in front of this house or passing down the street?"

"I'm just walking in, so I don't know," Beryl said.

"I need to make a quick phone call, and then I will do the inventory of the pantry."

I hope Jess answers her damn phone, she thought.

"Jessica, did James get there yet?"

"No, not yet, and I am pissed," Jessica responded.

"I thought I saw your car by my job when I was pulling up," Renee told her.

Jessica wasn't really paying attention to Renee because she was looking out the window and saw her car pulling up.

"Let me go — he just pulled up in front of the house. Later!"

As Jessica got into the car, she decided it was time to get to the bottom of a few things.

"James, what's going on with you lately? This is not like you. You don't call anymore. You don't answer your phone. You're coming late to pick me up. I told you I had a meeting today, so what's your excuse?"

"Oh, my God, Jessica. I was asleep last night, and this morning, I had to make a stop. I left the phone inside the car, and that's why I missed your phone call. I figured it didn't make sense to call because I was on my way here anyway."

"Was that stop in Hempstead?" Jessica asked.

"Why do you ask that?"

"Renee thought she saw you by her job. James, listen. I hate to do this, but I need my car during the week because I can't afford to be late."

"I understand, Jess. My car will be ready soon. I was not trying to take advantage of the situation. Call me later, and let me know if you are going to work late. I will pick you up, and you can have your car back then."

Jessica, feeling guilty, asked, "How will you get around until your car is fixed?"

"I will borrow my man's car. It's not a big deal. When I pick you up later, you can drop me off over there so I can pick up his car."

"I am sorry about this, James."

"Jess, it's OK. Go inside, and call me later. I love you, babe."

Jessica got out of the car feeling satisfied with the way the conversation had gone.

Inside the office, Charmaine was wondering where Jessica was until the phone rang and she heard Mike's voice.

"Good morning, Ms. Charmaine. Are we still on for this weekend on Broadway?"

"Yes, we are, but do you mind if I bring a friend and her boyfriend?"

"That will be fine, as long as I get to see you," Mike said. Enjoy your day, and I hope to speak to you soon."

Charmaine had been longing to hear from him and was disappointed that the conversation was so quick.

"That's it? Why the rush off the phone? I'm not busy because my boss is not here yet. She must be running late."

"No rush — it's just that I've reached my destination, and I have to go inside," he said.

"OK, Mike. I can't wait to see you this weekend. I will speak to you soon."

Mike had already hung up the phone, so she never got a response to her statement.

She got off the phone and started to call Desire, but Jessica finally walked in the door, ready for work.

"Hello, ma'am. Welcome to Dr. Carl's office. How may I help you?"

"My name is Desire Williams, and I have an appointment with Dr. Carl for my test results."

"Please have a seat, and we will call you in just a minute," the receptionist said.

As Desire sat down, the door to Dr. Carl's office swung open again.

Desire looked at this woman with *What the fuck?* eyes, because the door almost hit her.

"Hello. Is Dr. Carl in?"

Yes, but do you have an appointment?" the receptionist asked.

"No, but I need to see the doctor as soon as possible."

"Sure, fill this out, and have a seat. Someone will be with you shortly."

Both women sat silently in the waiting area until the sound of the receptionist broke the weird silence.

"Ma'am, are you ready with those papers?"

"Yes, I am. They are completed."

The nurse recognized the referring patient name and smiled pleasantly.

"Oh, you were referred by Renee Tyler. She was here not too long ago."

"Yes, she is a very close friend of mine."

Desire, overhearing the conversation said, "Excuse me, Miss. I don't mean to be in your business, but did you say 'Renee Tyler'?"

"Yes, I did. Do you know her or something?"

"Yes, I do, but it is not like that, so you can calm down. I mean her no harm. She works at my current address. She is a very nice person. I wasn't aware she used Dr. Carl also. That's all."

"Well my name is Kit, and Renee is my best friend. What's your name?"

"I am Desire. Renee has gone above the call of duty for me. She is trying to get me a job in her sister's office building."

"That would be a good job to get. Jessica has a lot of pull in that building," Kit said.

"I need anything that pays more than what I am getting now at this new job I am starting later on today," Desire said.

"I hear that. I am in the same position. Her sister's secretary isn't doing too bad for herself, either. We went to her house on Saturday to play some game called 'Pokeno,' and, of course, I won."

Desire, thinking that it couldn't be that much of a coincidence, asked, "Is her assistant named 'Charmaine Dupree'?"

"I know her name is Charmaine and that she has a nice studio apartment, but I don't know her last name," Kit responded.

Desire, smiling very hard, said, "Charmaine is my best friend."

"This world is too small. I am glad I didn't say anything bad about her. I know I just met you, and I shouldn't be all up in your business, but why are you living in the shelter?" Kit asked.

"I don't mind, but long story short, my kids' father left us flat broke. Hell, he is the reason I am here today."

"We have something in common. My man, I mean ex-man, is the reason I am here. Sometimes I wish God would have made me gay," Kit said jokingly.

Desire started laughing and shaking her head in agreement.

"You can laugh, but it's the truth," Kit said.

"God made us strong, so we should use it to our advantage when dealing with the men he put in our lives. Dealing with Jay, I had to borrow some strength from somewhere. Jay is the name of my headache," Desire added.

"Eric is the name of my ass pain," Kit added.

Both ladies were laughing at each other's misery until the nurse came out and called, "Ms. Williams, the doctor will see you now."

"It was nice to meet you, Kit. I hope everything works out for you, and maybe when I find a place, the next Pokeno game will be at my place."

"Nice meeting you, also. Good luck to you and your family."

Dr. Carl walked into the room where Desire was still smiling from her conversation with Kit.

"Hello, Ms. Williams. I suppose you want the results?"

"Yes. I have been so nervous about this."

"The good news is that you're negative for HIV, but you have chlamydia."

Desire took a deep breath of relief.

"You don't seem shocked by the news at all," Dr. Carl observed.

"I knew he was cheating on me, so there was always a possibility of catching something. I am glad that it's not HIV. I just want to get cured and move on with my life."

"Well, here is your prescription, and I will see you in four weeks to make sure you are all cleared."

Kit was still sitting in the lobby reliving her conversation with Desire when the nurse called, "Ms. Karter, the doctor will see you now."

"Hello, Ms. Kit Karter. I like your name," Dr. Carl said. "It is very unique and has a nice ring to it. So, what brings you in today?"

Kit briefly reflected on her talk with Renee on what to say when she spoke to the doctor.

She said, "My boyfriend of a year just told me that he is gay. I need to be checked for every disease out there."

Even Dr. Carl had to gasp for air after hearing that.

"I am sorry you have to deal with that. Let's get started with your exam. Is there any chance you might be pregnant? Speaking of pregnant, you did say you were referred by Renee Tyler, correct?"

Kit was so caught up in her drama with Eric that she didn't catch the subliminal hint from Dr. Carl about Renee.

"Yes, she is my best friend, and no, I am not pregnant."

Kit lay on her back with her feet in the stirrups, saying a silent prayer.

"Well, that's it. So, I will call you when I have the results," Dr Carl explained.

The moment she got in her car, she called Renee.

"Hey, Renee. I went to see Dr. Carl today. He was very nice. I met this girl in his office named Desire. She lives at the shelter."

"What was she doing there?" Renee asked.

"She said something about her kids' father. Did you know that she is best friends with Jessica's secretary, Charmaine?"

Renee responded very shocked and amazed, "No — get out of here! This world is too small."

"That's what I said. Her kids' father needs to be ashamed of himself. I have to go, but I will see you at home later."

Desire had the same idea to call her best friend and tell her what had happened at the doctor's office.

"Hello, Charmaine. Can you talk?"

"Yeah, girl. What's up?" Charmaine asked.

"I went to the doctor today before I went to work."

"Oh, that's right — you started today. How is it?"

"It's good but very boring. There's a lot of downtime, but back to what I was saying. I went to the doctor, and he said I have chlamydia."

"You *what?*" Charmaine exclaimed.

"That no-good bastard gave me chlamydia, and to top it off, he came by the shelter this morning talking about how he wanted to take the boys to school. He had the nerve to show up here driving his new woman's car."

"How do you know? Please tell me he didn't have her in the car with him," Charmaine said.

"No, she wasn't there, but I never saw that car before, so I assumed it was his woman's."

"Well, Dee. God bless her. Are you OK otherwise?" Renee asked.

"Yes, I'm good. While I was at the doctor office, there was a girl in there named Kit."

Charmaine blurted out, "I know her — she is my boss's sister's friend.

"She told me she knows you and how much she liked your apartment."

"She is the one I told you who won the game."

"She told me that, too. But did you know that your boss is the sister of the girl who works at the shelter? The one I told you was trying to get me a job?"

Charmaine stopped for a minute to think. "Are you talking about Renee? I didn't know she worked at the shelter. This world is so small."

"She also goes to Dr. Carl's office," Desire said.

"Maybe I ought to meet this Dr. Carl and complete the circle. He has been all up in everybody's business but mine."

The ladies enjoyed a small chuckle at the expense of Dr. Carl.

Out of curiosity, Desire asked if Charmaine had met Kit's boyfriend.

"No. Why? Should I know him?" Charmaine inquired.

"I just figured I would ask. She said he is the reason she was at Dr. Carl's office. Oh, well. Let me go do some work, and you, too," Desire said.

"Give me a call if you need anything. Love you, girl," Charmaine added before hanging up the phone.

Come on, Eric — answer your phone.

Eric saw the name "Mike" come across the screen of his cell phone and answered, trying not to give it away that he had been crying.

With a slight tremble in his own voice, Eric said, "Hello, Mike."

"Yo, Eric. I need a favor on Saturday. Are you crying?"

"Don't worry about it. I'll be alright."

"Yo — we are still boys, so tell me what's up," Mike said.

"I told my girl that I'm gay, and she took it really badly. Now I have to tell my best friend the truth about me, and I don't think he is going to take it well, either."

"Man, why are you telling everybody that?" Mike asked, sounding annoyed.

"I don't want to live a lie anymore, and you shouldn't, either," Eric said.

Mike became enraged listening to Eric say that about him, and he lashed out. "And me *what*? I am not gay or even close to it."

Eric, trying not to upset Mike, just said, "I don't want to go down that road again. So, what did you need on Saturday, Mike?"

"I need to borrow your car."

"Not a problem. Who are you trying to impress, and when will you be back?"

Mike answered, "By the next morning."

"Mike, you shouldn't play with these females' emotions."

"What are you talking about, E? I really like this girl."

"You really like them all until they start talking about being in a committed relationship."

Mike thought about it for a moment. "I tried that before, and I will commit again when I am ready and not before. That's the problem with women — they're always trying to force the relationship. If they'd just sit back and enjoy the ride, all that they wish for will come naturally."

Eric interjected his thoughts on Mike's theory by adding, "Or the man can suck up all they have to offer and leave them wondering what happened and why. That's where the saying is derived, 'Men won't buy the cow if they can get the milk for free.'"

"Damn, Eric. You just came out of the closet, and you sound like one of these emotional chicks already."

"Call me what you want, Mike, but I just realized how much I truly hurt Kit because I was lying to myself."

"Did you say 'Kit'? Is that your ex-girl's name?"

"Yes, and she didn't deserve this, but now she is free to be loved the way she gives love."

Mike was tired of listening to Eric whine like a woman, so he said, "I have to go. I'll be home later. I may need you to pick me up later."

"Why? What is wrong with your car?"

"I have to put it in the shop. That's the real reason I need your car on Saturday. I'll see you later, Eric — and stop all that crying shit."

Over at the accounting firm, Charmaine had just gotten off the phone with Kit and was going to try to find out why Jessica was late.

"Hey, is everything okay with you? Because it's not like you to be late."

"James had my car again, and he was late picking me up. Something is not right with him."

"Maybe he is just going through something that you can't help him with. Let him have some time to work it out, and he will be back to normal. Men need that room to breathe. Maybe if you come out this weekend with me and my new friend this weekend, it may help him relax a little bit," Charmaine suggested.

"The way he has been acting lately, I doubt I can get him to do anything. You may be on your own Saturday."

"If that's the case, then say a prayer for me that I don't give him a taste of dessert before I see what's on the menu."

Jessica looked at Charmaine with a puzzled look on her face and said, "What the hell are you talking about?"

"I don't want to sleep with Mike before I see what he's really about. It has been so long since I've been with someone, and this guy really turns me on."

"I have faith that you will make the right decision and respect your body," Jessica told her.

"You sound just like Desire. Speaking of Des, I didn't know that your sister worked at the shelter. My friend, Desire, whom I have been telling you about, met Renee's friend Kit at Dr. Carl's office. She said Renee had spoken to you about getting her a job in the legal department here."

"She sure did, and I told her to give me your friend's resume. How's she doing, anyway?" Jessica asked.

"She is doing better now. She has job as a file clerk for now until something better comes along."

"Renee is bringing me her resume on Monday, and I will do my best to get her something more beneficial to her future."

"That would be great. She can sure use some good news. Not only did he leave her with three boys to raise, but he also gave her chlamydia."

"Dear God, the poor woman. I hope I never meet a man like her children's father. So, is that why she was at Dr. Carl's office?" Jessica questioned.

Charmaine answered, "Yes. She is very happy to know that it's something that can be cured, so she can move on with her life."

"That is definitely a blessing. Speaking of Dr. Carl, I need to make an appointment myself."

"You use that doctor also? I was telling Desire that she should check him out just because."

"Yes, he is an excellent doctor," Jessica said.

"So I have heard. I haven't used my equipment in so long, the only thing he would find is cobwebs."

Jessica smiled at her and said, "Then, on second thought, maybe you should do a little dusting on Saturday. Just make sure you use a latex glove."

"Trust me, it has not been that long. I have not forgotten the basics of protection. I do not want to get up with something that I did not lie down with."

"I hear that. Let's finish up this day so we both can get out of here. Matter of fact, I'm going to try to call my sister to see if she is going to cook tonight."

Charmaine went back to her desk, and Jessica dialed Renee's number, still thinking about James.

"Hey, Renee. It's Jess."

"Jessica, let me call you back because I am trying to call Sam on the other line."

Renee switched back over onto the other line, anxious to talk to Sam.

"Sam, it's Renee. We need to talk."

"Okay, well, let me call you back because Eric is on the other line, and he sounds like something is wrong," Sam replied and then hung up the phone abruptly.

Renee thought to herself, *I know damn well he did not just hang up on me like that. What the hell has gotten into him? First, he goes out in the middle of the week and doesn't invite me, and now he is hanging up on me. When I catch up with his ass, he has a lot of explaining to do. I could have told him what's wrong with Eric.*

Sam answered his other line with genuine concern for his friend in his tone.

"Eric — what's up, man? You don't sound good at all. I was calling your job, and they said you haven't been to work in a couple of days," Sam said.

Eric responded, "I know. I wasn't feeling well. Have you spoken to Kit or Renee?"

Sam said, "That was Renee a few minutes ago, but I haven't spoken to her or Kit. I have been busy. I need to talk to you about a situation I havc. I think I am falling for someone else. She is so different than most women I talk to. She is beautiful and smart. She has goals and dreams, and she makes me want more out of life than just being a telephone technician, climbing poles all day."

"This girl sounds really special, Sam. Who is she, and do I know her? After you answer that, then I really need you to listen to what I have to say."

"Hey, man. What's up? Talk to me. We can get back to her later. What's going on?"

"I don't know where to start now. I told Kit a few days ago that we had to end our relationship."

Sam, responding out of shock, asked, "Why would you do something like that? Did you meet someone new also?"

"Something like that, Sam. Just listen, please, because this is very hard for me to say to you after all these years of us being friends."

"Yo, E. We are boys, and you can tell me anything, so just say it."

"Sam, there was a point in my life where I was confused. I tried to make a life based on what I thought was real. I now know that I can no longer lie to myself or my friends about who I am. Sam, I am gay."

Sam paused for a brief moment to reflect.

"Eric, about two years ago, I noticed a change in you. You stopped talking about all the girls you hit up for some ass. You started going out by yourself and not inviting me to hang out with you. Was that what that was all about?"

"Around that time, I was beginning to question my sexuality. I started noticing men in a different way. I couldn't understand why I was feeling that way. I believe that was part of the reason I got with Kit. I wanted to make myself believe that it was a passing phase. Those nights I went out by myself, I actually went to a gay bar. I wanted to see how it would affect me. I was so scared when I realized that I liked being there. I liked how I felt when I was surrounded by men who were just like me. The only difference was that they were free. They didn't hide who they were. That's why I am telling you this now. I want to be free."

"When you say 'free,' do you mean you have a boyfriend, E?"

"No, I don't have a boyfriend. If you want to know if have slept with a man, the answer is . . ."

Sam wasn't ready to hear that just yet, so he cut Eric off before he could answer the question entirely.

"No, I do not want to know that. That is your business. How did Kit take your news?"

"She hates me. I don't blame her — or you, for that matter. I would probably feel betrayed if someone was lying about who they were for all this time."

"I don't hate you, E. We have been friends since junior high, and more than anything, I am just disappointed that it took you so long to come clean and tell me the truth."

"I didn't *know* the truth until recently. I was denying every sexual act I performed with another man. I said I did it because I was drunk or high. Do you remember the guy I told you about, my deejay friend?"

"The one who was supposed to go out with us last weekend?" Sam questioned.

"Yes, well his name is Michael, and he is the reason I know the truth about who I am. He was the first man I made love to, and it was more real than any experience I have ever shared with a woman. I knew from that moment I could no longer just write it off as a drunken fling. This was real. The way I felt was real, and I wanted that feeling to last forever."

Sam was still confused and was searching for more clarification.

Sam asked, "He is the dude you said had just left his girl and moved in with you, right?"

"Yes, but we are not a couple. He doesn't want to admit that he's gay. He is still living that lie."

"What are you going to do now? Please tell me you're not going to start snapping your fingers and wearing tight jeans that hug your nuts," Sam said, laughing,

Both Sam and Eric were able to laugh briefly.

"Naw, man. I'm going to still be me. I just know that I like boys more than girls. The question is, what about us?"

"We are always going to be boys no matter who you sleep with. Just please tell me I am not your type."

Again, they both shared a laugh, and Eric responded, "You are definitely not my type. I was so worried about telling you the truth because I thought you would react like Kit. I wonder if Kit has told Renee already."

"She probably has, and that's why Renee keeps telling me she has to talk to me."

Eric felt a weight had been lifted off his shoulders because his friendship with Sam was still intact. He didn't skip a beat with changing the subject and talking like they would before he came out as being gay.

"So, now back to this girl who put that thang on you," Eric said, smiling.

Sam decided he didn't want to talk on the phone anymore, so he invited Eric out for drinks on Saturday, to tell him all about his new boo.

"I have to wait until Saturday," Eric said.

"The weekend will be here before you know it. You can wait until then. I want to call Renee back, but I don't want to hear the fussing in my ears right now. Maybe I will make *her* wait until the weekend also. Anyway, E, I'll see you on Saturday."

"Sam, thanks for making this easy for me. Later."

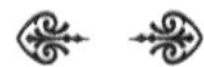

Jessica was thinking to herself, *Oh, my goodness! I can't believe it is Saturday already. I should call James to see if he wants to go out tonight.*

"James, I have been calling you because I really want to go with my secretary and her new boyfriend to the play today."

"Jessica, I have been really busy, and I really don't have time," James said. "The mechanic found something else wrong with my car, and I have to get the money together to pay for it."

Feeling insecure, Jessica said, "Have I done something wrong? All of a sudden, you have changed. Is it because of our conversation about starting a family and maybe moving in together?"

Realizing that Jessica was feeling insecure, James wanted to reassure her that everything would be fine.

James said, "No, I want that day more than you can imagine. I promise you, if you are patient, I will make this up to you. I love you, but I have to go now. I will call you later, and maybe we can have a Netflix night."

Hearing James say he loves her put Jessica in better spirits.

"OK, baby. I will make something special for dinner. Bye, and I love you, too."

Talking to herself aloud, Jessica said, "Well, let me call Charmaine and let her know that I tried."

"Hello, Charmaine. This is Jessica, and I am so sorry, but James can't make it tonight, so you are on your own. Call me when you get this message."

Charmaine was in her apartment preparing for that night as she ran into the living room trying to answer the phone.

"Hello. Hello" . . . *Damn, I missed it. There's no point in calling her back if she can't go. What the hell am I going to do*? she questioned herself as her phone began to ring again.

Well, damn. My phone has never rung this much before, Charmaine thought.

"Hello, beautiful. Did you miss me?" Mike asked, as she answered the phone.

"I guess I will let you know tonight when you pick me up, handsome," she responded.

"Are your friends going with us?" he asked.

"No, her boyfriend can't make it."

"Too bad, because I was looking forward to meeting them and showing them why you are going to fall in love with me."

"You are so sure of yourself. I might not ever want to see you again after tonight."

Still feeling very sure of himself, Mike said, "You might as well blame it on the rain, but you fell in love with me that night we met. You just haven't admitted it to yourself yet. Anyway, go make yourself more beautiful, and I will be there soon to pick you up."

"But I haven't told you where I live."

Mike laughed as he said, "That was my mission after I met you. I will be there soon."

Charmaine sat on the edge of her bed fantasizing about actually being in love with Mike and becoming his wife. Her daydream was interrupted by a knock at the door. She ran to the door, hoping to get rid of whoever it was so she could get ready for her date tonight. She opened the door without looking through the peephole first, and, to her surprise, there he stood.

"Mike, you are early."

"I wanted to watch perfection try to outdo itself," he said, trying to be really smooth.

His smooth talk made her smile light up the room as she invited him in.

As he walked past her, she said, "Would you stop?" as she blushed thinking about his compliment.

"Would you like a drink while you wait?" Charmaine asked.

"Only if you have one with me," he suggested.

To tell the truth, Mike, I am so nervous about tonight that I've already had two drinks to calm my nerves."

"So, make mine a double, while you sip on your third."

"How about you make yourself a double, and I'll go jump in the shower. Make yourself at home."

Charmaine turned to walk back toward the bathroom, and Mike couldn't keep his eyes off of her rump-shaker as it jiggled down the hall.

He was thinking to himself, *Baby girl, you won't be alone in that shower for long, because that thing is looking right.*

But instead he said, "OK, I will be here when you get out."

Charmaine closed the bathroom door but did not lock it while she prepared for her shower.

All the while, Charmaine was thinking, *Why did he have to bring his fine ass over here all early? Maybe I will take an extra-long shower with my "Mr. Pleasure," and that way, I can take the edge off temptation. Who the hell am I kidding? I want the real thing. Oh, hell, Mr. Pleasure — work your magic.*

Mike walked over to her bathroom door and peeked his head in, saying,"Ms. Charmaine, do you need any help in there? I could help you wash your back."

Oh, Lord Jesus — why? she thought.

"No, I am just fine, Mike. Thank you."

Oh, that you are, he thought to himself.

"Have a seat, and I will be right out."

"Charmaine, your phone is ringing. Should I get it?"

"No, just tell me whose name is on the caller ID," she yelled from the shower.

"It says 'Jessica Tyler.' Maybe I should turn it off so we won't be interrupted. I will turn mine off, also."

"That sounds like a great idea. I really want to enjoy this night with you."

The studio was set up in such a way that the bathroom and bed were toward the back of the apartment, separated by a Chinese room divider. Mike went and sat back down on the sofa on the other side of the room divider. He was still trying to engage in conversation while she was in the bathroom, telling her that she has a really nice studio apartment.

She didn't respond because she was about to reach her peak with Mr. Pleasure.

Because she didn't answer, he yelled, "Charmaine, I need to use the restroom."

"I am coming right now," she yelled back but whispered the word "*literally*" under her breath.

Charmaine opened the bathroom door wearing nothing but a towel.

Mike saw her and couldn't help himself.

"Lord, girl. What are you trying to do to me?"

She smiled at him and said, "Go use the bathroom, and wait in the living-room area."

When he finished in the restroom, he had to walk past her to get to the living-room area of the studio. He looked at her still wrapped in the towel and said, "Let me help you get dressed, by first helping you lotion your sexy body."

"Mike, I asked you to wait in the living room until I get dressed."

Mike walked up behind her, placed his hand gently on the back of her neck, and planted a soft kiss on her shoulder.

"Mike, go back into the living room," she moaned. Wait a minute — do that move again on my shoulder."

His voiced softened as he said, "You like that, huh? Well, let me do your whole body. I promise to be the perfect gentleman. You can trust me."

Still writhing with excitement from his touch but trying to fight the feeling at the same time, she said, "Mike, I don't know about this. Oh, God! That's the spot, right there."

Mike was massaging her shoulders and kissing her neck and, at the same time, slowly working his way down the center of her back.

"Mike, we should not be doing this, but your lips feel like butterflies landing on my back. I need to stop this, but it feels so good. I haven't been touched by a man like this since . . ." *Oh, God, what is he doing to me?* she thought.

He stopped her from talking by placing one finger across her lips.

"Relax. I want to try something with you, but you have to turn over on all fours. Don't be afraid, I'll be gentle. If it hurts, I will kiss it and make it all better. Trust me."

"I believe you won't do anything to hurt me, so you may have your way with me, she moaned sensually.

Oh, Lord — did his tongue just take a wrong turn on the Hershey highway? This man is good. How the hell did he take his clothes off while caressing my body with his tongue? Charmaine was thinking.

"I feel you getting nervous. Just relax, Charmaine. I just wanted to feel your skin against mine. I won't do anything you won't let me."

"Mike, I'm not nervous anymore. I am anxious for more."

Eager to please, Mike told her, "Well, I won't keep the lady waiting."

There he goes back on that Hershey highway. What is his obsession with the road untaken? Charmaine wondered.

"Charmaine, sweetheart, I am going to use my finger and apply a little pressure on your sweet spot. I want you to push out as you feel that pressure," Mike suggested.

Charmaine, still wondering where all of this was leading and feeling somewhat uncomfortable now, asked, "What the hell is this, a gyn exam?"

Mike, using a soft tone, trying not to kill the mood, made one request: "Charmaine, stop complaining, and go along with it. You are in the thick of things now, so you might as well try to enjoy."

In total compliance, she said, "OK, Mike. Whatever you wish."

"Do you feel that?" he asked.

"Yes, I feel it. Should I push now?"

"Yes. Whenever you feel a little pressure, push back gently."

"Mike, that finger feels more like a thumb."

"Do you want me to stop, Charmaine?"

"No, Mike, not yet. Should I push again?"

"No more talking. Just keep doing what I ask, and the reward will be great. Tilt your head to the side so I can kiss those sexy lips. I love the way you arch your back. I have one more question, baby."

"Yes, Daddy, anything," she said.

"Have you ever had anal sex?"

"No, Mike, and I am not ready for that experience yet."

"It's too late because you are already doing it. If you don't like it, I'll stop."

Mike started to thrust harder and faster.

"Mike, how could you? Charmaine said while moaning . . . hmmm! Hmmm! How could! Don't stop, Mike! Don't stop! I think I am about to — *Oh, God, Mike!*"

"Charmaine, baby, are you OK? I'm sorry that I tricked you, but I wanted our first time to be something you will always remember. This is going to sound like some sort of line, but this was the first time in my life that I climaxed with a woman at the same time she did."

Charmaine was lying on her back taking slow, deep breaths, staring at the ceiling and wondering what just happened.

"I can't believe I climaxed from having anal sex. I never knew I would enjoy anal sex. It is actually pretty damn good. That must be the secret among gay men. Now I have a request. I've waited so long to have sex that I just want to feel you inside me, the regular way."

Mike turned over, kissed her lips, and said, "Your wish is my command, but what about the play?"

Charmaine looked at him with the eyes of a horny teenage girl and said, "Two more times, and we can go see the play. I am going to make up for lost time here. For the record, you are right — I will never forget this."

Over at Nipsy's Lounge, Sam and Eric were meeting up to finish their conversation from the other night.

"Yo, Sam. It is crowded in here tonight."

"Do you want to go someplace else, E?"

"We're here now. Let's just find a seat so you can tell me about this new girl."

"Yo, E, man. I hope you don't judge me."

"Who am I to judge anyone, but from the way you sound, are you sure you really want to pursue this girl?"

"Eric, man, I already know that I love her. I know a man should never kiss and tell, but when we made love the first time, I knew I wanted to marry her."

Eric was caught off guard by hearing that Sam had already slept with the mystery woman. He asked, "You had sex with her already?"

Sam replied, "We tried not to take it there, but we could no longer control our feelings, and it just happened."

"The way you have been talking about her, she sounds like she may have what it takes to make me switch teams again," Eric said with a slight chuckle.

"Don't even play like that about my future wife, E."

Eric, realizing that Sam had not found his joke funny, said, "You are serious about this girl, but what about Renee?"

"I think Renee will understand. We are better off as friends. I need someone a little softer around the edges. Renee has been hardened by other men. There is no sweet, sensitive side to her, at least with me. She doesn't ask, she demands. She's lost that feminine quality that makes a man want to protect a woman. She is just too rough. She lacks that emotional nature about a woman. As a friend, I can deal with those qualities, but as my life partner, it just wouldn't work. Although she is a couple of years younger than me, I believe in my heart this girl is the one. Like Aaliyah said when she married R. Kelly, 'Age ain't nothing but a number.'

"Well, I hope for your sake that she is all that you say she is and that Renee will be that understanding person you think she can be. If it's anything like the way it was when I told Kit, you have major problems. When do you plan on telling her about this new lady?" Eric asked.

"I plan to tell her soon," Sam said. My phone is ringing, and I bet you the next round of drinks that it's Renee, because I have been dodging her. She hates being ignored."

As Sam looked down at his phone and they both saw 'Renee Tyler,' they both burst into laughter, and then Eric said, "Bartender — another round on me."

What the hell is going on with Sam? This is not like him to not answer when I call. He's got some serious explaining to do when I catch up with his ass, Renee thought.

Renee went downstairs to speak with her mother, who was looking in the freezer, trying to find something to cook for dinner.

"Ms. Tyler, you need to speak to your granddaughter. She is getting out of hand. She stayed out all night last night."

"Renee, if I have to tell you again to stop calling me that, you are going to be put out for good, not just one night."

"You are missing the point, Mother. Where is Tawana, and who is she spending time with? Do you even care?" Renee said.

"Did I put a leash on you when you were her age? The answer is, 'No, I did not,' and you turned out just fine. As long as nobody comes in here pregnant with no husband, it's alright with me."

Renee gave her mother a look that said, "That was the most stupid comment I've ever heard."

"You don't have to be married to have a baby, Mother."

"Listen to me good, Renee. If your last name is Tyler, and you live under my roof, then you have to be married, or you and my grandchild can go live in that shelter you work for."

Both Renee and her mother were speaking and putting emphasis on every word they spoke.

"Well, we are not talking about me. We are talking about Tawana and what if she gets pregnant?"

"Then she can get out, too. That's why they created shelters and social services. You should know that better than anyone," Ms. Tyler said.

"That is just wrong, Mother."

"Yeah, well — it's my way or the highway, as the saying goes."

Renee was sitting at the table, shaking her head at her mother's statement, when Tawana walked in the door.

"Hi, grandma."

"Hi, *grandma*?" Renee repeated. "Is that all you're going to say, as if you don't see me sitting here? You come strolling up in here like you're grown," Renee said.

"What are you talking about, Renee? Grandma knew where I was."

Renee turned to her mother with a disgusted look on her face and said, "You knew all that time, and you didn't say anything?"

Momma Tyler shot her back a look that said, "So what?"

"I don't have to report to you, Renee," her mother said. "If she wanted you to know where she was, she would have told you."

"See, Renee? That's why you should mind your own business," Tawana said, with a smirk on her face.

"You must be feeling yourself, talking to me like that," Renee said to Tawana.

Rolling her eyes, she snapped back, "Whatever, Renee! Grandma, thank you for understanding."

Renee stood to her feet and took a few steps toward Tawana in an aggressive manner, but just then, the door swung open to reveal Jessica standing there with a silly grin on her face.

"Good day to all the beautiful Tyler women. Why all the yelling? I am in a good mood, and I am going to cook a good meal — shrimp ala Jessica — so y'all need to work it out or get out of my kitchen."

Renee decided to go upstairs to her room instead of dealing with Tawana, her mother, and Jessica.

CHAPTER 5
Shedding Light

Four days later, Renee kept going over the conversation in her mind between herself, Tawana, and her mother. She decided she was going to address the issue with her niece.

"Tawana, I want to speak to you about the other day. I didn't mean to sound like that, but I was really worried about you."

"It's OK. I understand, but I need to talk to you about something."

"Oh, yeah. What happened with your friend's man?" Renee asked.

"He told me that he loves me and wants to be with me. We made love for the first time the other day."

Renee's voice was filled with disappointment as she said, "Tawana, why would you do something like that?"

"Because, Auntie, I realized that I love him, too."

"I told you to stop with that 'Auntie' mess, and how do you know that? How much time have you really been spending with this boy?"

"We have spent enough time to know that we love each other. My problem is how do I tell my friend?"

"If you guys are sure about this love that you say you feel for each other, then you should tell her together. Make sure it's someplace public so there's a better chance there won't be a scene."

"What is his name, and how old is he? Do I know any of his relatives?"

Renee was waiting for Tawana to answer her questions when her phone began to ring. She was willing to let it ring out just to hear the answer, but instead Tawana said, "Renee, your telephone is ringing!"

Renee ran up the stairs, still talking to Tawana on her way to her room. "Hold that thought, and I'll be right back. I have been waiting for Sam to call me all day, but I don't think that is him." The moment she heard Sam's voice, she screamed into the phone.

"Sam, what the hell is going on with you? I do not appreciate the way you have been acting lately! We need to talk, and it is very important!"

Sam, sensing her tone, asked, "Renee, why are you talking to me like that? That is exactly why . . ."

She interrupted him "Why *what*?"

"Never mind. What was it that you wanted?" he asked.

"First thing is, have you spoken to Eric?" she asked.

Not really interested in discussing his friend, he replied, "Yeah — *and*?"

"Kit said that he told her he was gay."

"I know already. Eric called me and told me all about it. I was with him last night, so when you called, that's why I didn't answer the phone."

Renee was sort of shocked to learn that he already knew, which led to a barrage of questions for Sam.

"You know? How long have you known he was gay, and why didn't you say anything to me? Kit is my best friend, and you let her fall in love with a man you knew was gay. Why would you do something like that?"

"First of all, Renee, he just told me a couple of days ago, and I am not like you. He is my best friend, and I will not turn my back on him for nothing."

"Nothing! Being gay is not *nothing*, Sam."

"I understand that your friend is hurt, but she will get over it and move on with her life. He is just trying to move on with his life, free from all lies and doubts."

"Sam, what the hell are you talking about? Oh, God — please don't tell me that you and he have been sleeping together!"

"Only you would think something like that, Renee."

"What the hell does that mean, Sam? This is what I mean: something is not right with you."

Sam felt his threshold for what he considered a level of stupidity had reached its peak.

"Just what I said, Renee! I have been wanting to tell you something for a while now. I am not happy with this situation anymore!"

Stunned by what she was hearing, she reacted by saying, "*Situation*! Did you just call our relationship a *situation*?"

Sam retorted, "Our relationship became a situation a few months ago when you started acting like a warden instead of a wife."

Still confused, she asked, "Are you trying to break up with me?"

"I think that would be best for both of us," he said.

Renee began screaming into the phone. "Do not speak for me! Don't ever speak for me! This doesn't even sound like you talking! Is someone else in this picture?"

"That is one of your problems. You seem to think that I am some idiot who can't think for himself. I knew I was not happy with you, and yes, I've found someone who makes me happy."

Still yelling at the top of her voice, she said, "You are just like the rest of them! You are worse because you were my friend."

"I think we should have stayed friends," was all that Sam could say.

A loud knock at her bedroom door distracted Renee for a brief moment.

"Renee, are you OK? We heard you yelling from downstairs."

"I am fine, Tawana. I will be down in a minute."

Hearing Renee respond to Tawana, Sam said, "I know you are upset, but can I speak to Tawana? I need her to do me a favor."

Renee again screamed into the phone. "She is my niece, and she won't be doing any favors for you. Go to hell, Sam!"

Sam, sensing her anger beginning to elevate, said, "I will give you some time to calm down and think, and we will talk again. Goodbye."

The knocking began on her door again. "Renee, open the door. Are you alright?"

"Give me a minute. I'll be OK."

Here I am, Lord, pregnant with this man's baby, and he tells me he wants someone else. Help me to do the right thing. Pull yourself together, Renee. You have been down this road before.

Renee finally opened her bedroom door. Tawana was standing there, with deep concern on her face.

"Renee, what happened?"

"Nothing I can't handle. Sam and I just broke up. He said he'd found someone new, and to top it off, he made it seem like it was as simple as saying 'I love you' and 'goodbye.'"

Momma Tyler started calling from downstairs for Tawana.

"Tawana, Sam is on the phone for you."

Tawana looked toward Renee as if to say with her eyes, *Do you want me to get it?* Instead, she said, "Renee, I am sorry."

Renee said, "Don't be. Go see what he wants, and if he asks you to do anything for him, just say 'No.'"

Tawana ran downstairs to get the phone and took it out onto the back steps of the house.

"Hello, Sam. I just heard what happened. Why would you do Renee like that?"

"I had no other choice, Tawana. She started with that bullshit, and I couldn't take it anymore. I need you to look out for her as best you can."

"*Me?* How can I help her? She is going to shut down and not want to talk to me — or anybody, for that matter."

"Well, don't let that stop you," Sam pleaded.

"No, I won't let that stop me, but it will be hard."

"I will see you later. Bye, Tawana."

Tawana came back into the house and went back upstairs to Renee's room, where she was sitting on the edge of her bed, staring at the floor.

"What did he want?" Renee asked.

"He wanted me to make sure you will be OK."

Renee rolled her eyes at hearing that.

"If he really wanted that, then he would not be leaving me for another woman."

"Is that what he told you?" Tawana asked.

"Yes. He said he'd found someone who makes him happy."

"Are you sure that is what he said?" Tawana asked, with a slight smile on her face.

"That is exactly what he said — and don't look so damn happy."

"I am not happy, Renee. I am in shock that he would say that."

Jessica came out of her room. She was standing in Renee's doorway and asked, "Did I just hear you right, Renee? Did you just say Sam broke up with you?"

Jessica didn't even give Renee a chance to answer the question. She just kept talking.

"Well, I think James and I might be having the same problem. He has become very distant and secretive lately."

Renee, still sitting on the bed, just shook her head at her sister's statement.

"James always had issues; you just chose not to see them."

Jessica, feeling attacked by Renee's comment, said, "Why do you always have to be so nasty even when someone is sympathizing with you?"

"That was not sympathy for me, Jess. That was you trying to gain sympathy for yourself."

"I don't need your sympathy because he has not left me like Sam did you."

Tawana nudged Jessica and said, "Jessica, that was a low blow and uncalled for."

Renee looked toward both of them standing in her door and said, "It's OK, Tawana. I can take it. Jessica had better not ever find herself in my shoes and look for sympathy coming from me. I will laugh in her face."

Tawana, trying to be the voice of reason, said, "You two need to stop because all you have is each other in the end."

Renee jumped up from the bed out of frustration, "You know what? I am tired of all this bullshit. I am leaving. Where are my damn keys?"

Renee pushed past Jessica and Tawana, running down the stairs and out the front door.

As she sat in the car, she started dialing numbers frantically on her phone.

"Kit, where the hell are you? I need you."

Kit, sensing the urgency in Renee's voice, told Renee to meet her at Nipsy's.

Before she could pull out, Tawana was knocking on her car window, asking, "Renee, do you want me to come with you?"

"No, I'll be alright."

"Again, I am sorry for everything you are going through," Tawana offered.

Renee sped off en route to Nipsy's.

The moment they were seated at a table, Renee started talking and couldn't stop.

"Kit, I can't believe this shit! I trusted him like no other! We were best friends for years. How could he do this to me? How could I not see this coming?"

"Renee, like you always told me, he is still a man. At least you lost him to another woman and not a man. As for your question about not seeing it coming, we only see what we want to see in a relationship. Can we at least get a drink before we continue with the convo?" Kit said.

Renee just kept talking. "And that's the worst part of this whole thing. I can't even have a drink because I am pregnant. I have been trying to tell him for days, but he was too freaking busy."

Kit was literally sitting there with her mouth wide open until she found a few words. "You are *what?*"

"I'm sorry to tell you like this, but you had your own problems."

With excitement in her voice, Kit said, "My little big-head niece or nephew comes before some gay man."

"Kit, don't get too excited; I don't think I'm going to keep it."

Kit's facial expression changed from excitement to disappointment.

"What do you mean? You can't let that stop you. This is a gift."

"Oh, Lord, Kit. Please do not start with that 'gift' shit right now. I refuse to be the mother to a child who was not wanted by both parents. If he doesn't want me, why would he want my baby?"

"So, he still doesn't know about the baby?"

"No, I was trying to tell him when he told me we should be friends."

"I think you should tell him — it might change his mind about things," Kit suggested.

Renee gave Kit a glance that read, "*Hell*, no."

"That's what I don't want. Why would I want to be with someone out of pity? He doesn't want to be there, so he shouldn't be. I am not keeping this baby. I have made up my mind."

"I think you should sleep on it. Have you told your family yet?" Kit asked.

"No one knows but you and Dr. Carl. I can't believe this is happening to me. I thought we were going to be happy together and that he would love this baby."

"Renee, let me school you on a few things. Not everything that we *want* is what we *need*. Maybe this is a blessing that he left you. You now have this baby to think about."

Renee replied, sarcastically, "The Lord should have found another way to bless me."

"All I'm going to say is, just think about it before you do something stupid that you will regret."

"Kit, you might be right. Maybe I should take a vacation to clear my mind. I think that, by the time I get back, I will have made a decision based on what is real and not so much about the hurt and disappointment."

Shaking her head in agreement, Kit asked, "Where are you thinking about going, and how long do you plan on staying?"

"I was thinking like one week in Jamaica. You can stay in the room and enjoy some privacy. When I get home, I'm going to book my flight."

"Thanks, girl. But I was planning on spending some time at my aunt's house because she had a stroke."

"Goodness, you didn't tell me that, Kit."

"I just found out today. My uncle said she did not want me to know. I will not be moving back in there, but he said he needed me to stay with her next week."

"Girl, I am sorry to hear about that. When it rains, it pours for some of us. I just need a break from this mess of a life. I am so tired that I just want a shower and some sleep. Let's go home," Renee said.

The night was short for Jessica because she was up most of the night thinking about James. She arrived at work slightly groggy to be met by a full-of-joy Charmaine.

"Jessica, I think I am falling in love with Mike. We have been spending so much time together. We don't even have sex all the time. He actually enjoys just watching television or playing Scrabble, hanging out, and talking. I love the fact that he doesn't make me feel like some sex toy or blow-up doll. We enjoy each other's company."

With envy in her tone, Jessica managed to muster up, "I am happy for you. I have not heard from James at all lately. Whenever I call, he says he will call me back, but he never does. I am convinced he is cheating on me. Speaking of cheating, my sister and her boyfriend broke up last week."

"Oh, wow. How is she doing? Breakups can be really hard."

"She is talking about going to Jamaica to clear her mind. I am thinking maybe I should go with her. We could both use a little pick-me-up. Two Stellas on the beach of Ochi Rios trying to get our groove back. Even the thought of that sounds pathetic."

Charmaine and Jessica shared a laugh at that idea.

Charmaine gave it a second thought and said, "It sounds like the perfect opportunity for you and Renee to bond as sisters. You guys are not that far apart in age, and yet you act like mother and daughter."

"Don't tell me who is the mother in that scenario. I love my sister, but she drives me crazy. However, I can't stand to know that someone has hurt her feelings."

Charmaine suggested, "I think you should ask her if she wants company on her trip and take advantage of the opportunity to get to know her and free your mind of the situation with James. I'm going to call my best friend and see how things are going for her. Have you heard anything from the legal department in regard to finding her a job with us?"

"They said there was nothing available by way of paralegal, but they may have a legal-researcher job coming up in the next few weeks," Jessica said. "See if Desire would be interested in that position."

"I can tell you if she would be interested in that position. How much does it pay?"

"Anywhere from $55,000 to $65,000 per year."

"Then, *hell,* yeah, she wants the job. That kind of money can get her out of the shelter. It'll be a struggle, but that's one giant step in the right direction for her and the boys."

"I will tell Tom to give her a call and set up the interview."

Feeling very grateful to Jessica, Charmaine said, "Thank you for helping her like this. God is going to bless you for this. Go call your sister and enjoy a well-deserved vacation."

Jessica started dialing Renee's number before Charmaine could leave the office. She was getting excited about the possibility of taking the trip to Jamaica.

When Renee's answering machine picked up the call, Jessica began to leave a message.

"Renee, I am truly sorry for what you are going through with Sam. If you are listening to this, pick up the phone. I want to ask you something important."

Renee was lying in bed rubbing her belly and decided she wasn't taking any calls from anyone.

Jessica, leave me alone. I don't want to be bothered by anyone right now.

Jessica continued with her message, "Renee, pick up the phone. Anyway, I wanted to know if you wanted company on your trip to Jamaica. I am going through a rough time in my life, and I need my sister."

Intrigued by Jessica's last comment, Renee reluctantly picked up the receiver.

"Alright, Jessica, you got me. Now, what do you want?"

Jessica, smiling internally, sat back in her chair and looked out at her view and said, "I want to come with you to Jamaica."

"Okay, Jess. I'll play along. Why?"

Jessica's mood changed as she swiveled in her seat to face her desk. She said, "I am convinced James is cheating on me, and I just want to get away."

Renee's defenses came down, and she had to admit to herself that the idea wasn't bad.

"To tell the truth, I would love the company. I don't think I want to be alone, anyway. I am booked tomorrow. Is that too soon for you?"

"That's fine. It'll cost me a lot more, but I could make it happen. I have enough time to cover all the bases at work."

"Well, let me ask you this, Sis: are you going to confront James about your suspicions before you go?"

"I can't even reach him. It's like he just disappeared."

"Well, damn. Did you go to his house?" Renee asked.

"Girl, that is the funny part. I went to where he said he lives, and some girl answered the door, but she had no idea who or what I was talking about. I don't even want to talk about it anymore. I have work to do, and I can't let this get me down. See you when I get home. Email me your itinerary so I can try to get a seat next to you when I book my flight."

"You need this trip more than I do. Sam at least had the decency to tell me he had someone else. Well, do some work, and I will see you later when you get home."

While Jessica was on the phone with Renee, Charmaine was at her desk giving Desire the rundown about her and Mike.

"Des, I am so happy. Mike and I have spent every waking moment together since we made love. It feels like he lives here with me. When I get home, he is there, waiting to serve me dinner. Some nights, he has my bathwater set, or he has the Scrabble game set up with my favorite drink, and we play all night."

Desire, sarcastically and with a touch of skepticism, said, "He sounds like a real prince."

"Are you trying to be funny?"

"No, not at all. He sounds like a prince with no job."

"Desire, would you stop being like that? He works from six to two in the afternoon. Since you are in hate mode, I will not talk about the man in my life until you have a man in your life. Anyway, Jessica said that the legal department has an opening coming up as a legal researcher. It pays $55,000 to $65,000, depending upon experience."

"Oh, *hell,* yeah — I'll take that. Does the position come with benefits?" Desire asked.

"I don't know. Tom from the legal department is going to call you to set up an interview. Just be ready when he calls. Now that I've given you some good news, can I tell you one more thing about Mike? He actually said he can picture me being the mother of his firstborn child."

Desire, doubtful and downright pessimistic said, "Wow — after only a couple of weeks of knowing you, he is talking about children."

"OMG, Des, you switch back to hate mode in an instant. Never mind. Maybe he has a friend for you. I think you need to get bitten by the one-eyed snake."

"That is the last thing I need," Desire said.

"You need something, and if the penis can't cure you, then you are a lost cause."

"Penis is not the answer to everything, Charmaine."

"See? You can't even take a joke anymore. You are letting your situation get the better of you. I will speak to you later."

Realizing that Charmaine may have a point, coupled with feeling a little guilty for not being more supportive of her friend, Desire conceded, saying, "OK, I am happy for you, but I am still very bitter about Jay."

"That is why you need something to help you forget about Jay and remind you that you are a beautiful woman."

"Charmaine, there is one thing that I learned for sure about being put in this position, and that is: I do not need a man to validate me. I know who I am, and I know that it is OK for me to be angry about the situation. I also know when to let go of that anger and live life."

"Every time I talk to you now, the conversation is so deep. All I want to do is laugh and have fun with my friend again. That dude stole your joy. Let me know when your interview will be, and I'll give you a ride. I'll call you later."

Feeling a little guilty, Desire said, "Thank you, girlie, and I am sorry about raining on your parade. I think it's just one of those days."

"OK. Well, feel better, and I will speak to you soon. Bye, Des."

Exhausted from her conversation with Desire, Charmaine wanted to hear a friendly voice of cheer, so she called the person who brings her joy.

"Hello, Mike. It's Charmaine. I just wanted you to know that we have a whole week to play house because my boss, Jessica, is going to Jamaica tomorrow for one week.

"Great news, Love Bug, but do you still have to go to work?" he asked.

His response made her smile. She answered, "Yes, if I want to, or I can take my vacation at the same time."

"Well, babe, I would love to practice for the real thing, but I think you should go to work, and we can plan a vacation together."

A little disappointed — but at the same time, understanding — Charmaine said, "I was hoping you would say, 'Don't go,' but I understand why you said 'No.' I will call you later."

"What time do you think you will be home?" he asked.

"I'll be there late because Jessica left early so that she can start packing for her trip. I have to stay and take care of some last-minute paperwork."

"I'm going to stop by my boy's house, then. Call me when you're ready," Mike said.

While Jessica was driving home, she was talking to herself in the car.

I can't believe James would do this to me. I'll show his ass what it feels like to disappear without a trace. How could we be talking about moving in together and having a family one minute, and then the next, you just up and disappear? That is a real punk move. Oh, shit! I am busy talking to myself and ran the damn light. When his punk ass finally calls me, I am going to make him pay for this damn ticket I'm about to get.

Sure enough, the next thing she heard and saw was a siren and flashing lights behind her.

"Hello, ma'am. License and registration, please. Do you know why I pulled you over?

Jessica replied, sarcastically, "To say 'Hello,' I hope."

Drake did a double take as he said, "Hey, lady — I almost didn't recognize you. This is going to sound really corny, but I was just thinking about you."

Jessica smiled as she said, "Well, then, maybe it was a good thing that I ran that light."

Drake, seizing the opportunity, offered, "I'll let that slide if you agree to have dinner with me."

"Unfortunately, I have to go home and pack, but I did enjoy your company last time we spoke."

"Well, that's unfortunate for me, but I hope you are going someplace nice," Drake said.

"I am going to play Stella on the beach of Jamaica with my sister."

Drake made a comment hinting at James not being the man she'd portrayed him as when they met at the club: "Let me guess — he didn't realize what a gem he has."

"I can't say that," Jessica answered. "I think I was the one who scared him off. I started talking about moving in with each other and starting a family. I was just trying to let him know that I was serious about him and our relationship. To make matters worse, I have not heard from him in God knows how long, now."

"If he can't be adult enough to talk about his fear of commitment, then, like I said before, he doesn't realize what he has, and he does not deserve to keep it," Drake said in a stern but caring manner.

Jessica caught herself just as he made that statement.

"Why am I always telling you so much — too much, in fact? I barely know you."

With a slight smile on his face, Drake said, "Deep down, you want to know me."

"There you go again, getting ahead of yourself," Jessica said, smiling back at him.

"I am going to start writing this ticket if you don't promise me that you will go to dinner with me when you get back. I am not trying to take advantage of you and your situation with your ex-boyfriend. I like our debates, and I would prefer to do it over dinner."

Jessica gave him a half smile — she'd caught that slick little comment about "ex-boyfriend."

She decided not to address it but instead said, "What if I said, 'Yes' and never called you when I got back?"

Drake laughed loudly. "Ha-ha! I thought of that, and I have your license-plate number, which means I can track you down and still give you that ticket. It will help me meet my quota for the month."

"Well, I don't want that to happen, so I will give you my number, but you can only use it one week from today."

"Why are you so specific with everything?" Drake asked.

"I really don't know. Could that be why I am on the verge of being single again?"

"I will answer that question at dinner. Until then, have a safe trip, and take it easy on those *Jamaican* men. I will speak to you soon, but I do have one question before I let you go: Do you even remember my name?"

"Of course, I do. It is something with a 'D,'" Jessica said, smiling a girlish smile.

"I am so hurt, Ms. Tyler."

Jessica nodded her head as a sign of reassurance to him.

"I know your name, Drake."

Drake smiled and tapped the top of her car as he said, "Now I feel better. Enjoy."

Jessica drove off feeling less tense and smiling on the inside. She began to sing — and laughed at herself because she knew she couldn't sing.

As she walked into the house, she yelled, "Hey, Renee — are you home?"

Tawana answered instead.

"She hasn't gotten home yet, but, Jessica, can I talk to you?"

"Not right now, Tawana. I have to pack. We can talk later. I promise."

Confused by her response, Tawana asked, "Are you going somewhere?"

"Yes, Renee and I are going to Jamaica for a week."

"I wish I could go. Is Renee feeling better?" Tawana asked.

The always-totally-positive Jessica said, "She will be fine. We are Tyler women, and we always bounce back."

"Maybe this trip is what she needs to clear her mind about the Sam situation," Tawana added.

Just hearing Sam's name angered Jessica.

"I think Sam is a piece of shit for what he did, but at the same time, if someone is unhappy, then they should not stay in the situation that is causing them pain."

Tawana asked, "Would you feel the same if James did the same thing?"

Instantly, Jessica became defensive with her response.

"James was not unhappy with me. I believe he just got scared that the relationship was getting too serious. There is a difference, little girl."

Tawana, in turn, became angry at being called a "little girl."

"I am so sick of you guys calling me that," she said.

"I don't care about you getting mad. That is what you are," Jessica snapped back. Now, where did Renee go?"

Still upset at being called a "little girl," Tawana answered with an attitude. "She went for a drive because she had to see someone before she left," she said as she walked away from Jessica.

Still talking loudly, Tawana continued down the stairs and said, "I am tired of this already. I'm calling my friend so I can get out of here for a while. I wish Renee were here."

Renee, in the meantime, was pulling into the parking lot at Dr. Carl's office building.

"Hi. Is Dr. Carl in?" Renee asked with urgency in her voice.

"Yes, he is, but he is with another patient. Did you have an appointment?" the receptionist asked.

"No, I just needed to ask him an important question."

"Is there something we can help you with?"

"No, I have to ask him directly. Is he going to be much longer?"

"I'm not sure, but you can have a seat, and I will let you know when he is available."

Before Renee could turn to have a seat in the waiting area, Dr. Carl walked up to the receptionist's desk.

"Oh, Dr. Carl — can I ask you a quick question?" Renee asked.

"Anything for my favorite Tyler girl," he said as he led her toward his office.

The moment she entered his office, she blurted out, "I was planning on going to Jamaica, and I wanted to know if it was OK for me to fly."

"Sure, you can. Was that it?" Dr. Carl questioned.

"Not really. I was thinking about having an abortion."

"Oh, really? Well, that is something different, but may I ask why?"

"Dr. Carl, I am just going through a lot, and I can't deal with a child right now," she told him.

Dr. Carl asked, "Is that what this trip is about?"

"Yes, I was going to weigh my options, however, I am leaning toward getting the abortion."

"Well, I think that is a good idea. Give me a call when you return, and we will take it from there."

"Thank you, Dr. Carl."

Renee got in her car still feeling conflicted in her thoughts.

I should tell him before I leave so he would have something to think about while I'm away. Why should I be the only one stressed the hell out? Screw him! He left me for someone else. Let them figure out what they are going to do with me as a baby mama. That's what she deserves for stealing someone's man. Renee, you are getting yourself upset for no reason. You are bigger than that. Just get rid of the problem, and move on with your life. Show him what he will be missing. Oh, shit! Too late now — I'm here.

Before she realized it, she was pulling up to Sam's apartment.

"Lisa, is Sam here?" Renee asked Sam's sister Lisa.

"No, he went out with his friend."

"You don't have to lie, Lisa. I know all about the other woman."

"Are you OK with it?" Lisa asked, sounding perturbed.

"It's not like I have any other choice. That's the decision he made. I just want to talk to him face to face for the sake of clarity."

"I would be ready to kill somebody, if I were you!" Lisa added. "You are definitely better than me. Excuse me — I have to take this call, but I will tell him you came by."

Renee gave Lisa a half smile; then, instead of bidding Lisa a simple "Goodbye," Renee added, "Take care," sounding very phony as Renee went back to her car.

On the way back home, Renee thought, *Do you really want your child to be a part of that family? She is phony as hell. Trying to act like she cares about me. If she really cared, she would have told me who the bitch is. That gives me an idea. I should get Tawana to see if she can find out who he is messing with. For his sake, I'd better not know this bitch.*

Lisa had lied to Renee — there was no incoming call. She was looking for an excuse to have Renee leave.

"Sam, you need to figure something out, because Renee was just here looking for you. I told her that I had to take a call so she would leave. By the way, did you tell her that you had another girl?"

Annoyed with her question, Sam said, "Lisa, you're my sister, not my mother — so stay out of my business."

"Well, if she pops up over here again, then I'm going to tell her."

"Lisa, stay out of my fucking business!" Sam yelled into the phone. "I need to make a call. See you later."

I have to put a stop to this, Sam thought to himself as he pressed the digits on the numerical pad on his phone.

When a voice answered the phone, Sam found himself going right into the meat and potatoes of the conversation without saying "Hello" first, just as Renee used to do with him.

"Tawana, when can we tell her the truth about us?"

"I can't hurt her like that. She has become like my best friend."

Sam said, "It is too late for regrets."

"I don't regret being with you. I just hate that it happened this way. Our happiness will cause so much pain. When she finds out the truth, it will seem as if her world has come to an end."

"The longer we wait to tell the truth, the harder it will be for all involved."

"How will we tell her?" Tawana said.

"We can invite her out to some place public," Sam said.

"That shit works only in the movies. I will tell her when we are alone."

"Tawana, I don't think that's a good idea. What if she flips out?"

"Then I will deserve it," Tawana said humbly.

"I don't want you to get hurt. I think we should do it together," Sam insisted.

"I don't want to get hurt, but if I tell her in public with you there, it will be a whole lot worse. Sam, are you sure that you love me? I know that I love you, as sure as I know that I love myself. I need to be sure before I destroy someone's life, Sam."

"You need to tell her soon so we can move on with our lives, Tawana. I love you, and I'll be there soon."

"OK, Sam. I will see you later, and I love you, too."

Tawana hung up the phone feeling guilty and happy at the same time. Twenty minutes later, she received another phone call from Sam telling her to meet him around the corner.

Tawana yelled upstairs to both Jessica and Momma Tyler that she would be back soon.

Five minutes after Tawana had run out the door, Renee came into the house yelling, "Tawana, I'm home, and I need a favor."

Jessica yelled back, "Tawana went out with her friend. Are you ready to go?"

"Almost. We have to get Kit to drive us to the airport in the morning, but she has been taking care of her aunt, so I don't know if she can make it."

With desperation in her tone, Jessica said, "Well, call her!"

"Damn! Give me a chance to get into the house first. What is your hurry all of a sudden?"

"I am just ready to think about something other than James. I want to worry about falling while climbing Dunn's River. I want to shop and eat, jerk everything."

Renee found that to be hilarious.

"You are stupid. I will call her now."

She was laughing as she dialed Kit's number.

"Kit, do you have to take care of your aunt tomorrow?" she asked without saying "Hello" first.

Kit just shook her head, because she knew and accepted this rude behavior from her friend.

She answered, "I can get my uncle to do it if you need me to."

"We need a ride to the airport."

Kit asked, "Who is 'we'?"

Renee said, "Jessica decided to go with me because she is stressed over James."

Kit gave a fake giggle and said, "That is so cute. You two are acting like loving sisters. What time do you need me there?"

Instead of answering the question, Renee asked another question. "If your uncle is taking care of your aunt, then why can't you just come home?"

"Oh, I forgot to tell you that I got that apartment in Jessica's secretary's building," Kit answered joyfully.

Renee was happy and upset at the same time. She said, "How could you forget to tell me something like that?"

"They just called me today. I just didn't get a chance to call you today because they needed a lot of shit. They really put you through it to get up in that building."

"Girl, anything is better than you staying on Terrace. I am so happy for you."

"Yes, girl, it was a close call because Terrace Avenue Apartments called me, too. I didn't have to think twice about my decision."

"Maybe I could have Sam help you move while I am away. Wait — what the hell is wrong with me? Did you hear what I just said?"

Kit said, "I made the same mistake and called Eric to give him the news. Some guy answered his phone and brought my ass right back to reality, real quick. Hell, *I'm* the one who needs a vacation."

Renee laughed, saying, "It's not too late to join us on the trip."

Kit thanked her for the invite but said, "I need to save my money because this move is going to take all that I have. I am starting from scratch here. I don't even have a bed."

Renee offered some sound advice. "Don't sweat the small stuff. It will work out."

"Anyway, I'll see you tonight. Let me tell my uncle I can't watch the wicked bitch of the east. Do you know she had the nerve to formulate the words 'Get out of my house'?" I wanted to push her ass down a flight of steps. I know God won't bless me if I use this opportunity to seek revenge for all her years of torment."

"Kit, have you ever thought that maybe God is smiling on you, and that is why you found a place in Charmaine's building instead of that godforsaken other place?" Renee asked. There is no point in blocking your blessing with evil thoughts about your aunt. That stroke is her punishment for all those years."

"We will talk more when I get there," Kit said.

Over at Eric's apartment, Mike was telling Eric about a phone call he'd answered.

"Yo, E. I think your ex-girl called you."

"What did she say?" Eric asked.

"When I answered, she just started talking. She sounded really excited — something to do with an apartment. As soon as I said 'Hello' again, she hung up."

"Damn, Mike. I can only imagine what she is thinking right now. What did you say to her?"

"Man, relax. I didn't say anything to her. She hung up too fast."

Very annoyed, Eric asked, "Why are you here anyway? I thought you had a new girl."

"I do, and she is great, but I needed to do something tonight."

Assuming he knew where the conversation was going, Eric said, "Whatever it is, I need my car. You use my car so much I'm starting to think it's your car. Matter of fact, I think you are using me and taking me for granted. I love you, Mike, but I will draw the line if I feel I am being taken advantage of."

"Yo, man — chill! I am not taking advantage of you or anybody else. I just need to make a run," Mike said.

"Why can't you use her car?" Eric asked, still very upset.

"I can't be seen in her car where I'm going."

"One day, James Michael Frazier, your deceitful ways will catch up to you."

Mike was caught off guard by hearing Eric call him by his full name.

Mike asked, "How the hell did you find out my full name?"

"I was cleaning your room, and I found your birth certificate crumpled on the floor. What is the big deal?" Eric asked nonchalantly.

Mike became enraged, grabbed Eric by the arm, and yelled, "Don't ever go through my things again!"

"Mike, let me go! You're hurting my arm."

"Shut the fuck up! Do you hear me? Don't ever touch my things again. How would you like it if I touch your things? Matter of fact, take your fucking clothes off now!"

Eric was frightened and paralyzed with fear as Mike started tearing at his clothes.

"Mike, what the hell are you doing? Mike, stop before this gets ugly!"

Mike managed to get Eric out of his pants and flipped him over on his stomach.

"Shut up and turn over! Isn't this what you wanted all along?"

Before Eric could say anything, Mike said, "Shut the fuck up and take this dick."

Eric began to cry, trying to get Mike's attention.

"Mike, please stop it! You are hurting me. Don't do this, Mike!"

Mike began to moan with pleasure. "Uh, uh, uh, that's what you like, huh, E? Yeah, E, take that dick from Daddy. Be a good boy, and tell me that you like it. Say it — now!"

Trying not to upset Mike any further, Eric went along with it. "I like it! I like it!" he shouted.

"Yeah, that's it. Daddy is about to nut. Can you feel it? Turn over — I want to put it on your face. That's it, nigga. Now, how do you like it when someone gets all up in your shit?"

Eric sat on the edge of the bed with cum on his face and tears in his eyes, screaming, "Get your shit out of my house! You are a rapist!"

"Rape! I didn't *rape* you. You *wanted* it. In fact, you damn near begged me to give it to you. Besides, a man can't get raped. If you weren't such a pussy, you would have fought back if you didn't want it. Where are the keys to the car?"

"On the table. Just take them and go!" Eric yelled.

"I'll be back, so go clean yourself up," Mike said as he tucked his dick back in his pants and adjusted himself before walking out of the room.

Mike jumped in the car and called Charmaine to tell her that he really missed her and just wanted to hear her voice again.

Charmaine sat at her desk swooning over Mike and the reason he was calling, but she had to snap out of it because she had been trying to reach Jessica regarding an account, but Jessica wouldn't answer her phone.

Jessica was holding her phone in her hand while looking at the caller ID.

I just want everyone to stop calling me. The one person I want to talk to won't call or answer his damn phone. Oh, shit, speaking of the devil!

"Hey, Jess. How are you, baby? I have really missed you."

"You should, James. You have not come by here or called in weeks," Jessica responded, holding back her anger.

James sensed the tension and tried to mellow things out by tugging on her heartstrings.

"I told you I was going through a really rough time in my life, and I just needed some space."

She felt no sympathy for him and said, "Good. Well, you got it — because it is over."

"Don't be like that, sweetheart."

"*Sweetheart*, my ass! What happened to 'Pumpkin'? Are you getting your women confused, James?"

"What are you talking about? I have no other women. I only want you. Don't you remember our plans of moving in together and having our firstborn child together?"

"James, stop playing with me! Planning a baby is a little hard to do when the supposed father is not around. I don't have time for this. I am going away. If I feel like it, I will call you when I get back."

"Pumpkin, why wouldn't you tell me that you were going away? Where are you going?" he said in a really somber tone.

Jessica knew that tone of voice meant that he was trying to soften her up any way he could, but she tried to remain strong in her disappointment and anger.

"I am going away with my sister."

"OK. Where are y'all going?" he asked in that same soft tone.

"Like I said, I don't have time for this. You want to call questioning me about where I am going. Why don't you start telling me where you have been!"

James, growing frustrated with the negative attitude, snapped back. "Oh, so now we are playing a game of tit for tat."

"No games need to be played if you would just get off my phone," Jessica said.

"How can you talk to me like this? I explained the situation last time we spoke. I love you, Jessica, and if you love me, then you would not let it end like this. I am almost there, so we can talk face to face."

James was lying the entire time, because he was sitting in the car on the side of the house.

Jessica said, "I do love you, James, but you need to understand I will not take shit from any man again. I will ask you one question, and I expect the truth."

She paused before asking, "Have you been seeing or sleeping with someone else? But, hold on before you answer that question. Let me go get the door."

As Jessica opened the door, James was standing there holding the phone in his hand. He looked her square in the eyes and said, "Jessica, no. My heart is with you. I have been stressed out. I can't even think about having sex, let alone dealing with another woman."

Jessica was determined to play hard to get as she disconnected the phone line, turned her back, and proceeded to walk up the stairs, with James following behind her.

When her bedroom door closed, she turned to him, looked him dead in the eye, and said, "Prove it!"

His eyebrows rose with bewilderment, and he asked, "How do I prove that I was not with someone else?"

With a sexy-but-deviant look in her eyes, she said, "Make love to me right now — and remember: I can tell by how much love juice you produce. I can also tell by your touch and your smell if you've been with someone else."

Although he thought her suggestion made no sense, he agreed to her demands.

"I will make love to you because I have missed you and want to show you how much — but not as some sick test."

Jessica aggressively pulled him toward her and said, "Whatever, James — kiss me."

James became aroused by her touch and said, "Jessica, you are going to mess around and wake up the sleeping giant. Look what you've done."

Jessica started to take her shirt off and lay down across the bed saying, "Well, bring that thing over here, so I can see just how much you missed me."

"OK, but let me use the bathroom first, and you can't be grabbing on him like that."

That statement sent up red flags for Jessica.

"James, if you are trying to prove that you were not with someone else, never ask to use the bathroom before sex. All that makes me do is think that you want to wash the scent of the other woman off. How about we get started working on that baby we were talking about and let me feel you and only you inside me."

"OK, but take it easy on me. That thing is so hard, it hurts," he said.

"You just take your time, because if you have not had any, you will cum quick, and I need this right now," she warned.

James questioned what was going on with her.

"Are you still testing me, Jess?"

Jessica was now hot and ready for action and was growing impatient.

"James, please stop talking and work that thing for Mommy. Oh, yes, baby," she moaned. "Did you miss Mamma?" she whispered in his ear before using her tongue to stimulate his nipple.

"Oh, God, Jess — that thing is good. I should stay away more often. Work that thing, girl. I think you missed Daddy, too. Tell me that you missed Daddy."

"Oh, shit! Yes, I missed Daddy! I missed my Daddy! James, it's happening! Don't stop — keep that thing right there! Oh, James, I've missed you!"

James was pleased with his performance and happy to serve his woman.

James said, "That's it, baby. That's my Pumpkin."

Jessica, feeling very sexually satisfied, lay on her back, gazing up at the ceiling. She said, "I wish things were different."

"What you mean, Jess?"

Jessica answered, "As good as that was to me, I could not help but notice that you did not cum. I can't say for certain that you were with someone else, or if you just don't enjoy being with me anymore."

"I just wanted you to get yours. I didn't want to be selfish — that's all, Jess."

She turned on her side to face him, and, the moment she looked at him, she felt that sinking feeling in her stomach.

"Thank you, but I am still confused about what is going to happen between us from this point on. I still feel something is not right."

James decided to deflect from addressing the issue and flipped it.

"Let's start by telling me where you are going and for how long?"

"I am going to Jamaica with Renee for a week so we can clear our minds."

"Maybe that is a good thing. That could be what you need to realize you are jumping the gun. Maybe when you get back, we can talk instead of arguing."

Jessica thought that was the perfect moment to put him on high alert.

"That means you have a week to get your shit together, or when I come back, there will be nothing to talk about."

He completely ignored her statement and just asked his follow-up question.

"When are you leaving?"

"We are leaving in the morning. Kit is taking us to the airport."

"I'm surprised she's not going. I heard she's having a hard time right now."

"She is doing better. She got an apartment in my secretary Charmaine's building."

"Oh, really? Good for her," James offered, sounding genuinely happy for Kit.

Jessica added, "God is handing out blessings all around us. I think it was a blessing that you came here right before I left the country."

James said, "Either it's a blessing or perfect timing. I have to go. I borrowed a friend's car, and I have to return it. I will call you later. I love you, Jess, and I hope you'll be good out there in Jamaica."

"Go home and take a shower first, because you smell like sweaty butt cheeks."

"Oh — you got jokes now that you got yours off. I see how we're doing this, Jessica."

Jessica's laughter filled the room as she got up to get dressed and walk him to the door. As she said "Goodbye" and told him that she would talk to him later, she watched as he drove off down the street.

Moments later, Kit strolled through the door. "Hey, ladies. Kit is in the house."

"Kit, you are truly my daughters' friend," Momma Tyler said. Why do you girls have to announce yourselves when you come into the house?"

Kit smiled in her direction and laughed as she said, "The presence of greatness must be recognized."

Jessica loved the quick comeback statement Kit gave her mother and gave Kit props for it.

"That's a good one, girl."

Kit continued to laugh and asked, "Are you guys ready to go away and sit on the beach waiting for Dexter to walk by? I am going to pray that the Lord sends you guys each a version of Morris Chestnut, because the real man is for me. By the way, was that Eric I just saw driving away from your house?"

"Why would Eric be here? Sam does not come here anymore since he broke up with Renee, so he has no reason to come here. That was James who just left. He borrowed his friend's car," Jessica said.

"It looks just like Eric's car. What did James want?"

Jessica stepped back as if to say, *Why would you ask me something like that?* "He wanted me, of course."

"Well, where has he been?"

"He said he was trying to clear his mind."

"Did you really believe him, or did you just give him some because you needed to get off?"

Jessica shook her head in agreement. "I gave him some because I needed to get off. He can't fool me. He didn't even cum. If he was not with anyone in all this time, that negro would have bust all over me quick, fast, and in a hurry."

Kit burst out in laughter. "Jessica, I've never heard you talk like that."

"I am in rare form tonight. I can't wait to get to Jamaica. No, but for real, last time we couldn't do anything because I had a yeast infection. He came so fast and hard, it looked like cottage cheese. He got him some, and it was recent. I look at it like this: that session was one for the road."

Kit continued to laugh at Jessica's expense.

"You are talking a lot of shit right now, but it sounds good."

"Watch what happens when I get back. On another note, guess who I saw when I was coming home?"

Kit was intrigued and asked, "Who?"

Jessica held her in suspense for a brief moment.

"The bouncer from the club that night. He's a cop, and he pulled me over."

Kit interrupted: "You'd better had given him your number in exchange for the ticket."

"Kit, I ain't no fool — you know I did. He is cool, but I am not ready for that right now."

"He is cute though, Jess. Where is Tawana? I thought I saw her earlier with Sam. Speak of the devil, and in she walks. Hey, girlie — where are your loyalties?" Kit asked.

Tawana, caught off guard by Kit's comment, asked, "What are you talking about, Kit?"

"I thought I saw you with Sam earlier."

With a really distasteful tone, Tawana responded, "Yeah — *and?*"

"What the hell do you mean?" Renee snapped back.

"Renee, calm down. I got this. Why would you want to hang around a guy who hurt your aunt the way he did?" Kit questioned.

"First of all, Kit, you should mind your own business. I was with him because he was concerned for my aunt, thank you very much."

Kit was not buying her answer and asked, "If that is the case, why get so defensive?"

Tawana decided not to engage in conversation with Kit any longer and said, "Whatever, Kit."

She turned her attention toward Renee and said, "He wanted me to tell you just how sorry he is for hurting you like that. He did not want it to come out like that."

As Tawana was speaking, she looked around and noticed the suitcases in the room.

"Wait a minute. Is somebody going somewhere?" Tawana asked.

Renee was over hearing about what Sam wanted, so she said, "Listen, Tawana. Do me a favor, and tell him to stay away from me and my family. On another note, Jessica and I are going to Jamaica for the week."

"I need to talk to you before you leave," Tawana said.

"OK, we'll talk later. Right now, I need to talk to Kit in private."

Kit and Renee went upstairs to their room.

"Kit, don't be so hard on her. She thinks she is doing the right thing because she wants to see us together."

Kit, still angry from her brief interaction with Tawana, blurted out, "She is feeling herself. Whoever she is screwing has got her mind all twisted. She is lucky she is your niece. Anyway, how is my niece or nephew doing in that belly?"

"The baby is fine. I haven't told anyone here yet, so keep it down."

"Keep the baby, and forget about Sam's stupid ass," Kit said.

"Anyway, how are you and your situation? Have you gotten the results yet?" Renee asked, trying to change the subject.

"I am fine, so far. I have to go back to Dr. Carl to make sure everything is clear, but I am feeling better."

"That's good, Kit. I am glad you are dealing with it better. Anyway, I can't wait to leave, and Jessica is so excited she is making me sick. James is a piece of shit and does not deserve her or her forgiveness."

Kit smiled as she said, "That is one of the nicest things I've ever heard you say about your sister."

"She is my sister, and I always want what's best for her, even if I don't tell her. This baby makes me tired all the time. I need a nap."

"Well, go to sleep. I'm going to mess with the new-and-improved Jessica," Kit laughed as she walked out of the room.

Renee found it funny also when she responded, "She has changed since she decided to go on this trip, hasn't she?"

"Yeah, but I sort of like it. See you in the morning." Kit closed the door and burst into Jessica's room, but she was on the phone.

"Charmaine, this is Jessica, I saw that I'd missed your call, so call me back."

Charmaine was on the phone with Desire when Jessica was calling and decided not to switch over.

"Charmaine, sweetheart. I am home."

"Hey, babe. Hold on one second. I'm coming." She whispered into the phone, "Desire, I will call you later. Mike just came in."

She put the phone down and ran toward the front door.

"Hey, baby, gimme kiss. Oh, Mike, where are you coming from? You smell really foul."

"You are the second person to say that to me today. I am going to get in the shower."

"Please do. I will start dinner while you do that."

Mike looked at her and put his hand on his chest across his heart and said, "That's why I love you. You make life so easy."

"You love me? Yeah, right — since when?" Charmaine said, smiling all the while.

As he closed the bathroom door, he said, "We will talk about that over dinner."

The phone started ringing just at that moment.

"Hello, Charmaine. It's Jessica. How are you?"

"Oh, hey, Jess. I am fine. Mike is here, and I am about to cook dinner. What's up?"

"I just wanted to apologize again for such short notice on this trip," Jessica said.

"It's fine. I decided I am going to work instead of taking off with you. Mike said this is not a good time for a vacation."

"Well, maybe when I get back, you two can go somewhere romantic."

In the distance, Mike called out, "Charmaine, baby, can you come help me wash my back?"

Jessica asked, "Was that him?"

Charmaine answered proudly, "Yes, that's my man."

"He almost sounded like James for a minute. He just left here trying to plead his case. Anyway, I'm going to bed and rest up for my trip in the morning."

"You have a safe trip, and I will see you when you get back."

Charmaine disconnected the call and rushed into the bathroom.

"Hey, baby. I am here to scrub you down."

She looked down at the floor where Mike had undressed and at the pile of his clothes there.

"Now, Mike — you know you are too big for that mess."

"What did I do?" he asked.

"You have Hershey squirts in your drawers. How the hell did you get them on the front of your briefs? That is just nasty. I am throwing these out."

"I don't care. Take your clothes off, and get your sexy self in here."

"What about dinner, Mike?"

"Turn it down, and come take a shower with me."

"Say no more. Be right back," Charmaine said.

CHAPTER 6

No More Secrets

"Renee, I am so glad you agreed to let me come with you on this trip. Look at the sand and the water. It is so beautiful."

"Jessica, would you please calm your happy ass down? Can you just do that long enough to for us to find a spot on the beach?"

"Please, I am here to clear my mind, and that is what I intend on doing. There are two lounge chairs over there under that tree near those guys."

"Jessica, please find another set of chairs. We just got here, and I don't feel like being hit on already by Bob Marley's offspring."

"Renee, you know you are just wrong for that. Let's go over here by the beach band then."

"No, I don't want all the damn noise in my head."

Jessica gave her the side-eye and said, "What the hell is wrong with you? If you are going to complain about every little thing, then you find the seats."

"Those two over there close to the water, under the big beach umbrella. Let's go before someone gets them."

Jessica laid her towel down on the chair and took a deep breath.

"Finally, I need a drink. Oh, they have servers to go to the bar and bring your drinks to you," Jessica noticed.

"I am going to take a quick nap. When they come, get me water."

"A water! We are in Jamaica surrounded by water, girl — get a drink," Jessica shouted at Renee.

"I just want water. Why is that a problem for you, Jessica?"

"What is the matter with you, Renee?"

"I am pregnant, stupid. That's what's wrong with me."

Jessica jumped up from her lounge chair, elated.

"Oh, my God. I am so happy. I am going to spoil her rotten. 'Auntie Jessica' — I can hear her now."

"Get off of me and pump your brakes. I don't know if I'm keeping the baby. That is why I am here — to clear my mind and make my decision."

Shocked and disappointed at the same time, Jessica yelled, "Renee! Where would you be if mommy decided to throw you back into the unknown?"

Sarcastically, Renee answered, "I would not be here faced with the decision of whether I should keep a baby with no baby daddy — that's for sure."

Pissed at her response, Jessica said, "Damn him! You have your family and friends to see you through this!"

"I am still very young, and I could wait for the next time, when the father will stick around," Renee replied.

"Is that the reason he left?" Jessica asked, sounding very concerned.

"No, he doesn't know. I was going to tell him when he told me he wanted someone else. I just kept it to myself because I didn't want him to stay with me for the baby's sake. I don't want to be a victim of pity love."

"I understand that. I am not in your shoes, but I would love to have another member of my family to share my love with."

"Jess, don't make this any harder for me. That's why I didn't tell anyone in the family, because they are going to react like you."

"Well, does anyone know?" Jess asked.

"Kit knows and Dr. Carl, but that's it."

"Nee, let me ask you this: Do you want the baby?"

Renee placed her sunglasses on, lay back in her lounge chair, and thought for a brief moment before she answered.

"I do want it. I just thought that I would have the whole package when I finally decided to bring forth life. Without that package, I don't think I could do it on my own. I don't want to do it on my own."

"Oh, damn, Renee. You threw a monkey wrench into my plan of becoming the next Stella."

"Don't let me stop you, Sis. You can get your groove on if you want to."

"No, I have to take care of my little sister. Besides, I got mine before I came down here."

"Oh, yeah — I heard," Renee said sarcastically.

Renee slid her sunglasses down to the tip of her nose and turned toward Jessica, saying, "Jessica, I want you to know that I do love you, and I want what's best for you. I just don't feel James is the best person for you."

Feeling confused and defensive, Jessica asked, "What is your thing with him? Did he ever try to hit on you or do something to you?"

Renee sucked her teeth, making the sound of saliva squeezing in between each tooth.

"No, nothing like that. He just has something about him. My gut tells me he is no good."

"What did your gut tell you about Sam?"

Renee fixed her glasses on her face, while Jessica adjusted her lounge chair to lie all the way back.

"You got that, Jess, but Sam was different. He and I were friends long before we became lovers. James came from who knows where. There was that time when we went out to dinner, and Sam even said sometimes James acts funny. I hate the fact that he came into the picture, using your car like he'd paid the note on it. He just seemed like a user. I just want you to think hard before you forgive him."

Jessica wanted the conversation to end, so she jumped up, saying, "Enough of the serious talk. I want to ride the Jet Ski. I'll be back."

Back in the States, Desire was overjoyed with great news.

"Hey, Charmaine — guess what? I got the job! Please tell Jessica I said 'Thank you,'" she screamed into the phone.

Ms. Millie stepped out of the office because she thought something was going on in the shelter. Millie whispered "Congratulations" and signaled for her to keep it down with her hands.

Charmaine was just as happy as Desire at the good news.

"Congratulations, girl. Why didn't you call me? I told you I would take you to the interview."

"I didn't want to bother you. You have bent over backwards for me and the boys. I just wanted to do this on my own."

"Well, good for you. Now we just have to find you an apartment. There was a one-bedroom apartment available in my building, but Kit got it."

"That's OK, because I need a two-bedroom, but I will take a one-bedroom and make it work on the couch if it means I get out of this shelter. I don't need privacy, because no man is coming between me and my kids — ever."

Charmaine shook her head at the phone as if Desire could see her.

"There you go, sounding bitter. You need someone like Mike in your life. He has got to be the sweetest man alive. This morning, he made me breakfast in bed and cut all the fruit into heart-shaped pieces."

With a pessimistic tone, Desire said, "That all sounds really nice. Maybe one day God will send me a Mike of my own. Right now, all I want is a place of my own and peace of mind."

Charmaine said, "Anyway, I'll let you know if something else opens up. What are you doing right now?" she asked Desire.

"Nothing. The boys are in school, and I was hanging around the shelter trying to think of my next move."

"You didn't have to work today at the file-clerk job?" Charmaine questioned.

"I took the day off so I could go to the interview. Why are *you* not at work?" Desire asked.

Charmaine exhaled slowly when she answered. "Mike wanted to spend the day in bed. Des, I want you to meet him. Take a cab to my house, and I will pay for it."

With some hesitation, Desire said, "He wanted to be alone with you today. Perhaps we will meet another time."

Reassuring her friend that it would be OK for her to come over, Charmaine said, "He won't mind. We can make lunch, play Scrabble, and have some mid-day drinks. It will be fun."

"OK, cool. Sounds good. I'll be there soon," Desire said.

Excited to tell Mike, Charmaine flopped down on the sofa next to him and snuggled up under his arm.

"Mike, baby, I invited my friend Desire over to hang out with us for a little while."

Mike said, "You never mentioned her before."

"We have been friends for years, but she got with this guy who wouldn't allow her to see her friends or family. Long story short, she has three kids, and she is living in a shelter because he left her. I just figured she could use some fun in her life."

"Are you talking about that shelter in Hempstead on Main Street?" he asked.

"Yeah — you know it?"

"I heard someone else talk about it before. What time is she coming?"

"She should be on her way now. I told her to take a cab."

Mike, sounding concerned, said, "Wow, it sounds like she has been through a lot. I will go get some Apple Martini from the liquor store. I know how you ladies love that drink."

"I knew I could count on you. Thank you, babe."

Mike gave her a kiss and headed out the door. Ten minutes later, the doorbell rang, and Charmaine thought that Mike had forgotten something. When she opened the door, she saw that it was Desire.

"Damn, girl. It seems like I just got off the phone with you. Did you fly over here?"

"What's up? Where is that man of yours?" Desire asked.

"He went to go get some drinks for us. I wonder which liquor store he went to, because he has been gone way too long now."

Just then the phone began to ring, and Charmaine asked Desire to answer it because she was closest to the phone.

"Hello. Charmaine Dupree residence. How may I help you?"

Because no one answered, Desire kept saying, "Hello . . . hello . . . I guess they didn't want to talk to me," she said as she hung up the receiver.

"Who was on the phone?"

"I don't know. They wouldn't say anything when I answered," Desire responded. There it is again. Do you want me to get it again?"

"I'll get it. Hello. How may I help you?" Charmaine asked.

Mike answered, "Charmaine, sweetheart. I am sorry. My boy called while I was in the liquor store and said he needed my help moving some equipment. I will be home later. Tell your friend I hope to meet her soon. I am sorry for leaving like that, but I figured you girls could have a ladies' day."

Charmaine was disappointed and said, "I wanted my two favorite people in the world to meet."

"We will meet another time — I promise. Enjoy your day with your friend. I love you, baby."

"Love you too, boo."

Charmaine turned to face Desire, standing in the kitchen area of the apartment, looking in the direction of Charmaine as she got off the phone.

"He's not coming, but he said he can't wait to meet you."

Desire was more concerned with the drinks. She asked, "What about the drinks? Please tell me you have something to drink in here."

Charmaine answered, "I got a half bottle left in the fridge. We can drink that while I bust your ass in a game of Scrabble. So, when do you start work, Des?"

"On Monday, at nine."

"That's good, but what about the other job?"

"They said I can work part-time on the weekend."

"Jessica will be back from her trip on Monday. I think you guys will hit it off well. I hope she is having fun on her trip. But on another note: Girl, I think I need to see a doctor. I don't know whether it's because I finally started having sex on a regular basis or what, but it just doesn't smell the same down there anymore."

Desire spit Apple Martini across the floor at Charmaine's statement.

She was laughing really hard as she tried to speak. "What do you mean?" she asked, while she patted the dribbles of Apple Martini off her lips.

"It smells like old garbage down there!"

Still laughing uncontrollably, Desire said, "You are stupid! If it was that bad, I would smell you from here."

"I'm gonna go see this Dr. Carl who has been all up in everyone's hot pocket, next week sometime, because I can't take this smell."

"Speaking of Dr. Carl, how is Kit?" Desire asked Charmaine.

Charmaine said, "I guess she is fine. We are really not friends like that. Actually, the night we hung out was the first night we met. I haven't even seen her since she moved into the building. I've got an idea: When I do see her, I will invite her over for dinner or something to welcome her to the building. It would be great if you were living here also, Des"

"Charmaine, I think you are doing all this talking to try to distract me from this Scrabble game. I may be a little buzzed, but I know that ain't no word."

Both Charmaine and Desire looked down at the Scrabble board and burst out in laughter.

"So, do you have any pictures of your beau?" Desire asked.

"He took the camera and said he was going to get them developed at Walgreens, but he accidentally erased all the pictures. He is not electronically inclined at all," Charmaine offered.

Desire looked at her watch and realized that time had gotten away from her.

"I should be getting back, because the boys will be home from school soon."

"I would take you home, but Mike took my car. His car is in the shop, or maybe he said he let his boy use it. Something to that effect — I can't remember."

"That's OK, girl. I will call a cab. Come wait with me downstairs."

"Perhaps Mike will come back before the cab gets here."

While they were standing outside her building waiting for the cab, Charmaine started to reflect on the goodness that had happened for them thus far.

"I pray the Lord keeps smiling on us, Des. He has sent me a good man, and you are on your way up the ladder again. We are going to be at the top of our game in a minute."

Desire shook her head in total agreement, as she looked down the street and spotted a car headed in their direction.

"Well, girlie, here comes my cab. I love you, girl. I will call you later. Tell that man of yours I won't accept a rain check next time."

As Charmaine turned to go back into her building, she spotted her car parked toward the end of the block.

She thought to herself, *That is strange. How did Mike get to his friend's, if my car is still here?*

In the meantime, Mike was back at Eric's apartment, banging on the door.

"Hey! Yo, E! Yo, Eric, open the door! What the fuck did you change the locks for? Come open this door before I break this motherfucker down!" Mike yelled in the hall.

Eric walked toward the door, saying, "Mike, just go away and leave me alone!"

"Man, open the door. I ain't gonna do anything to you. Stop acting like a bitch."

Eric stood by the door with his hand on the lock, saying, "Please just leave. I will take your things over to your girlfriend's house."

"What the fuck are you talking about, E?"

"I know all about her! Does she know all about you?" Eric yelled at the door.

"Open this damn door, or when I catch your ass, it will be worse than last time."

Eric sensed that he meant that threat and felt he couldn't control this situation any longer.

"I am calling the police. Just leave!"

Mike pounded on the door after hearing Eric say he would call the police on him.

"That's how you are gonna play me! Yo, E, man, I will see you again — trust me on that. You forget I have your keys to the car."

"I called and reported the car stolen. So if I were you, I would leave the car here and go."

"You can have that piece of shit. I don't need your car, but I will see you, Eric. You think that the police can save you?"

Eric tried to talk some sense into Mike through the door.

"Things don't have to be like this, Mike. You did what you did, and it's over. Do not come back here again, and we can leave it like that."

Mike tried to lower his tone to give the illusion that he had calmed down.

"All I wanted to do was talk to you man to man, but you're in there still acting like a bitch."

Realizing that Mike was not calm at all, Eric said softly, "That is exactly why I won't let you in. Mike, please just leave me alone and go away!"

There was silence in the hallway, so Eric decided to take a peek through the peephole. Mike used his fingers to form the shape of a gun and pretended to fire a shot at the door as he walked away. Eric jumped away from the door as if it were a real gun, clutching his chest. He ran to the phone and dialed Kit's number, but then he realized that he could no longer call her. He sat on the sofa and cried.

Kit was preoccupied with happy thoughts of moving into her own place. She went to the Tyler residence to pick up some of her things to take to her new apartment. As she entered Renee's room, she instantly wished she could unsee what was transpiring before her eyes.

"You trifling little bitch! I should whip your ass, for your aunt! She is the reason why you are here, and this is how you repay her? Do you have any self-respect? How could you do this to her, in her room? In her bed, no less! Matter of fact, you and this punk-ass negro, get up and get out of my sister's room!"

"Kit, you don't come in here and talk to my grandbaby like that! You are a guest in this house also."

"Ms. Tyler, do you see what is going on in here? You knew about this and let it happen?" Kit screamed at Momma Tyler.

"This is still my house, and you have no right to come in here and question me about anything I do under my roof, little girl."

Kit felt deep down inside that she'd lost all respect for Momma Tyler.

"No wonder your daughters are in need of therapy," Kit shouted.

"How dare you talk to me like that? You can get the hell out of my house! I don't care whose friend you are! Get the hell out!"

Kit realized she'd been disrespectful toward her best friend's mother and the person who'd put her up when she had nowhere else to go.

"No problem, Momma Tyler. I meant no disrespect, but how could you violate your daughter's feelings like that?"

"My daughter is a grown woman who can handle her own affairs. This is a family matter, and, therefore, none of your business."

Kit thought, *Fuck it. I have nothing to lose. I am moving out anyway, and this lady is crazy.*

"Renee is my sister, and I am glad you are not my mother."

"You went too far, Kit. Don't talk to my grandmother like that," Tawana said.

"You and your grandmother are fools. How do you think Renee is going to feel when she hears that her mother was allowing her niece to have sex with her ex-boyfriend in her bed?"

Sam felt it was his turn to speak, and he said, "It is not your place to tell her anything."

"You shut the fuck up, Sam. You are the worst kind of piece of shit-ass negro out there, and I will be damned if I keep this a secret!" Kit screamed in Sam's direction.

She turned to look Tawana dead in her eyes and said, "You need to be dealt with. I would put my hands on you, but neither one of you is worth my freedom."

Kit shook her head in Sam's direction as she said, "Sam, she really loved you. You were her best friend besides me. How could you do this to her?"

Sam, feeling ashamed, tried to plead to Kit's sensibility.

"Kit, please understand, I didn't mean for any of this to happen. I knew that I was not happy anymore with Renee."

Kit couldn't believe the audacity of him talking about Renee not making him happy.

She interrupted his thoughts, "So, you decided to sleep with her niece! I am sure that made you really happy," she said sarcastically.

Sam was determined to justify his action. "I love Tawana. I want to spend my life with her. I imagine myself with her in ways I never saw myself with Renee."

Kit began to clap her hands as loud as she could.

"Oh, how romantic! Who gives a fuck! The bottom line is you don't cross those lines!"

Momma Tyler grew tired of the yelling and cursing in her house. She said, "Kit, I told you to get out of my house!"

"I am leaving, but all of you can be certain that I am calling Renee to let her know as soon as possible."

Kit jumped in her car and immediately dialed Renee's number, but it went straight to voicemail.

Renee and Jessica were lounging in their hotel room in Jamaica, blissfully unaware of what was happening back home.

Jessica mentioned, "This has been a beautiful trip. Were you able to clear your head, Renee?"

"Yes, I think I want to keep my baby. Life is too short to worry about whether or not he will be there. If he doesn't want to be a part of the baby's life, then that's his loss."

Completely excited for her sister, Jessica shouted, "Oh, shoot! You do have your mind made up!"

"Since today is our last day here, we might as well just get some rest before we head back to our confusing lives," Renee said.

Jessica's phone rang. She looked down and saw that it was her mother calling.

"Hey, Mommy is calling me. I wonder what happened."

"Well, if you answer the phone, you will find out," Renee said with a slick undertone.

"Hey, Ma. You calling to check on your beautiful daughters?"

Jessica couldn't understand a word her mother was saying because she was talking fast and furious.

"Ma, slow down. I can't understand you. Kit did *what* to you?"

The moment Renee heard Kit's name, she snatched the phone from Jessica.

"Hello, Mother. What happened with Kit?" she asked with urgency in her voice.

Momma Tyler was able to calm herself down just long enough to answer Renee.

"I threw her out of my house. She is disrespectful, and I don't want her back here again."

"What are you talking about?"

"She came in here and cursed me out stink. If it wasn't for Tawana, I don't know what would have happened."

"That doesn't sound like Kit. What exactly happened, mother?" Renee questioned.

Momma Tyler shouted, "Are you taking your little girlfriend's side over your own mother's?"

"That is not what I'm saying, but it just doesn't sound like Kit."

"Well, does this sound like Kit? She said, 'You old fool. I am glad you're not my mother!'"

Still unsure, Renee asked, "Kit said that to you?"

"Yes, she did, so I threw her ass out of my house."

"Don't worry about that, Ma. I will straighten that all out when I get home," Renee said before she hung up the phone.

Jessica couldn't wait to hear what had happened, so before Renee could put the phone down, she was already repeating the words, "What happened? What happened?"

Renee repeated her what her mother had told her about the situation.

"Ma said Kit disrespected her, and she threw her out."

"Sis, I know that she is your friend, but has she lost her mind?" Jessica asked, sounding pissed off.

"She won't be my friend for long once I get back. See, we haven't even gotten on the plane to go home yet, and the drama has started," Renee added.

Jessica decided that it might be best to hear both sides of the story before she became too angry with Kit. She made the same suggestion to Renee.

"I love our mother, but maybe you should hear Kit's side of the story before you jump to conclusions."

"What side does she have? When her aunt was getting flip at the lip, I held my tongue. I don't care how bad of a mother she is — she is still my mother. Kit could have waited until I came home so I could handle my mother. I let her handle her aunt."

Jessica asked, "Are you going to call her now?"

"Hell, no. It is too expensive, but as soon as I touch American soil, it is on."

Renee's phone started to vibrate in her hand at that moment.

"Look at this: Kit is trying to call me now."

As the phone was ringing, Kit was talking to herself out loud. "Renee, please answer the phone. I don't want you to walk into that mess when you get home."

"She is so lucky I am pregnant, or I would whoop her ass when I get home."

"Uh, Sis — you have to put those thoughts behind you now. You are going to be a mother."

Jessica said, "I know you are right, but I don't want to hear that right now. Look — she is calling me again. I am not going to answer for the sake of this baby because I don't want to work myself up too much."

Kit was standing outside her new apartment building, staring at her phone, as James was approaching her. She finished up leaving a voicemail message for Renee.

"Renee, when you get this message, please call me. There is something I need to tell you, and it is very important."

James walked straight toward her, smiling an uncomfortable smile.

"Hey, James. How are you, and what are you doing here?" Kit asked.

"Hey, Kit. I am doing well. I was visiting one of my boys. What are you doing here?"

"I just moved in. I got a one-bedroom upstairs. You come around here a lot?"

"Yeah, I'm here often. My boy and I go way back."

"Have you spoken to Jessica since they have been away? Speaking of Jessica, have you ever met her secretary? She lives in this building also."

James said, "I wouldn't know her if I saw her."

"I am sorry to bombard you with all these questions. It's just that I am trying to get hold of Renee. There is a situation that needs to be handled right away."

"Can I help with something? After all, that is my family, too," James offered.

"It has more to do with Renee than with Jessica," she said.

Kit looked off into the distance and spotted Charmaine walking up from behind James.

"Oh, here comes Jessica's secretary, Charmaine. Maybe she has spoken to her."

James didn't wait for Charmaine to catch up to them before he started to walk off.

"Well, I have to go. I hope whatever it is works itself out," James said.

Charmaine picked up the pace as she started walking in their direction.

"Hey, Charmaine. Have you spoken to Jessica?"

"No, but they should be back tomorrow. Was that guy trying to get with you, and was his name Mike?"

"No, that was Jessica's soon-to-be-ex-boyfriend, James. He was visiting a friend who lives in this building."

Charmaine said, "From the back, he looked like my boyfriend, Mike."

"So, why would you think that he was trying to get with me if he is your boyfriend?" Kit asked.

"Men will be men, even when they have a good thing. I make it a habit not to put anything past them."

The ladies shared a giggle with each other in agreement.

“I hear that. Now that I am living in the building, maybe we can hang out or something. I could use a hand painting and decorating. I’ve never had an apartment before, so I don’t want to jam everything together,” Kit said.

Charmaine responded quickly, saying, “No problem. I have skills. We can go shopping for furniture whenever you like.”

Kit nodded her head in disagreement, saying, “Girl, funds are limited. We can go window-shopping. I can’t wait for my girl to get home. Let me go. I have to try and call her again.”

As Kit walked away, her phone rang. She thought it might be Renee calling her, but the caller ID said it was Sam.

Kit thought to herself, *He’s got a lot of damn nerve calling my phone. Fuck him. He can’t talk me out of telling my friend.*

Sam disconnected his call to console Tawana.

“Tawana, baby — stop crying. I just tried to call Kit to see if I could talk her into letting us tell Renee, but she didn’t answer the phone. Everything will be alright. It is better now that things are out in the open. We are free to explore our love on the next level.”

Tawana, trying to talk through her tears said, “I wanted to tell her myself. This is bad, really bad. I don’t know if I can go on with this relationship, Sam.”

“What does that mean, Tawana? Have we gone through all of this for nothing? I hurt my best friend in the name of loving you, and you just want to leave.”

“I don’t want to leave. I just want to think. I will call you later. Sam, I do love you.”

“Tawana, I am in this for the distance. Things will work themselves out. Renee and I were best friends at one point, and if that was real, we will be friends again someday.”

“Sam, Renee and I are family. How do we repair that?”

“You let time take care of all the pain this may cause her. She will heal in her own time, and when she does, it will be OK. You can’t control this. It had to come out.”

“I understand what you are saying, Sam, but I just feel so bad.”

"I feel bad also, but I still have my life to live, and so do you. We can't make ourselves miserable just to make her happy. Think about it: how happy would she have been with me? I knew that I did not feel for her as deeply as she needed me to. Eventually, she would have felt it, too, and things would have gotten really bad. The only thing we can do to make it a little easier on her when she comes home is not to flaunt our relationship in her face. At least until some time has passed and Renee has gotten used to the idea of us being together."

Tawana questioned, "Do you think we are going to hell for this?"

"God knows our hearts were in the right place. We didn't set out to hurt anyone. I think we would have his blessing. Get some rest. We will talk tomorrow."

Sam kissed Tawana on her forehead before he left the house. Tawana went to bed but not before saying a prayer.

Heavenly Father, my aunt will be home tomorrow, and I pray to you that she receives this news with an open heart and mind. Amen.

When the plane landed, Renee and Jessica reflected on life back in New York.

"I am glad to be home. The vacation was good, but something about coming home just feels right," Jessica said.

Renee, sounding very pessimistic, answered, "I am still stressed out. I am pregnant with a baby by a man who does not know, and I have to cut my best friend off for disrespecting my mother. Please tell me what is so good about coming home?"

"Well, I learned not to put all my eggs in one basket. James is just a man, and I was making him out to be a god of some sort. I felt I needed him to love me because I wanted to take my life to the next level. I wanted a child and a husband and a great career. The way he has been acting lately shows me that he might not be the one for me. I realized during this trip that I was not having fun with him. I wasn't myself. I was just trying to please him. Hanging out on the beach, I met so many men who just wanted to make me laugh, and I realized that James and I don't laugh. I spent most of this relationship trying to encourage him, reinforcing his ego, and pushing him to strive to be more. He should want that for himself. My husband and future baby daddy needs to possess these qualities, or I can't be with him. This trip was everything I needed to open my eyes."

Out of all that Jessica had just said, Renee had heard only one part.

"You were trying to start a family with James?" she asked.

"I asked him to move in with me and be my baby's father."

Renee asked, "Did he go running out the door? You sound so desperate."

Jessica responded as if Renee's feelings had some merit.

"At the time, I thought it was special — a woman wanting to give that much of herself to someone. Maybe he saw it the way you did, and that is why he gently turned me down."

"Jess, when it comes to topics like having children and moving in together, always let the man bring that up. I believe it shows his intent in the relationship. If a man goes two years or more without ever suggesting it or mentioning it, then he has doubts about you and a long-term relationship. I personally think two years is too long to wait to know if he is serious about a future with someone."

"You go, Sissy. I think that baby is making you wise."

"No, Sis — it's just a lot of heartache and pain, and, obviously, I still don't have all the answers. Here I am alone again, but now I have a baby on the way. I have faith that I will get it right one day. Don't you wish sometimes that you knew exactly what went wrong at the moment when it went wrong?"

"That's every woman's wish. I know I'm home now. There goes my job calling me," Jessica said, as she shrugged her shoulders.

"Well, you take that call, and I guess I should call Kit."

Renee was dreading to have this conversation with her best friend as she dialed her number.

"Oh, my God, Renee. Where have you been? I have been calling you like crazy. First off, how is the baby thing going?"

Renee answered, "The baby is a keeper, but I need to ask you some things. Did you disrespect my mother, and have you lost your fucking mind?"

Caught way off guard by Renee's tone, Kit said, "Renee, you need to calm down and listen to me. Where are you? Can you come to my new place so we can talk?"

"I am in an Uber, on my way home."

"Why would you take an Uber when you know I would've come to pick you up?"

"To tell the truth, Kit, I didn't know what or how I would feel seeing you after my mother told me what you did."

Once again, Kit was shocked. "What *I* did? What about what *she* did? I know that is your mother, but she is foul."

"Kit, watch your mouth. That is my mother you are talking about. She may not be the best, but she is all that I have. Make no mistake: I will defend her at all costs. That includes if I have to lose a friend over her."

"Hold up! Who do you think you are, talking to me like that, Renee? We have been friends for too long for that shit. You are considered a sister to me, and you should know that, for me to violate anyone in your family, there must have been a good damn reason."

Renee raised her voice slightly, saying, "What fucking reason could there have been for my mother to call me in Jamaica, crying hysterically, because of something you said?"

Kit felt disheartened by her friend's reaction and decided not to tell Renee anything at all.

"So that's how it is going to be, Renee? Fuck what I say, huh? You know what? Maybe you do deserve what is coming to you! Goodbye."

Kit slammed the phone down and started pacing the floor of her new apartment.

Jessica turned to Renee, giving her the *What happened?* look.

Renee was absolutely furious, but she still tried to remain calm for the sake of the baby.

"I don't know what the hell she is talking about. She had no excuse for what she did. I just want to get home, forget about everything, and start making plans to be a single mom."

"Speaking of that, are you going to tell Sam?" Jessica asked.

"I decided I am not going to tell him. I want a clean split, with no attachments."

"So, you are just gonna let him think that the baby belongs to some other man?"

Renee answered, "He can think what he wants to. I owe him no explanation, nor will I answer any questions about my baby."

"Alright, girl. We are home. Are you ready to deal with the rest of your life?" Jessica asked.

Renee said, "I got this," as she stepped out of the Uber.

They opened the front door, yelling for their mother and Tawana. When no one answered, they looked at each other and said in unison, "Where is everyone?"

As they both reached the top of the stairs, they saw their mother sitting on her bed.

"Mother, why didn't you answer? I know you heard us come in," Jessica said.

With slurred speech, Momma Tyler said, "How are my babies?"

Renee peeked into her room and shook her head.

Renee began to shoot off a flurry of question directed at her mother, who did not answer any of them.

"Were you drinking? Why are you talking like that? Are those tears? Jess, is she crying? What the hell is going on in the world? I am tired. Jessica. *You* deal with her and her issues. Just fill me in later. I want to lie down."

Renee went into her room, closed the door behind her, turned on the television, and jumped onto her bed.

Momma Tyler looked at Jessica standing in the doorway and said, "Tawana is not here. She is with Sam."

Jessica stepped into her mother's room and partially closed the door behind her. She whispered, "With *who*? Why is she with him? What the hell is going on here? Why are you drunk and crying?"

"I didn't know what to do when she told me. She is my granddaughter. I thought my daughter would understand and move on to find someone who truly loves her," Momma Tyler mumbled.

"Mother, what are you saying? Are you trying to tell me that Tawana is the reason Sam and Renee broke up?"

Momma Tyler slurred her way through the words. "I knew, and I couldn't say anything."

Jessica asked, "Is that what happened with Kit?"

"Yes, she found out and tried to fight Tawana."

"Do you know what this will do to Renee when she finds out? How could you betray your own daughter like that?"

"Please don't start, Jessica. I feel bad enough."

"When are you going to tell her?"

"It wasn't my place. I told Tawana she had to be the one to do it. If she was bold enough to sleep with her aunt's boyfriend, she can tell her to her face."

"I agree with that statement, but that does not excuse you as a mother," Jessica said. "There are so many things you guys just don't know. Renee's frame of mind is not the same. Please ask Tawana not to tell her just yet."

"I told Tawana she should tell her as soon as possible, because the longer she waits, the worse it will become."

"Oh, Mother — she needs to wait! I have to see if I can reach her on the phone."

Jessica was overwhelmed with everything she'd just heard, and she didn't know who to call first — Tawana or Kit. She decided to call Tawana but accidently dialed Kit's number instead. When she noticed her mistake, she quickly hung up.

Kit, meanwhile, was still pacing in her apartment.

What the hell is wrong with Renee talking to me like that? I was just trying to look out for her. Maybe that bitch's hormones were getting the best of her. You know what? Screw her. I should've told her and let her feel the pain. As a matter of fact, I am going to tell her.

Just as Renee got comfortable in her bed, her phone rang.

Lord, I just want to rest. I am tired. Who the hell is calling me?

Renee saw that it was Kit calling, and, with hesitation, she answered.

"Oh, Kit. I'm tired, and I don't have time for this shit right now."

"I just wanted to tell you something," Kit said.

"What is it, Kit? And please be quick."

"You and I have been friends for a long time now. I wouldn't want anyone to hurt you. I know your situation, but I feel you should know."

Kit took a long pause before she let the words slip from her tongue.

"Your niece is the woman Sam left you for."

Renee sat up from the bed instantly.

"Kit, don't say shit like that to me!" Renee yelled into the phone.

"Ask her and your mother. They can't deny it, because I caught them. They were in your bed. I stood there in shock and watched as they changed positions. She saw me first, and then he asked me to excuse myself from the room. That is why I was so angry and said those things to your mother. I love you, and if you hate me after this, then I will still love you. I am here for you always."

Renee sat still on the bed and couldn't close her mouth, because her jaw had literally dropped at hearing this information.

"Renee, are you still there?"

"I am here. Can you come over? I really need a friend right now. I feel like I can't breathe, and more than anything, I just want this baby out of me."

"Renee, take it easy. You don't mean that. Take a deep breath. I am coming. Is Tawana there now?"

"No. She's probably with him."

"What about your mother?"

"I will handle her. Please hurry. I don't think I can . . . I have to throw up . . . bye!"

Renee hung up the phone and ran out into the hallway, headed toward the bathroom.

"Renee, are you OK?" Jessica asked when she saw Renee's face as she ran past her.

"Jess, I think something is wrong. You won't believe what Kit just told me. My stomach is cramping badly."

Momma Tyler entered the hallway, looked into the bathroom, and said, "Renee and Jessica, is everything alright in there?"

Renee screamed at the top of her lungs, "Stay away from me! Because of you, I may be losing my baby!"

"*What* baby? Renee, I didn't know!"

Jessica looked back at her mother and screamed, "Mother, call an ambulance — she may be having a miscarriage!"

Momma Tyler was still standing there, pleading her case.

"I didn't know, Renee."

Renee shouted back in her direction, "If you would have known I was pregnant, would you have stopped her from sleeping with him in my bed with you right across the hall?"

Jessica screamed at her mother, "Call the ambulance now!"

Renee squeezed Jessica's hand and said, "Call Kit, and tell her to meet us at the hospital. Please, Jess."

Momma Tyler came back into the hallway, saying "I'm going to ride in the ambulance with my baby."

Renee fought through her pain to say, "No, I don't want you near me. Stay the hell away from me. I was cursed the day God put me in your body. Go to hell, and take your granddaughter with you. I wish you were not my mother."

Jessica placed her hands over Renee's mouth to stop her from talking.

"Renee, you don't mean that. You are just upset right now, and you really need to calm down."

Momma Tyler yelled up the stairs, "The ambulance and police are here, and there is some guy out front asking for you, Jessica."

"Well, let them in!" Jessica yelled back."

Jessica was helping Renee down the stairs when she spotted Drake.

"Drake, what are you doing here?"

"I was with my man when the call came through on his radio, and I recognized the address. I just wanted to make sure you were OK."

"I am fine, but my sister may be having a miscarriage."

"Is there anything I can do?" Drake asked.

"Actually, there is. I am very nervous, and I don't want to drive. So, if you are not busy, can you take me to the hospital?"

"I will do better than that. I will stay with you at the hospital, if that's OK with you."

"I could use the company. Thank you."

As the EMTs loaded Renee into the back of the ambulance, Tawana jumped out of an Uber, screaming, "Oh, my God, Jessica! What is going on?"

Renee screamed from the back of the ambulance, "You little bitch. You'd better hope I don't lose my baby. I will kill you *and* that sorry son of a bitch."

Tawana ignored Renee's comment and looked to Jessica for her next move.

"Jessica, what should I do?"

"Tawana, just stay here and take care of Mommy."

Tawana ran into the house, passing her grandmother. She dialed Sam's number.

"Sam, did you know that she was pregnant?"

Bewildered and confused by what he was hearing, Sam couldn't find any words except, "What?"

"Yes, Renee is pregnant, and she may be losing the baby because of us."

"What do you mean, 'because of us'?"

"Kit must have told her, or somebody told her. I can't stay here. When she comes home from the hospital, I can't be here, Sam!"

"I'll come get you."

"No, don't come here. We have to stop this, Sam."

"What are you talking about? I love you, Tawana. I did not know anything about that baby. The only person I could even imagine having a child with is you. I know I have made a big mistake, and this is all my fault. I have mistreated a few women in my life, but what I feel for you is more than I have ever felt for any of them. I know that, someday, I have to pay for how I treated those women, but don't let today be that day. Tawana, please don't be my karma. Please don't leave me now. I will come get you, and we can talk about it then."

"How long will it take you to get here?"

"I am on my way right now."

Tawana walked into her grandmother's room to find her sitting on the bed with a drink in her hand.

“Grandma, Sam is coming to get me. Are you gonna be OK?”

“You go, baby. I will be fine. I don’t want anything to spoil your happiness. Renee will see that things happen for a reason.”

“Are you sure? She is very angry with you, and it’s all my fault.”

“I’m a grown woman, and so is she. More than that, I am her mother. We will work things out when she gets home. I made the same mistake when I was a young girl. I settled for a man who treated me like — excuse my language — pure shit. I loved him more than he liked me, and all I wanted was him. He cheated on me several times, and I accepted it because I just knew that, one day, he would love me enough to stop. I didn’t want that for my daughter, so if Sam loves you, then he will make you happy. He would’ve made my daughter miserable. I didn’t know about the baby, but I would’ve made the same decision. Go live your life with a man who loves you.”

Tawana reached out for her grandmother’s hand and held it tight.

“He does, grandma. He really does love me. I didn’t mean for any of this to happen. I love Renee, and I didn’t mean to hurt her.”

“I don’t want any more fighting in this house over this matter. We are all adults, and we can sit down and discuss the matter as adults. When she comes home and things calm down, I will call you so we can sit down and talk.”

“Grandma, Sam is here. I will call you soon. I love you.”

Momma Tyler grabbed onto her grandbaby and held her close and tight. Then she whispered into her ear, “Make sure he is everything you dreamed of in a man, and if he falls short, don’t hesitate to leave. I’ll be fine as long as my daughter is OK.”

I can’t believe my mother would violate her own child, and now I am sitting in a damn hospital. Jessica’s deep thoughts were interrupted by the touch of a hand.

“Drake, I really appreciate you being here with me. You don’t even know me or my family.”

“It’s no problem, but this is not the date that you promised me. How was your trip?”

"We had a good time. That's when she told me about the baby. I hope everything is OK. When she told me, all I thought about was holding my niece or nephew. I don't think I will ever have children of my own, so I looked forward to her reproducing."

"You are still young, and this is not the time to have that conversation. Did I tell you how beautiful you look when you are stressed out?"

His comment brought a smile to Jessica's face.

"Something is seriously wrong with you, but at least you made me laugh."

Kit came rushing in frantically and interrupted their conversation.

"How is she doing?"

"Hi, Kit. They are still in there. Here comes her doctor now."

The doctor had a somber look on his face, which said it all before the words even came out of his mouth.

"I'm so sorry. She lost the baby."

Kit just wanted to see her friend, so she asked, "Can we see her?"

"Yes, we gave her something to keep her calm. Try not to get her upset."

They all rushed toward the room.

"Hey, Renee. I am so sorry about the baby."

"I'm not. I am happy I dodged that bullet. Can you imagine having a baby by your niece's boyfriend?"

No one in the room responded to her comment.

Jessica asked, "Do you need anything?"

"I need to go home, pack my things, and move out of that house."

"Sis, where would you go?"

Renee turned to face her friend. "Kit, can I stay with you for a little while?"

Kit did not hesitate to answer. "Of course, you can."

"Do you really think it's the best thing to do right now?" Jessica asked. "This is the time you need your family."

"'Family'? Jessica, *really!* If I stay in that house, I will end up in jail. My own mother betrayed me. How can I live under the same roof with her and the little girl who she let betray me? *Family* put me in this hospital."

Jessica had to concede her point of view.

"I guess I see your point."

Renee looked around the room and finally noticed there was a guy in the room.

"Hey, aren't you the bouncer from the club?" Renee asked.

"I'm sorry. My name is Drake. I'm sorry for your loss."

"He drove me here. I was a nervous wreck, and I didn't think I was going to be able to drive," Jessica said.

"It's good to see you are doing well," Drake said. "Ms. Jessica, I see you are in good hands, so I will leave now."

"Thanks again, Drake, and I owe you big time for this one."

He gave her a smile and a wink as he said, "I will call you, so you can pay up."

He wasn't even completely out of the room when Renee said, "Jessica, you should get with him. That's the kind of man you need in your life."

Kit chimed in, saying, "That's the kind we all need in our lives."

Jessica responded, "I have to give James a chance. Besides that, you don't even know him."

"Give him a chance to do *what*, exactly?" Renee said.

"Drake doesn't even know you, and he's here with you."

"Listen, Renee. We are here for you. Besides that, I am a big girl. Let me handle this."

"Well, just don't be stupid with love. Can you do me another favor? I need you to go home and pack some of my things and give it to Kit, because I don't want to go back to that house when I get out of here. Can you believe my own *mother* let some man do this to me?"

Jessica was trying her best to defend and justify her mother's actions.

"You know Mommy did not mean to hurt you. She was stuck between the love of her grandchild and her daughter."

"And it's obvious she chose her grandchild. I don't want to talk about this anymore. I'm gonna put this mess behind me and move on with my life. Didn't that doctor say not to upset me?"

"Oh, so you're gonna milk this. That may be a good attitude to have, but, in all honesty, Sis, you still have to grieve first," Jessica added.

"Yeah, yeah, whatever! I dodged a major bullet, and I am happy. You need to take a page from my book and leave James's ass in the dust."

"Alright. Well, Kit and I are gonna leave on that note. I am actually looking forward to work on Monday. Goodnight, Sis."

CHAPTER 7

Drama

"Good morning, Charmaine."

"Hey, Jessica. This is my friend, Desire Williams, that I have talked about so much."

"It's good to finally meet you. I hope you like it here. My sister speaks highly of you."

"You know your sister's friend Kit moved into my building."

"Yes, I heard. My sister is going to be staying with her for a little while. We will talk about that later. I am expecting a phone call from James. If I'm in a meeting, put the call through anyway. Desire, it was nice to meet you. Maybe we can all do lunch later. I have to play catch-up now."

"Okay, no problem, but you know he always calls on your direct line," Charmaine said.

"I know, but, just in case, put it through."

"I'll talk to you ladies later. I want to check on my sister before I go in there. I have to make a good impression."

As Charmaine and Desire exited Jessica's office, she was dialing Renee's number.

"Hey, Sis. How are you? Just wanted to check on you before I start my day."

"I'm fine. They are releasing me today. Kit is coming to pick me up. Your mother has been blowing up my phone."

"You should talk to her. She is your mother."

"The doctor said I shouldn't be stressed out, so, please don't get me started. I sat in this hospital and did a lot of thinking. I am through with your mother and your niece. I'll call you later."

Renee hung up the phone, Sitting up in the hospital bed, she decided to be real with herself because she couldn't show weakness to her sister or best friend.

God, why didn't you take my life? I was falling in love with the idea of being a mom. I feel so empty now. There's no reason to live. Renee, snap out of it. You know better. There is nothing on this earth worth contemplating suicide over. It hurts now, but you will get through this. You are strong, and you will make it. What the hell is taking her so long? I am ready to leave this damn hospital.

Kit walked in while Renee was still thinking everything through.

"Hey, lady. Are you ready? I was talking to James. He was coming out of my building again."

Curiosity made Renee ask, "What was he doing there?"

"He was visiting his friend. Some guy who lives in the building. He said he is supposed to meet Jessica after work today for dinner."

"He is a sorry-ass negro. He should be at work. How much money can you possibly make as a part-time deejay?"

"Wow — you really don't like him."

"Right now, I hate all men."

Kit tried to make Renee laugh by saying, "You are crazy! You're not thinking about switching teams on me! I have issues with that lifestyle."

"As Jay-Z would say, *'I got ninety-nine problems/but a bitch ain't one.'* Besides, you have issues only with that one person living that lifestyle."

"Speaking of him, he called me the other day to tell me something about Jessica. I just hung up the phone on his ass."

"Why would he call you to tell you anything about Jessica? He doesn't know Jess like that. What could he have to tell you about my sister? What's his number? I'm gonna call him, because I want to know what he has to say about my sister."

Kit was trying not to give this conversation about Eric any life.

"That was just his way of trying to get me to talk to his ass. I wouldn't call him back."

The ride back to Kit's apartment was a continuous barrage of questions regarding why Eric would want to talk to Jessica.

When they finally arrived at the apartment, Renee was tired and decided to take a nap. Kit decided to go to the store while Renee was napping.

Renee was unable to take a nap because Kit's phone kept ringing back to back, nonstop.

Maybe if I answered this damn phone, whoever it is will stop calling. Please don't let this be my mother calling me over here now.

"Hello!" Renee yelled into the receiver.

"Kit, I need to talk to you."

"This is not Kit. Who is this?"

"This is Eric."

"Eric, why are you calling here? You know she does not want to talk to you."

"I wanted to tell her something, but maybe I should just tell you."

"If you are about to start that shit about my sister, then don't, because you don't even know her."

"I don't have to, but I know someone she knows," he said.

Growing impatient with the suspense Eric was trying to create, Renee said, "Stop playing this cat-and-mouse game, and just say it then!"

"This is hard for me, Renee!"

Kit walked in and saw Renee on the phone.

"Girl, I thought you said you were going to take a nap."

"I was, but your ex-boyfriend kept calling."

Kit screamed from across the room, "Hang up the phone on him!"

Eric was on the phone, trying to keep her attention.

"Renee, don't hang up! Renee, are you listening to me? I said I have been sleeping with her man! Renee, are you there?"

Oh, no! She did not hang up on me! I am just trying to help a bitch out. That's alright — they can all get what they deserve, Eric thought.

Renee was sitting there holding the phone because Kit had already disconnected the call.

"Kit, that was just wrong. He was in middle of telling me what he wanted with Jessica."

"He can go to hell. Tomorrow, I'm changing my number. Go to sleep, Renee, and don't think about his stupid ass."

"I am still gonna take a nap, but I want to call Jessica before she leaves work so I can tell her what happened."

"What are you gonna tell her? He didn't tell you anything," Kit said.

"I am going to tell her anyway. Oh, well. I guess it has to wait because her private line is busy. Alright, I am going to take a nap for real this time."

Charmaine walked into Jessica's office just as she was hanging up the phone.

"Ms. Tyler, I need a favor, if you can. Mike just called and said he is stuck in Manhattan and won't be back in time to pick me up. Can you give us a ride to my place after work? He said that he should be at the house by the time I get there, so I can take Desire home after that."

"That shouldn't be a problem — and cut the shit with that 'Ms. Tyler' stuff. I could check on my sister while I'm there. Did James call your desk looking for me?"

"No. Does he know that you're back?"

"I told him when I'd be back as I was leaving. Maybe he just forgot."

"If that's the case, then just call him," Charmaine said.

"I will do just that. Meet me at my car in fifteen minutes."

Jessica dialed James's number, but the phone just kept ringing.

Oh, James, if you only knew how close you are to being cut off, then you will surely answer your phone and have a good explanation.

Just as she was about to hang up the phone, James answered.

"Hey, baby. I was just thinking about you. I was on my way to your job to take you out for a surprise dinner."

"Oh, so you were just going to show up? Why haven't you called me all day?"

"I was busy, but I knew I was going to see you later."

"I wish you would have called first, because I told my secretary Charmaine and her friend Desire that I would take them home. Her new boyfriend has her car."

"That's fine, babe. I will meet you at your house afterward."

"Let's just meet at Red Lobster. I feel for some fried broccoli. Let's say about seven o'clock."

"That's fine. I can't wait to see you," James said.

Jessica rushed out to her car, where Charmaine and Desire were waiting for her.

"Hello, ladies. Ready to go?" Jessica said as she walked up to her car.

"That must have been a good conversation," Charmaine said.

"Yeah, we are going out to dinner later."

Desire thought she recognized the car but wasn't really sure.

"Jessica, do you know a guy by the name of Jay?"

"No, I don't know anyone by that name. Why?"

"One day, my stupid kids' father came by the shelter driving a car that looked like this one."

"No, I don't know him," Jessica said nonchalantly. "How much longer do you have to stay there?"

"I am trying to find a place now. It's not easy looking for a place and telling the new landlord that you are living in the shelter. All they hear is the word 'shelter,' and automatically, they think 'ghetto people.' Hell, no."

Showing genuine concern, Jessica said, "I'll keep an ear out. That is no place to raise children."

"It's actually not that bad. Your sister could tell you. Did she tell you that, when we first met, it was not pretty?"

"She never said anything about that. She only asked me to help you find a job at the firm."

Desire laughed under her breath.

"She asked me if I had HIV, and I just lost it. I know that was her job, but it really pissed me off. We managed to work things out. Matter of fact, how is Ms. Renee? Ms. Millie said she was sick."

"She wasn't sick. She was pregnant, but she lost the baby, so she may be out for a little while longer."

"Send her our best," Charmaine said.

Changing the subject, Charmaine said, "Desire, guess what? On top of that smell I was telling you about, now, I'm feeling a little itchy." I can't wait to go see this Dr. Carl. He has to tell me something about what is going on with my snatch."

Jessica started laughing. "TMI — too much information."

"We've all had a yeast infection before," Desire said, laughing.

"Yeah, but I didn't broadcast it," Jessica said.

"Oh, please, Jessica. We are all women here," Charmaine snapped back.

"I see your car is here. Did you tell your man that you have a yeast infection?" Jessica asked.

"Uhh, no. Some things you just don't share with your man. They always think it's something that you can catch or give them," Charmaine responded.

Desire was laughing loudly in the back seat.

"How stupid are they?" Desire questioned.

Jessica changed the subject when she asked if Charmaine knew which apartment Kit lived in.

"Sure, I'll show you. Desire, before I let you in, let me call Mike to see if he is decent. We like to walk around naked, just in case we get in the mood."

Jessica covered her ears and said, "Again, you are just filled with all this I don't need to know information today."

Charmaine laughed as she said, "Shut up, hater! Mike, are you dressed? I have my friend Desire with me."

Mike advised, "No, wait a minute. I'm about to get into the shower. Just give me two minutes."

"Okay, Mike. I'm going to take Jessica to Kit's apartment. I'll be right back," Charmaine said.

All three ladies headed toward Kit's apartment.

"Hey, Kit. How is Renee doing?" Jessica asked.

"She's fine. She is in the room taking a nap. She said she was going back to work in a couple of days."

Kit noticed and remembered Desire from the doctor's office.

"Hi. I remember you from Dr. Carl's office," Kit said. "Did everything work out?"

Desire sidestepped the question about her visit with Dr. Carl and asked, "Is Renee really OK?"

Kit looked over at Jessica and shook her head.

"Jess, say that you did not tell her. No offense to you, Desire, but Renee is a very private person," Kit said.

Renee heard all the voices in the living room and decided to get up from her nap. She entered the room just as Kit was scolding Jessica for telling Renee's business.

"Yes, I am. And what did you do, Jessica?"

Jessica's voice sank, like a child who was about to be put into time-out.

"I told Charmaine and Desire about the baby."

"I can't cry over spilt milk, but I will talk to you later," Renee said.

"Renee, all my best. I know what it's like to lose a baby," Desire said. "I won't say anything back at the shelter."

"Thank you, Desire. I will be back at work in a few days. I will see you then."

Desire turned to Charmaine and said, "I have to get back to the shelter, so I can pick up the boys."

Charmaine walked into her apartment calling for Mike, but he was still in the shower.

"Mike, where are the keys? Do you hear me? Never mind — I found them. I wanted you to meet Desire."

Mike called out from the bathroom, "Next time."

"Why do you sound like that?" Charmaine asked. Are you brushing your teeth? Let me in."

Before Mike could respond, Desire called out, "Charmaine, I really have to go."

Charmaine told Mike, "I will be right back. I'm going to take her home."

As soon as Desire got to the shelter, she was hoping the door had been left unlocked, but she had to ring the bell.

"Hello, Ms. Millie. Sorry I'm late."

"Today is the only day that I will let those boys in the house without you being here. You had a visitor come by here, also. I informed him of the rules, and he left his number," Millie advised.

Desire was taken aback at hearing there was a visitor looking for her.

"Who was it? Was his name 'Jay'?"

Millie answered, "No, his name was Eric something."

"Hmmm, I don't know any Eric."

"Well, just call him, and see what he wants."

"Thank you, Ms. Millie, and thanks again for letting the boys in."

"By the way, how was your first day on the job?" Millie asked.

"It was really good. I finally met Jessica, the lady who hooked me up with the interview. I think everything is gonna work out."

Meanwhile, Jessica was sitting at a table at Red Lobster, waiting on James to walk in. As he sat down, Jessica wanted to get straight to the point.

"James, the real reason I wanted to meet you here instead of at my house was because I wanted us to talk instead of having sex and forgetting about our problems."

"Jess, I know we have issues, but they would've worked themselves out. All I needed was time to myself, just to clear my mind."

Feeling confused all over again, Jessica said, "Was I smothering you? Because you made me feel like *I* was the problem."

"Not at all. You are on the fast track with your career, and I just wanted to be able to stand next to you and hold my head up as a man. I didn't want people thinking I was living off of my wife."

"Your *wife*! When did you start considering me your *wife*?"

"I've *always* considered you my wife. You are the first woman who made me feel like I wanted to be more in life. I wanted to prove to you that I can make you happy."

"I was happy with you, James. I just wanted us to share a home and possibly flirt with the idea of having children. I know you don't have any children, and it would be nice to share that whole experience with someone."

"That conversation is what made me realize that I had nothing to offer you, Jess. I probably couldn't afford the place that you would've wanted to live in. Do you understand what I am saying?"

Jessica reached across the table for his hand to reassure him.

"I saw potential in you the moment we met. That's why I wouldn't have a problem with footing the bills because I knew you were going to be someone we both could be proud of. Who the hell cares what other people think about us? As long as we are happy, what difference would it make? Those same people don't care what we think about who pays the bills in *their* house."

James slowly moved his hand away from hers.

"I don't care what people say, but that's what I think. It was about how I felt like less than a man."

"Well, James, what are your plans — so you won't feel like less than a man by being with me? Most men would've jumped at the chance to have a woman hold them down."

James became agitated because he felt like she wasn't listening to him or hearing what he was saying to her.

"I am not 'most men'!" he said, raising his voice slightly

Jessica sat back away from the table and gave him a look of disbelief.

"No, you are so special. You almost had me going with all that bullshit, but I just realized you'd stopped calling. You would not return my calls, and I did not see you for days."

"Jess, how many times do I have to say I just needed time to myself?"

Jessica leaned forward in total confidence about what she was about to say.

"That is bullshit, because you could have talked to me about all of this just like you just did. If you loved me like you say you do and claimed you wanted me to be the mother of your firstborn, then you would have talked to me. I think there is more to this story. You said you wanted to be a better man. Well, tell me: what did you come up with while you were away? What would make James a better man, because you have not answered that question yet. My sister thinks you are cheating."

James became a little irate at hearing that.

James snapped back, "*Renee* thinks! She couldn't tell that her man was sleeping with her own niece under the same roof."

"How the hell do you know about that? I didn't tell you, and if you ever speak about my sister like that again, you will never hear from me again."

James realized that they were in a public place and that they both needed to calm down.

"I am sorry, but you want to tell me about what someone else thinks I'm doing, and I can't defend myself."

"How about you answer the question, instead of worrying about who said what?"

"You want to know if I am cheating?"

"Yes, please, and who told you about the Renee, Sam, and Tawana situation?"

"No, no, no! I am not cheating! I love *you* Jessica, and you should know that. I saw Kit, and she told me that Renee is staying with her."

"OK, James, but I'm telling you now that if you ever do something like that to me again, I am cutting your ass off."

"I will never put you through that again," James promised.

Jessica wanted to put the question on the table again because James had never answered it.

"So, again, I ask: what are your plans?"

"Glad that you asked. I have decided to go back to school to become a musical engineer. With the connections I have from doing parties, I can make a killing. That is why I decided to take you up on your offer of holding things down for a little while. I'm going to need you big time, if I'm going to make this happen."

Sounding totally supportive, Jessica asked, "Have you registered for classes yet?"

"Not yet. I have to raise another $2,000."

"I can give you the money, so you can get started right away. You are going to be the next music mogul."

James smiled from ear to ear hearing her words.

"That's my baby. I love you so much, Jess. Can we please go back to your place so I can show you just how much? That thing is backed up."

"I was only gone a week, but I need you, too, James. One other question: I went to the address you gave me, and some woman answered the door, but she didn't know who you were."

"Wow, that was fast! They rented my apartment quick," James answered. "During the time I was away, I moved into a smaller place so I can save money."

"Kit told Renee she sees you leaving her building a lot. Is that where you moved to?"

"Naw, my boy lives in that building. He is the one who was talking to me about going to school. He's going there also."

"Then he is the type of person you need to be hanging out with. Why don't I know any of your friends?" Jessica asked.

James tried to change the subject by asking, "When are we going to eat? Because you seem to be full of questions tonight."

"I just realized how little I know about you. I've never really asked about your goals in life."

After Jessica made that statement, she was thinking to herself as James was rambling to find answers to her many questions.

Damn, Jess! Are you making a mistake? Did you fall in love with the man, or was it the idea of being in love? Are you making another mistake by offering to bankroll his career without knowing who he is?

"Hey, why did you get so quiet all of a sudden?" James asked, breaking her thoughts.

"I was just thinking. I don't feel good. Can I have a rain check on the lovemaking session tonight?"

"I miss you, and I really need to be with you, but if you're not feeling well, then OK. I will walk you to your car," James offered.

"What are you driving?"

"I have my boy's car. Speaking of him, I have to bring his car back. Maybe we can get together tomorrow. Goodnight, Jessica. I love you."

Charmaine was driving back home after dropping Desire off at the shelter, hoping to speak with Mike when she got back to the apartment.

"Mike, are you still here?" she called out as she entered the apartment.

Where does this man disappear to all the time? Charmaine thought.

Mike walked in the front door just as Charmaine was ending the conversation with herself.

"Hey, baby. Who are you talking to?" Mike said as walked toward the back of the apartment.

"I was just talking to myself. Where were you?"

"I went to the store to buy you these."

Mike handed Charmaine a dozen long-stemmed red roses.

"They are beautiful. You are spoiling me," she said, as she inhaled the aroma of the flowers.

"You deserve it and so much more. I have to be honest with you about the real reason I brought those flowers. I have been cheating on you with your best friend."

Charmaine stopped dead in the middle of a deep sniff and gave him the look of death.

"What did you just say?!"

Mike said, "I'm just playing with you. Relax. That was meant just to soften the blow for when I asked if you can spot me $2,000, so I can buy a new laptop. I have a party, and my computer crashed. The party pays $4,000, so I will give it back when I get home."

"Mike, don't play with me like that. I have some serious issues — and you don't want to wake that side of me. Anyway, I don't have that kind of money in cash lying around, but I can put the computer on my credit card. The mall closes about nine or ten. We can go now."

Mike jumped up like a child, excited and eager, and said, "Let's go then, and thank you so much, baby. And I'm sorry about the joke."

"It's OK. The next time you buy me flowers, it had better be for no reason at all."

On the way to the store, Charmaine decided to fill Mike in on all the drama surrounding her friend and new neighbor.

"So, babe. Finish telling me about when your boss's sister moved into the building," Mike said.

Charmaine said, "That is some drama for your ass. She found out that her niece was sleeping with her boyfriend in her own bed, and her mother let it happen. Not to mention the fact that she was pregnant."

"Wow — did she get an abortion?" Mike asked.

"No, she lost the baby after she found out what was going on."

"That's crazy! You're right — that's way too much drama for me."

"I also think my boss's boyfriend is cheating on her."

"Why do you think that?" he asked.

"Because she is constantly asking if he called. She used to spend a lot of time on the phone with him at work."

Mike didn't think that Charmaine's theory had any value or merit.

"Why does that mean he is cheating? Are you just being over the top?"

"Listen, when a man deviates from his routine like that, there is something wrong."

Mike thought about her statement and disagreed with her conclusion.

"That statement is more for a woman than a man," he said.

"I can see where you might say that, but most men don't even notice when the change occurs in a woman. That's why men are so shocked when they find out that their woman has been cheating on them."

Charmaine's phone rang before she could finish explaining her thought process.

"Sweetheart, excuse me, but this is Desire. I have to take the call."

While Charmaine was talking to Desire, Mike went into the store, looking at the computers.

"Sir, how long do I have before I can return the computer if she doesn't like it?" Mike asked the sales rep.

"You can get a full refund within seven days, as long as you have the receipt."

"What about if we purchase on a credit card; do you give cash back?"

"No, we can only return it to the original card, or we issue a Visa Debit Gift Card for the refunded amount."

"How does that work?" Mike asked the sales clerk.

"For example, if you returned a $1,000 laptop, then we'd issue you a card with a $1,000 cash limit, with a Visa logo, so you can use it anywhere they accept credit cards."

Charmaine walked up behind Mike just as the sales rep finished explaining how the Visa gift card worked.

"Oh, honey. That was fast. What happened?"

"She wanted to know if I knew anyone named 'Eric,' because he called the shelter looking for her."

"Why would she think you knew him?"

"Because in his message, he said we had a friend in common, so she thought it was me."

"Well, do you know him?" he asked with suspicion.

"Are you jealous?" she asked, smiling at the thought.

"No, I'm not," Mike said and then changed the subject quickly. "I like this one," he said, pointing to an Apple laptop. "It's a little more expensive than the one I originally saw, but it has more to offer," Mike said.

"How much more does it offer for $3,500!?" Charmaine screeched.

"Don't be like that, babe. You're getting your money back."

"For this amount, I ought to charge you interest."

"Please, baby! You won't regret it. When we get home, I am going to make my first interest-only payment."

"Good. Let's go home, because I fully intend to take advantage of this ding-a-ling payment."

"I can't wait. but I need to use the car for a quick run, and then I am all yours."

"Well, Mike, I can just come with you."

"No, I need to take care of this myself."

"Okay. I'm tired, so hurry up. But if I fall asleep, you'd better wake me gently."

"I will. See you in a little while. Try to stay up. I know you have to work, so I won't be long."

Mike drove straight to Eric's apartment, and he even ran a few lights. He knew Eric wouldn't let him in willingly, so he ran the bell and knocked on the door, as most delivery men would do.

"Yeah, hold on. I'm coming. Who is it?"

Mike disguised his voice and said, "Chinese food."

Walking toward the door, Eric yelled, "You must have made a mistake. I didn't order anything tonight."

Eric opened the door wide without checking the peephole.

"Oh, shit! What the fuck!" Eric shouted.

Mike grabbed him by the neck, pushed him back into the apartment, and used his feet to close the door behind them.

"What the fuck are you doing trying to call Desire?"

"Mike, I can't breathe."

"Fuck you, nigga. Die slow, bitch."

Eric was struggling to breathe and talk as Mike continued to put pressure on his throat.

"Mike, please. I am sorry."

"You will be sorry, faggot-ass nigga. I will make sure your ass won't talk for a long time, bitch."

The phone rang, and Eric tried to reach for the receiver, but Mike pulled him away, still holding onto his neck and squeezing tighter.

I wonder why Eric is not answering his phone? Sam thought to himself.

"I wanted to check on Eric, but he is not answering his phone," Sam told Tawana.

"Sam, I feel uncomfortable being here. Your sister knows my aunt, and, before, she thought we were just friends."

"Would you relax? She does know about us. Why are you always so concerned with what people think? Make yourself at home. This is my apartment. Remember one thing: my name is on the lease, and if my sister disapproves, then she can leave."

"In that case, can I answer the phone?" Tawana asked.

"Of course, you can. I have nothing to hide," Sam said.

The phone rang again, as if on cue.

"Speaking of the phone, you can start now," Sam said.

Tawana was very happy to oblige.

"Hello. Perry residence," she said.

"Yes, is Mr. Sam Perry available? This is the nurse at South Nassau Hospital."

"Is there something wrong?" Tawana asked, with fear and concern in her voice.

"We have a Mr. Eric Wright admitted here. According to his insurance company, Mr. Sam Perry is listed as the emergency contact person."

Tawana's hands were shaking as she passed the phone to Sam.

"He is here. Hold on. It's a nurse at the hospital. Something about Eric."

"This is Sam. Is Eric OK?"

"He should be fine. His mouth is wired due to a fractured jaw bone. His eyes are swollen shut, and he has several broken ribs, but he should be just fine. The worst of his injuries were to his rectum. We found the telephone lodged in his rectum. He may require the use of a colostomy bag when he fully recovers."

"Oh, my God! Can I see him?"

"Visiting hours are about to end, so get here as quickly as you can."

"Do they know what happened to him or who did this to him?"

"It appeared he had been severely beaten during a robbery attempt, according to the police."

"Thank you, Ma'am. I'm on my way."

"Sam, do you want me to come with you?" Tawana asked.

"No, you stay here. I'll be back soon."

Tawana was nervous but felt she needed to call and tell Kit about Eric.

"Hello, Kit. This is Tawana. Please don't hang up. It's about Eric. He's in the hospital. Somebody beat him really bad."

Kit became angry just hearing Tawana's voice on the phone line. She asked, with an attitude, "Is he going to die?"

"They said no, but he's in really bad shape. Sam just went to the hospital. Kit, is Renee OK?"

Making sure that Tawana understood that she was not in her good graces, Kit said, "Thank you for letting me know about Eric, but everything else is off limits to you."

Before Kit could hang up the phone on Tawana, Renee asked, "What happened to Eric?"

"He's in the hospital. Somebody beat him up."

Renee, sounding sympathetic to what she'd just heard about Eric, said, "Kit, I know you're mad at him, but do you want to go?"

"I feel like I should, but then again, why would I?"

Renee shook her head at having to be the voice of reason in this situation.

"Because you are a good person, and no matter how much he hurt you, you're not the kind of person to see someone hurt and walk away. You once loved him, and no one deserves what happened to him."

Kit rolled her eyes at Renee, because she knew if the shoe was on the other foot, she wouldn't listen to her own advice.

"You talk that mess now, but if it were Sam, would you go?"

"Yes, I would, because we were friends, and I would want to see up close what karma looks like."

Kit shook her head and laughed, "That's cruel."

"I will come with you, if you like. I am sick of sitting in the house anyway."

"It has only been a day, Renee."

"Whatever — let's go."

As they were walking out of the building, James was coming in.

"Hey, James. Hold the door. I know you saw us coming."

"What's up, Kit?" James replied.

"What is your problem? You don't see me standing here?" Renee said.

"I don't have nothing to say to you. Matter of fact, who the hell are you to tell Jessica that I'm cheating on her?"

Renee made sure he knew that she was not afraid of him and that she would not back down from him, either.

"Are you feeling guilty about something, James? That is my sister, and if I feel like telling her that her half-ass man is probably cheating on her, then I will."

Kit intervened and stepped in between them.

"You two, stop it!"

James refused to let it go and said, "You are jealous of your sister because she has a good man, and you ended up with a guy who screwed your family in your bed and made you lose your baby."

Renee considered those to be fighting words, but she knew she couldn't physically beat him, so she used her words as she stepped closer to his face.

"What the fuck did you just say to me? You good-for-nothing, half-ass son of a bitch, who can't get a real job, so you try to live off of women. I will not let you use my sister. You no-good, piece-of-shit-ass motherfucker."

James couldn't find any other words, so he said, "I will slap the shit out of you, bitch."

Renee tried to step even closer to him, but Kit wouldn't let her.

"Try it, faggot. I will have your ass under the fucking jail."

Kit grabbed her by the arm and pulled her out the door.

"Renee, let's go. You don't need this right now."

Renee kept talking over Kit.

"Nigga, I will make sure my sister never speaks to your ass again."

"Jessica is my woman," James fired back.

"Yeah, bitch, but she was my sister before she ever thought about being with your sorry ass."

"Call me a 'faggot' or 'bitch' again, and you'll see what will happen to you."

Renee didn't get a chance to respond because Kit ushered her toward the car.

"Renee, please. Let's go."

Renee got into the car, still pissed about James and what had just transpired.

"That motherfucker has a lot of damn nerve trying to tell me what I can and cannot tell my sister."

Now it was Kit who had to be the voice of reason.

"You just lost your baby, and you don't need the stress of arguing with some idiot. Do you still want to go to the hospital?"

Renee snapped back, "I'm out here now. Let's go. He just really pissed me off."

They made it to the hospital in record time, but, because of the argument with James, Kit never got the chance to tell Renee that Sam was at the hospital.

"Renee, don't get mad at me, but Sam is here. You can go back to the car and wait. I'll be right behind you."

"Too late, Kit, because he is right behind you. Exactly what I needed today — a fight with a jackass and seeing you," Renee said, looking directly at Sam.

Sam looked at her with sympathetic eyes and said, "Renee, I just want to know if you are OK. Why didn't you tell me about the baby?"

"I tried to tell you, but that's when you decided you wanted to tell me that you were in love with someone else. Remember that?"

"I guess I deserve your anger, but I also deserve to know the truth about my child. You were not the only person who lost someone here."

"Cut the bullshit — you didn't want the baby. You wanted my niece, and now you have her. Go make another baby, and leave me alone. My baby is gone because of you and that little whore, so go to hell, and don't try to play the loving-baby-daddy role with me."

Kit had to remind her that there was a time and place for everything.

"Renee, you are in the hospital, and we did not come here for that. Make it another time."

Renee knew she wouldn't be able to maintain her composure around Sam for much longer, and there were a few things she wanted to get off her chest.

"Don't ever say anything to me. You and that little whore niece of mine. Burn in hell, the both of you!"

She turned to face Kit and said, "Tell Eric I wish him the best, but I'm going to wait in the car."

Sam didn't want to end the conversation like that, so as she was headed toward the door, he shouted in her direction.

"At least let me tell you why it happened!"

Renee turned around and walked back at a rapid pace.

"Why the hell would I need to know that? You screwed my niece, and that was that. Is this an attempt to clear your conscience? Sam, I know exactly what it was — new pussy versus old pussy. It's the same story with every sorry-ass black man."

"It was not about that. She let me be a man, and you took that away from me. You wanted to be the man *and* the woman in the relationship."

Renee interrupted him before he could finish his statement.

"Correction — she let you rule her. I've been down that road before, and it leads to nowhere."

"That was another problem, Renee. You were making me pay for what some other man did to you. I had nothing to do with that."

"Yeah, well, now you do. But let me set you straight: you could have just talked to me about whatever you were feeling. But, no — you had to sleep with my niece in my bed to prove that you were unhappy.

I hope you get what you deserve. I hope she makes you pay for being stupid. Mark my words, she's going to leave your ass. She is young and feeling herself. Somebody else will come along and offer her more than what your sorry ass has to offer, and she will leave."

Sam realized there was nothing he could say to make her understand, and he figured he was wasting his time.

"There is no point in talking to you," he said, as he turned to walk away.

Renee stood there for a few seconds and then said, "Good. Then don't, because there is nothing you or she can say that can begin to ease the pain you caused me."

He kept walking, but he briefly turned around, while walking backwards, to respond.

"Alright, Renee. You win. I will leave you alone. Kit, I will take you to his room when you are ready."

Renee ran to the car in tears.

Kit followed Sam to Eric's room.

"Oh, my God, Sam. You could have warned me or something!" Kit yelled.

"Yeah, whoever did this worked him over really bad."

"Do you think it was one of his lovers?" Kit asked.

"I don't know. The police think it was a robbery."

"Can I have a minute alone with him, Sam? Please?"

"Sure. I'll be back soon."

Kit stood over Eric, staring at his battered face as she spoke aloud in a soft voice.

"Hey, Eric. I know I am the last person you thought would come see you in the hospital, but I had to see for myself. I wish your eyes were open so you could see me, but I know you can hear me. I think whoever did this to you should have cut your dick off. I came here to laugh in your face and to tell you that this is good for you. You deserve so much more pain. Karma is a bitch, so I am glad that I am here to see you in this hospital bed with your face all twisted. I know the next time you decide to lie about who you are and what your preference is, you'll think twice. Goodbye, you selfish piece of shit."

Sam walked back into the room because he thought she might be taking seeing him like this really hard.

"Kit, is everything OK?"

"Yes, everything is fine. I'm about to go."

"I'm sure he would have appreciated you coming up here to see him."

"I'm sure he would. When he comes around, make sure he knows that I was here, in case he thinks it was a dream."

"I will. Kit, I want you to know that I didn't mean to hurt Renee. She was my best friend."

"Sam, I can't speak to that. I will say this: family is family. You just ripped that family apart. Are you sure you love Tawana? Because if not, then none of this was worth it."

"I do believe I love her, and I would do it all over again. Well, not hurting Renee, but choosing Tawana. I would do it again."

"Then you have to make things right with that family," Kit added.

"You heard her. How am I supposed to do that?"

"It's gonna take time. Right now, things are still too new, but whatever you do, you need to make things right again."

"I hear you. It was good seeing you, and take care of her."

"I will do my best. Later, Sam. Make sure you let him know I was here."

Kit and Renee drove home in silence.

As they were getting settled in the apartment, there were several knocks at the door. They could hear Jessica's voice in the hallway, saying, "Renee, open the door!"

"I am coming!" Renee yelled back.

Renee assumed that James had called her and that's why she was there.

"Jessica, did that piece of shit you call a boyfriend call you?"

"Well, damn! Hello to you, too, Sis. And no, I have not spoken to James yet. Why?"

"I saw that bastard coming out of my building, and he had the nerve to tell me not to be filling your head with nonsense. Then he had the nerve to try to throw Tawana and Sam up in my face. You need to check him for real! Then after dealing with your jackass, I ran into Sam at the hospital."

Jessica became a little nervous hearing that Renee had been at the hospital.

"Are you alright? Why did you have to go back to the hospital?"

"Yeah, I am fine. Kit's ex-boyfriend got beaten up really bad, and he's in the hospital."

Jessica turned to face Kit and asked, "Your boyfriend's name is 'Eric' — right, Kit?"

"No, Jess. My *ex*-boyfriend's name is 'Eric,'" Kit said, with a little sass in her tone.

"I think he called me, but I don't know him like that. He left a message saying he had something to tell me that was very important, about a mutual friend of ours. Is everything OK with you, Kit? Because that would be the only person I know of who we have in common," Jessica said.

Renee chimed in, "This dude has been calling around the world for you. He called Kit's house, but Kit hung up the phone on him when he was trying to tell me what he wanted with you."

Kit asked, "You think maybe he knows James?"

"I doubt it. That clown did not have that many friends from Long Island," Renee said.

Jessica agreed with Renee about James not having many friends in Long Island.

"That's true. I wonder what the hell he wanted with me, then?"

"Well, you won't be able to ask him, because when he finally wakes up, he won't be able to talk much, since his mouth is wired shut," Kit said with a smile on her face.

"Damn! They really whipped his ass, huh?" Jessica asked.

"I didn't see him because I was too busy arguing with that other jackass, Sam."

"I still want to know what he wanted with me," Jessica said.

Renee wanted to change the subject quickly, so she said, "Enough about that loser. Have you spoken to Mr. Drake again?"

"I've already explained to him that I just wanted to be friends. I need to give James a chance. I really do love James."

"What does that have to do with anything?" Renee asked. "I didn't say *sleep* with the man. I just asked if you'd spoken to him."

"No, I have not, and one thing always leads to another," Jessica responded.

Kit chimed in with, "'Another' might not always be a bad thing. You should try it."

"Here you go with the BS. I am good for now, thank you. When it's time for me to let go, then I will know it," Jessica said responding to Kit's comment.

"Don't wait too long, sister."

"Well, I was just stopping by to check on you. I'm out," Jessica said.

"I will speak to you later, then. Thanks for stopping by."

The moment Jessica walked out the door, Kit had to ask the question.

"Why are you trying to push that man on your sister?"

"I just feel he would be good for her. Hell, he may be good for me. I forgot I was back on the market. So, are you, for that matter?"

Kit was not having it.

"I told you I don't want to be bothered with anyone for a least a year."

Renee laughed at her own joke before she even said it.

"That damn thing is gonna close up and dry out by then."

Kit laughed also and said, "That's OK, because the next man who touches this is going to have to pay to turn the water back on."

"Oh, so now, you're getting on some 'show me the money' shit."

"You're damn right! Love got me nothing last time but a gay man and a case of chlamydia."

"You are stupid as hell," Renee said, laughing loudly. "I know I'm mad now, but my next man has to think all of my friends and family look like the boy in the movie *The Mask*."

Kit stood up and did a twirl as she said, "You ain't never gonna find anybody, then — because I look good."

Over in Charmaine's apartment, Mike was coming unglued.

What the fuck have I done? That faggot motherfucker is going to wake up and tell what happened. I gotta get some money and get out of here.

Think, man, think! I have to call somebody. Mike pulled out his phone and started dialing numbers frantically.

"Hello. What time do you close today? I need to return a computer."

The voice on the phone said, "We close at ten o'clock."

"I'll be right there." Mike jumped in the car and called Charmaine.

"Hello, Charmaine, sweetheart. I will be a little late tonight."

"What happened to you today? You forgot to pick me up."

"A friend of mine was in a bad car accident, and he's in the hospital. That's where I am now."

"Okay, send him my best, and I will see you later."

Charmaine hung up and dialed Desire's number at the shelter, but the line was busy. The other woman at the shelter had just hung up the phone as Desire was walking by, and the phone began to ring again. She picked up the phone, and, before she could say "Hello," the person on the other end began to speak.

"Hello. May I speak to Desire Williams?"

"This is Des. What can I do for you?"

"I just wanted to apologize and let you know that I was thinking about you and the boys."

"Jay, how did you get this number? I can't believe you have the nerve to call here after our last conversation. You sound like such a fool right now."

"Don't be like that. I found you a place to live and raise our boys. That's why I am calling. I don't want to fight with you."

Desire was in complete shock at what she'd just heard.

"*What*? You did *what*?" she said.

"It is a two-bedroom apartment already furnished. The best part is that you can move in as soon as possible. There is one catch. You have to pay just the broker's fees. You don't have to worry about the first month and security, because I've already paid all of that."

"Jay, are you serious?" she asked, still shocked.

"Yes, I told you that I love you and the boys. I just needed some time to get myself together, and that's why I left. I know you think I was up to no good, but I have been busting my ass trying to raise the money to get you back. I have a steady income now. I stayed with a friend and attended school for computer programming, and I have a good job now. Will you please come home? We need our family back together. I don't know what I will do without you and the boys."

"Jay, I just can't believe what I am hearing. Are you sure?"

"Yes, baby. I love you so much, and I never meant to hurt you."

Still not trusting his words, Desire wanted to cover all bases before agreeing.

"Is this a scam?"

"Why would I do that to you? If you say 'Yes' and you have the money, we can move in tonight."

"*Tonight*!?" she screamed into the phone.

"Yes. You don't have anything there but clothes, so it should be an easy move. I can come get you and take you to the bank so you can get the money. Then we can take it to the broker."

"Alright, Jay, slow down. First of all, you never said how much it is."

"All you need is $3,000. I already paid $6,000 upfront. I figured you should have it since you have been staying there for free."

Desire sat on the bench in the hallway of the shelter, holding the phone, trying to think of the next question she could ask that would make her believe this was real.

"I do have it, but don't you think we should at least see the place first?"

"It's real nice, and you would love it. Please don't make me lose my money, because I already put the money down on it."

"Are you sure this is not a scam? Why would you lose your money?"

"They are holding this place for me when they could have been showing it to other people. I will lose $3,000 if I back out of the deal."

Desire finally was able to get excited about having a place of their own again.

"Jay, thank you for thinking of your family, and yes, you can come get us. I will give the boys the good news. They are going to be so happy to see you and to know we'll be a family again. Jay, I will tell you this: If this is a joke, I will make you regret it."

"No time for threats. Get my boys ready, and I will be there shortly."

Before Desire went upstairs to tell the boys the good news, she wanted to share the news with her best friend, so she called Charmaine.

"Hello, Charmaine. I know you are probably busy, but I have great news. Jay called, and he found us an apartment."

Bewildered by what she was hearing but trying to remain outwardly happy for her friend, Charmaine reacted like any reasonable person would.

"'*Jay*'? What do you mean, '*Jay*'?" she said.

"He said he loves us, and he only left so that we could have a better life. He found a better job, so he can give us our family again. He even put the down payment on the apartment for us. Charmaine, it's really happening — we have a home again."

Still trying not to rain on her friend's parade, she had to ask, "Can you afford the apartment if he decides to leave again?"

"He is not going to leave again!" Desire yelled at Charmaine. I believe him when he says he loves us. We had a good thing when we were together."

"Desire, excuse me for having a selfish moment, but what about our friendship? He stopped you from hanging out with me the last time."

"Charmaine, I did learn something from having gone through this. I won't let that happen again. I am not quitting my job or anything like that, either."

"Des, I have to ask: why do you believe him?"

"Because he's on the way to pick us up now and take us to the apartment. I will call you with the address."

Charmaine wanted to make sure her friend had heard her warning before they ended their conversation.

"Don't trust him, Des!" she warned. This doesn't sound right."

"Why aren't you happy for me? Do you want me to live in this shelter forever?"

"Stop asking stupid questions, Des. You know damn well that is not the case. However, I am worried that you are so desperate to move out of the shelter that you would accept anything — even from the person who put you there in the first place."

"I have to go. He's here."

"Don't be a fool, Des!"

God, help my friend, Charmaine thought.

Desire thanked Ms. Millie for everything and promised never to return to the shelter before she walked out the door. The boys went running to the car screaming, "Daddy! Daddy!

Jay opened the car door, and the boys jumped in, totally excited to be in his presence.

"How are my boys doing? I missed you guys so much. We are going to our new home." He leaned over and gave Desire a peck on the lips.

"Daddy, we love you. You can't leave us again because mommy had us living in the shelter."

"Don't worry about that anymore. Daddy is here for good. Desire, what bank are we going to?"

"I'm with Chase," she answered.

"I'm going to take you guys to the apartment first. The agent is supposed to meet us there."

On the way to the new apartment, the kids were telling Jay all about life at the shelter.

As they pulled up to the apartment building, Desire lowered her voice to say, "Thank you, Jay, for this. I really appreciate it."

"Are we here? Is this it?" the kids started screaming from the back seat. "Yay, Daddy — we are here."

They walked into the apartment, and the kids went running through the house.

"This place is beautiful. Boys, do you like your room? Jay, I love the furniture. The colors are perfect. Where is the agent?"

"He should be here soon. Give me the bank card, and I will go get the money. You can wait here for the agent. There's food in the fridge."

Her instincts about not trusting him kicked in, and she figured that, if he took the boys with him, then he would have to come back.

Jay said, "Let them stay and hang out in their new room. I will be right back. Don't worry. I am never leaving my family again."

His words and the look he gave her told her that she should trust him, and she said, "OK, here is the PIN number."

“When the agent gets here, tell him I will be right back with the rest of the money. I love you, Des.”

“I love you, too, Jay.”

“Here are the keys, just in case you want to take a walk around the block. I have to go, so I can catch the bank.”

Because the boys never answered her when she asked the first time, she asked again, “Boys, how do you like your new home?”

“We love it, Mommy!”

The doorbell rang, and her eldest son ran to open the door.

“There’s a man at the door dressed like a lady,” he said as he came running back into the room, telling his mother.

“I’ll go see who it is. Hello, you must be the realtor. Jay will be right back; he went to get the rest of the deposit.”

“Oh, no, honey. I was looking for Ms. E. Is she here?”

“‘Ms. E’?” she questioned.

“No, there is no one by that name who lives here. We just rented this apartment.”

“I was here just last week, and I left my wallet. She said she put it in the drawer in the kitchen.”

Desire said, “I will check, because the place did come furnished. Here it is. I am sorry for the mix-up.”

“Thank you, dear, but if you see Ms. E. around, tell her I enjoyed myself and want to hook up again.”

Mocking the obviously gay man, she said, “Yeah, I will do just that, Ms. Thang.”

Desire thought, *Lord, what is this world coming to? Where is the phone? Oh, shit! I didn’t get Jay’s new cell-phone number. Matter of fact, what the hell is taking Jay so long, and where is the realtor?*

As she was looking around for the phone, it began to ring, but her son was closest to the phone.

“Jamal, get the phone. It might be your father.”

He answered the phone assuming it was his father. He said, “Hello, Daddy?”

The voice said, “I am looking for Mr. Eric Wright.”

"You have the wrong number, mister," Jamal said.

Desire yelled out, "Who was it?"

"Some man looking for Eric Wright."

"OK, son. Go into your room, and unpack your clothes."

A minute later, Jamal screamed, "Mommy, there is some man's clothes in these drawers!"

She screamed back, "Just take them out! The old owner must have left them behind."

Desire started to worry about Jay because he had been gone so long. She decided to see if she could track him down at the bank.

"Yes, is this Chase Bank? I have an account there, and I sent my husband to take out some money, but he left his cell phone. Is there any way you can page him to come to the phone?"

"No, ma'am. We don't do that. This is a bank, not a bar."

"I am sorry, but he has been gone for a long time, and I am just worried something may have happened to him."

"I can check to see if the money was withdrawn. Maybe that will give you a time frame."

"Oh, yes, please. Could you do that? That will help a lot."

"OK, I see there was a withdrawal made today at five minutes to six, in the amount of $4000. Your account balance is $5."

Desire had to hold on to the kitchen counter to keep from falling over. She didn't even disconnect the call because she'd dropped the phone while trying to keep herself upright.

She thought, *Oh. God! How did I let him do this to me again? He said he loved me and the boys. Why, lord, why? I can't go back to that shelter. I won't go back. I will fucking kill you, Jay.*

"Boys, get in bed. You have to go to school in the morning, and I have to go to work," she yelled from the kitchen.

Desire went right back to talking to herself.

This is my home, and I am not giving it up, in the name of Jesus. My new house needs a woman's touch. I came too far to let him take my life all over again. The smiles on my kids' faces is worth the $4000, you son of a bitch.. I hope you burn in hell.

She reached down to pick up the phone and began to dial out.

"Hello, Charmaine. I know it's late, but I had to tell you that you were right."

"Right about what, Desire? What's going on? Wait a minute — Mike just walked in. Hey, baby. Where have you been? I was worried. I'm talking to Desire. I'll be off in a minute. Des, go ahead — what happened?"

"He left me again, stranded with the boys and penniless. He cleaned out my bank account and left me in this apartment. I don't even know who owns this place."

"Oh, my God, Des! I am so sorry. Do you want me to take you back to the shelter?"

"I am not going back there. My kids are in their room getting ready for bed. I can't put them through that again. Having to tell them that Daddy won't be here and that we are going back to the shelter would kill them. I am staying here. This is my home now. Maybe he really did get this place for us. Maybe he really does love us but just can't live with us. I don't know what he is going through, but I am not leaving my home."

Charmaine sensed that her friend was losing touch with reality and needed to be brought back to her senses quickly.

"That is not your house. You have to get out of there. What happens when the real owner comes home? You are not thinking straight."

"This is my home, and I have the keys to prove it, Charmaine! Goodnight, and I will see you at work."

Charmaine was still talking, but Desire had already ended the call.

"Des, don't do this!" Mike, my friend is in trouble, and I don't know what to do. I don't know where she is living now, and I can't call her back."

"What happened?" Mike said, trying to sound concerned.

"She was living in the shelter because her kids' father left her, and now, he called telling her some bullshit about still loving her. Then he claimed he got her an apartment but instead took all her money and left her again. Now she won't leave that apartment. What do I do?"

"Babe, the only thing you can do is wait and go to work tomorrow, and maybe by then, she will have come to her senses. I know a way to relieve some of that tension," he said, extending his hand and leading her toward the bed.

"You are right, Mike. Here I come, Daddy."

CHAPTER 8

Love Stops Here

"Renee, Sam called this morning and said Eric died last night."

"Kit, are you OK?"

Very cold and uncaring, Kit replied, "I am fine. He was not my boyfriend anymore. Let someone else deal with the loss of a loved one."

"Well, since you are taking that approach, we still don't know what he wanted to tell Jessica."

"Why do you care so much about that bullshit? He is dead, and whatever he had to say died with him. I am going to work. See you later."

"Well, I decided I am going back to work today also."

"Good. Refocus your thoughts, and move on with life. See you later," Kit said.

"Wait a minute. I'm leaving, too. Go hold the elevator," Renee ordered.

The met up with Charmaine in the elevator, on her way to work.

"Hey, ladies. Good morning. Renee, it is good to see you."

Renee was instantly annoyed. "Are you one of those crazy morning people, or did you get some last night?"

"I am both, not to mention the fact that I am in love," Charmaine added, showing all her pearly white teeth.

"Oh, please. Love is an excuse to be stupid. Relationships are hard work. People should work smarter, not harder. Love and relationships should come as easy as breathing," Renee clapped back.

Kit joined in, stating, "If that's the case, then I had a bad asthma attack, bronchitis, COPD, and every other chronic breathing disorder, during my relationship. I was in love with a gay man, for Christ's sake."

Renee started laughing by herself and added, "I must have had lung cancer. My boyfriend slept with my niece."

"You ladies are way too deep in the morning. Have a good day," Charmaine said as she stepped off the elevator.

"I don't really know if I like her," Renee said, making a stink face.

"Don't start your shit. Go harass somebody at the shelter."

Kit spotted James on the side of the building and decided to tease Renee.

"Oh, look. There is your buddy, James," she said.

Renee rolled her eyes at Kit and walked off in the opposite direction, saying, "I am gone. I can't deal with that mess this morning."

Kit was parked in the front of the building, so she just hopped in her car and sped away.

Charmaine had to walk to the corner, where Mike was parked, waiting on her.

"Mike, why didn't you meet me in front of the building?" she asked.

"I saw you with those girls, and I just didn't feel like meeting anybody today."

"Mike, just please be on time when you pick me up today."

Trying to appear understanding, he said, "I will, sweetheart. I promise. Try to enjoy your day, and talk some sense into your friend. Give me a call later and let me know how it goes."

"I love you, baby, and I will call you later."

Charmaine went straight to Jessica's office upon entering the building.

"Hey, Charmaine. How is your morning?"

"It is great. I saw your sister this morning. She was headed for work."

"That's good to hear. I hope she gets her life back on track. As for me, I am trying to give James a chance, but he is doing nothing to earn that chance. I am so sick of trying to make this work."

"I hate to be the one to say this, but maybe it's time to move on."

Jessica swiveled in her chair to face the floor-to-ceiling windows, looking out at the view.

"You might be right, Charmaine. My sister thinks I should call that bouncer from the club. Oh — it's my private line. This might be James. I will speak to you later. Hello. This is Jessica. How may I help you?"

"Jessica, it's James. I need to know if you are still going to help me with the money for school?"

"Yes, I said I would. Just meet me for lunch. I will meet you at the Spanish restaurant by my job. Speak to you later."

Desire walked into their office as if everything were normal.

"Hey, Charmaine. I just wanted to say, 'Good morning' and ask you if we were going to eat lunch together today."

Charmaine gave her the head-tilt, sympathetic-head-nod gesture. "Of course, we are, but we need to talk first."

"If you are going to ask about my new place, then we have nothing to talk about. However, I will cook dinner for you and Mike this weekend if you guys are not doing anything."

Charmaine could no longer hold back her frustration with Desire and the situation.

"You are starting to sound like a crazy person. That is not your place, and you are not doing those boys any favors by pretending that it is."

Desire, still sounding disillusioned, stated, "OK, then, you don't have to come over. I have to go to work. Bye," turned her back to Charmaine, and proceeded down the hall.

"Desire, come back so we can talk."

You are really starting to piss me off, Charmaine whispered under her breath.

Charmaine was so deeply bothered that she decided to call Mike.

"Hello, Mike. I just tried to talk to my girl, and she won't listen. She insists that it is her place, and she had the nerve to invite us over for dinner. I think she's having a breakdown. That son of a bitch drove her crazy!"

Mike was trying to take it all in, but she was talking so fast, it came out as one long sentence.

"Would you slow down? Try to talk to her again. I will be there later. Now, go do some work."

In the other office, Jessica decided that she should make a call that might change things with her and James.

"Hello. May I speak to Drake?"

"This is Drake. Who am I speaking with?"

Because she was nervous, her words came out quick and nonsensical.

"This is Jessica, and I'm hungry."

"Well, hello, stranger. How is your sister?"

"She is fine, but I will tell you all about it over lunch. Can you meet me?"

Drake responded, smiling, "It just so happens that I can. I work the midnight shift tonight. Where do you want to meet?"

"At Red Lobster on Old Country Road at noon, if that's okay with you," Jessica replied.

"That is perfect, because I have some running around to do over near there anyway."

"See you then," Jessica said and then quickly hung up the phone.

Jessica was flip-flopping with emotions as she thought to herself.

I almost feel bad, but fuck him. He deserves to feel how I felt every time he stood me up. I deserve better than him.

"Charmaine, I am going out for lunch. If James should call, just tell him I am running late."

"Got it, Jess. Enjoy."

Still feeling a little guilty, Jessica needed reinforcement, so she called Renee.

"Hey, I'm about to go have lunch with Drake. Are you proud of me?"

"Hell, yes — and ask him if he has a brother or cousin. Hell, I will take a co-worker at this point."

"You are not ready for all of that. Ain't no man gonna put up with you and your bitter ass."

"Listen to you, who is about to cheat on Mr. Wrong," Renee said, laughing.

"It's not cheating if he is the wrong man. It's called a breath of fresh air."

"Funny you say that. I was talking to your secretary this morning about just that. I have to admit, sometimes she gets on my nerves. Did she tell you that her friend, Desire, moved out of the shelter last night without notice? She is stupid. This is not the best place to be, but it's a roof over your head in the rain."

Jessica was shaking her head while listening to Renee speak.

"See what I'm talking about — bitter? I have to go. Good to know you are back at work, Little Sis."

"Oh, wait — did you hear that Eric died?" Renee said before she let Jessica get off the phone.

Jessica required a memory refresher and asked, "Eric was Kit's boyfriend, right? He was the one trying to call me? Wow, how did he die?"

Renee explained, "He was basically beaten to death. You know he was gay?"

"Did they find out who did it?"

Renee further explained, "They think it was an attempted robbery, but I think it was someone he forgot to tell he was gay."

"It doesn't matter why they did that to him; I just think that is no way to die. How is Kit taking the news?"

"She is acting like it didn't bother her, or maybe she truly just doesn't care," Renee said.

"I will come by your place later, and we'll talk then. I just got to Red Lobster."

Drake met her at the door. When Jessica saw him this time, she was looking at him with a different set of eyes. She really noticed just how handsome he was.

"Hello, Ms. Jessica. I was very happy that you called. I have been waiting for this for a long time."

"Yeah, well, I am very nervous. I find you very attractive, but I know that my heart belongs to another man."

"I understand. I just wanted a chance to talk to you again. I really enjoyed our first conversation. How about this: how has your day been so far?"

"I am having a weird day. I know you don't want to hear about this, but I didn't hear from him for days, which felt like weeks. Then he called, telling me how much he loves me. At first, I wanted to believe him, but something was bothering me. One day, he called out of the blue, and within days, he was asking me for money. I've been down this road before, where I let a man use me by telling me he loved me. I saw the signs, and at first, I said 'Yes,' but I just couldn't let myself go down that road again. So, now I'm here, having lunch with you, fighting the urge to give him the money, because I do believe I still love him. My heart is telling me to stay and give us a chance. but my mind is saying, 'Run!'"

Drake took a long swallow from his drink, wiped his mouth, and said, "I think you're right. I did not want to hear that. I am a patient man, and I believe you are a good woman, so I will listen and not judge, but you need to realize that you deserve better than that. Your mind is telling you the right thing to do, in my opinion. And, I am not just saying that because I am very interested in getting to know you and possibly assisting you in making him part of your past. Let me ask you this: did you share the story about your past relationship with him?"

"Yes, I did. I told him how low my self-esteem was, and that's how I damn near bankrupted myself, trying to buy love."

"That is where a lot of women make mistakes. They share too much of themselves with a man without really knowing him and his true intentions. They make it easy for him to take advantage of them by giving him the ammunition he needs to control her mind."

Jessica was intrigued and wanted to hear more.

"What do you mean?"

"If I were less than an honorable man and you told me that story, I would first tell you how beautiful you are every day. That would break down all your defenses with regard to low self-esteem; then I would have you right where I wanted you. You would be so concerned with the fact that I make you feel pretty that you would accept or deny all of my not-so-credible behavior."

"Wow, Drake — you are really taking me to school. I have never thought of it like that."

"You wouldn't, because you are a victim of it. He knew what he was doing. I am sorry you had to go through that, but be proud of yourself for learning from your mistakes. It shows, because you are here with me instead of rushing to give him the money. Also, because you actually heard your inner voice, aka, your gut, telling you something is not right. Most women ignore that inner voice. You also need to know that I will never take advantage of you."

"Every time I talk to you, I feel stupid, but I always walk away feeling glad that I talked to you," Jessica said.

"Well, enough of that. Why don't you tell me about your sister?"

"She is fine. She went back to work today. She is still very bitter about everything."

Drake said, "That is understandable. Has she spoken to the rest of your family yet?"

"No. In fact, she moved in with her best friend and has sworn to stay away from men and my family. She did ask if you had a friend, but in a joking way."

Drake smiled and said, "She hasn't written men completely off yet, if she is still asking about them. That's a good sign. I enjoyed lunch with you, but I know you have to go back to work. Maybe next time, it will be dinner."

Jessica gave him a smile that said "Definitely," but the word that came from her mouth was "Maybe."

"Don't make me wait so long next time. I am patient, but not that patient."

"You got that, and thanks again, Drake."

The police were over at Eric's apartment building, questioning visitors and residents all day.

"Hello, sir. Do you live in this building?"

"No. I was coming to visit my cousin."

"There was an assault in this building a few days ago, and we were trying to find anyone who may have heard or saw anyone or anything suspicious."

"Sorry to hear that, but if you have a card, I will give it to my cousin, just in case he heard anything."

That bitch Jessica stood me up. I could have been out of here by now. That bitch thinks she is going to play me. I got something for that ass, James said to himself.

Jessica was on her way back to her office when Renee called.

"Hey, Jess. I was just calling to see how lunch went."

"Lunch went very well. I think I really like him."

"Enough to cut off that other idiot?" Renee said.

"Enough to take a step in that direction. I did tell James that I was going to meet him for lunch today, and I didn't show up."

"You are crazy. What happens if he shows up at your job acting stupid like he did with me the other day?"

"James is not a violent man. He is just not the man for me anymore."

"I'll be damned!" Renee yelled. "He looked like he wanted to take my head off the other day."

"Well, you can get under someone's skin. Do you know what else is so nice about Drake? He always asks about you."

Renee laughed. "Maybe he is using you to get to me."

"Whatever! Bye!"

Jessica hung up the phone and stepped out into the reception area to speak with Charmaine.

"Charmaine, what time are you leaving today? I can give you a ride if Mike has your car."

"He's coming to pick me up, for sure."

"Are you sure? Because I'm going your way. I'm going to see Renee."

"That's OK. Thanks, anyway. I had planned on giving Desire a ride, so Mike and I could try to talk some sense into her."

"Alright, then. I may stop by after I leave Renee's."

"You should, so you could meet my Mike."

Charmaine's phone started to ring, which interrupted their conversation.

"Charmaine, this is Desire. I won't need that ride home today. You are not happy for me, so I really don't want you to know where I live just yet."

"Des, I just want what's best for you and those boys. Please don't let this happen again. We just started a new friendship after you let Jay come between us."

"Well, Charmaine, there's no man this time. I have a home for me and my kids, and, no matter how I got in, I just wanted my friend to be happy for me."

Charmaine felt that she had tried being sympathetic and she'd tried being understanding, but now she just had to be raw with realness.

"You are letting Jay play you all over again. He left because he said he loved you, and he came back because he loved you. Jay does not love anyone but himself, and I don't know why you can't see that. You don't know who the real owner of that apartment is. What if they come home and find you there? They may charge you with trespassing, and then where will you be with your kids?"

Desire never raised her voice. She just simply said, "I doubt that, because almost every drawer in the house was empty. The only thing in there was a little food, DVDs, and the furniture. Like I said before, maybe he did the right thing for the wrong reason."

Anger and frustration were rising within Charmaine.

"So, he got you a furnished apartment for the price of $3,000! You really think that makes sense?"

"It may not make sense to you, Charmaine, but my boys are happy, and if you were truly my friend, you would be happy for me, too. I have to go. See you around, Charmaine," she said and abruptly hung up.

Jessica stepped out of her office ready to shut it down for the day.

"Alright, Charmaine. It's quitting time. See you tomorrow, girlie. Is he here yet?"

"I just called him. He said he is a few blocks away."

"Alright, then. See you."

Jessica ran into Desire walking out of the building, and she noticed her glow.

"Hello, Ms. Desire. Congratulations on your new apartment. You have really taken lemons and made lemonade. It's good to see a woman grabbing the bull by the horn, so to speak. Do you need a ride home?"

Desire accepted her offer, saying, "Sure, Jessica. Thank you so much."

Jessica tried to keep the conversation upbeat in the car.

"So, how do you like the job? I heard they really like you."

"I like the job, but I still may have to get a third job just to afford my new place."

"How much is the rent?" Jessica asked.

"I really don't know yet. My kids' father found us the place. He took care of those details."

Jessica could no longer keep the conversation light because of what she already knew surrounding the apartment.

"I hope you don't get offended, but Charmaine told me a little about your situation. I thought he was the reason you were in the shelter to begin with."

"He was, but he said he'd changed, and I wanted to believe him for my kids' sake."

Desire was happy that they made it to her new apartment before she had to answer any more questions.

"Well, anyway, thank you for the ride."

"This is a nice place. Your kids should be happy here. Goodnight, Desire."

"Thanks again, Jessica. Here is my number if you want to come by sometime."

The moment Desire got out of the car, Jessica's phone began to ring. She saw his name on the caller ID, and she braced herself before answering.

"Jessica Tyler, didn't you tell me to meet you at the Spanish restaurant today?"

"I am sorry, but I got stuck at work."

"Jess, do you really want me to believe that? You don't think I call your job when you didn't show up? I'm gonna ask you straight up: are you fucking somebody else?"

"James, I got stuck at work, and I went and got a sandwich from the deli. Maybe that is when you called and they told you I was out."

"Are you trying to play me? I know I messed up when I disappeared on you, but you said you would give me a chance to make up for that."

"I was going to give you a chance, but when you finally called, all you wanted was money. I started to feel like the only reason you called me was because you needed money. I will not let myself be used by another man in this lifetime."

James realized his charm was not having the same effect on Jessica, and he spoke out of desperation.

"Jessica, Jessica, listen to me! I love you, and I wouldn't use you. I wanted you to be the mother of my child. Do you remember that?"

"James, that was all said before you left."

"But, Jess, I wasn't gone that long. If you loved me then, why don't you love me now?"

"I never said I didn't love you, James, but I will not be played by you."

"Sweetheart, where are you? I will meet you so we can talk face to face."

Jessica felt her empowerment returning with every word she spoke from that moment on.

"I don't think I want to talk anymore. I am going to see my sister, and then, I am going home. I just want to be left alone for tonight."

James sensed that he'd lost control over her and changed his tone completely.

"Yeah, right. That other nigga coming over there?"

"I don't have time for this. Goodbye!"

As she proceeded to hang up on him, she heard him saying, "Jessica, wait. I am sorry. I know you are not that kind of girl, and I know I hurt you, but we are good together. Are you really ready to throw all of that away?"

"I didn't. You did, when you decided to disappear. You left me with nothing but time to think. When I was in Jamaica, that's all I did, while watching my sister grieve over the loss of a man she thought she loved. I told myself that I would never let anyone put me in that position. You didn't want what I wanted in this relationship, so you left. Now I don't want what you're offering in this relationship, so now I am leaving. What is that old saying? 'Do unto others as you would have them do unto you.' James, I am going to be honest with you. I've met someone else, and I like how it feels so far. This is your fault. You let this happen to us."

Hearing Jessica say she'd met someone else angered James to the point where he was now screaming into the receiver.

"*I* made you fuck some other dude!?"

"See — you heard what you wanted to hear. I did not say I slept with him. He is just different from you. Like I said, I believe I am moving on. Whether this thing with Drake and me goes anywhere or not, I would rather be alone at this point in my life if it doesn't work out. I am here at my sister's, so I have to go upstairs now. I am sorry it had to end like this. Bye."

James sat in the car, holding his phone and trying to think of his next move.

I don't need you, because I am going to have the last laugh, bitch, he said to himself.

Jessica walked into Kit's and Renee's apartment feeling vindicated.

"Hey, ladies. I feel like I could use a drink. I just broke up with James."

Shocked by the news, Renee screamed out, "Get the hell out of here! How did he take it?"

"Typical — he thinks it's because of Drake."

"You told him about Drake?" Renee questioned.

"Drake, the bouncer?" Kit questioned.

"Yeah, we went out to lunch today, and I think he's good for me."

Kit offered her what she believed was sound advice.

"Go slow, because you know how you get."

"Shut up, Kit!" Renee said. I just can't believe you broke up with him. What brought it on finally?"

"Honestly, my trip to Jamaica. After tonight's conversation, I know I made the right decision. I don't think I ever heard him raise his voice before today, and the dumb shit that he was saying really pissed me off."

Renee reflected on her confrontation with James and added, "I told you he was like a different person when I got into it with him."

Kit sat there thinking deeply for a moment and then blurted out, "We are three single women abandoned by love."

"Speak for yourself. I am on the fast track to becoming Mrs. Drake McNeil," Jessica said, smiling hard.

"Well, just in case you forgot, Sis, just about two years ago, you were trying to become Mrs. James Frazier."

"You've got to admit that 'Jessica Frazier' had a nice ring to it," she giggled to herself. "On another note, you know Mommy has been asking about you. Tawana and Sam came by the other day, and she asked them to leave just in case you came by."

"Well, she might as well give them my old room, because I will never come back to that house."

"At some point, you are going to have to talk to her. She is your mother."

"Someday, not anytime soon, and Tawana can kiss my ass for the rest of her life."

"She is still your family," Jessica said.

Renee was done talking about that topic.

"I think this visit has come to an end. Goodbye, Sis."

Renee walked toward the door and held it open for Jessica to exit.

"You two really get on my nerves," Kit said. "I am going to bed."

"Before I go, let's do something this weekend," Jessica said. "How about another ladies' night? There is this card game I bought at Walmart called Phase 10. We can have some fun — just the girls."

"Alright, just get out. Later!" Renee said loudly.

Jessica ran into Charmaine on the elevator, looking really upset.

"Oh, hey, Charmaine. Are you just getting home?"

"Girl, don't ask. When I get into the house, he'd better not be there."

"Are you gonna be OK?" Jessica asked.

"I'll be fine, but I can't say the same for him if he is in this house."

Jessica said, "Don't hurt him too bad. Goodnight."

Charmaine walked into the apartment and slammed the door behind her.

"Mike, are you here? You'd better have one hell of an excuse for leaving me!"

When she looked into the bathroom and saw he wasn't in the apartment, she immediately called his phone.

"Mike, you son of a bitch, you'd better bring me my damn car now."

"Baby, calm down. I can explain when I get home."

"Mike, I don't want to hear your shit. Just bring me my damn car!" she screamed as she hung up the phone.

This bitch is losing her mind, he thought to himself.

Charmaine began looking around the apartment and realized certain things were out of place.

What the hell is going on? Wait a minute — where are all his clothes? What the fuck happened to my jewelry box? Oh, my God! Tell me he didn't just do this to me! Oh, my God! Oh, my God!

Charmaine began to call his phone repeatedly.

"Mike, answer the phone! Answer the phone, Mike!" *Oh, God, what happened? What did I do wrong? Why would he do this to me? I can't be here. I have to go.*

She picked up the phone and dialed the shelter, looking for Desire.

The woman who answered the phone said, "Desire no longer lives here."

Shit! I forgot she'd moved, Charmaine thought.

Charmaine went banging on Kit's apartment door.

"Hold on. Wait a minute! Who the hell is it?"

"I am so sorry to bother you ladies, but I have a problem."

"First of all, calm down. You are hysterical. What happened, Charmaine?"

"He left me! He just up and left me!"

"*Who* left you?" Kit asked.

"Mike! He took everything and left. I just bought him a computer, and we were talking about kids. What the hell happened?"

"Were you talking about kids before or after you brought him the computer?" Renee questioned.

Kit felt the question was insensitive.

"What difference does it make?"

"It makes a big difference. If you talked about children right before he asked for the computer, then he was just softening you up for the kill," Renee said.

"He was not like that. He loved me. I must have said or done something wrong," Charmaine said, as tears began to form in her eyes.

"No wonder you get along with my sister. You are just as stupid as she is. Why would you blame yourself for his shortcomings?"

"Renee, the girl is going through it. Don't be so hard," Kit said.

"She needs to hear it raw."

"Did you want to hear it raw when I tried to tell you about Sam?" Kit asked.

"That was different."

"How? An affair of the heart is an affair of the heart, Renee."

"Exactly. There is no easy way to break someone's heart or deal with a broken heart."

Charmaine was sitting on the sofa, with her face in her hands, listening to them banter back and forth.

Kit asked Renee, "Are you dealing with your broken heart by moving out of your mother's house and not speaking to her or your niece?"

"Kit, that is totally different, and you know it!"

"Was that not a matter of the heart? Kit asked rhetorically. "Leave that girl alone, and let her deal with it as she sees fit. She will come to her own realization when she is ready. We all blame ourselves at first. You did it, I did it, and Jessica and Tawana will soon do it, too. You can't tell me that you didn't ask yourself at least one time, 'Why did he choose my niece over me?' It took a long time for me to finally stop asking myself, 'Was I not good enough? Why did he come out of the closet after being with me? Did I make him turn to men?' I finally came to my senses after seeing him in that hospital. I know it had nothing to do with me. It was his self-hate that kept him in the closet. I knew it was his issue, not mine, that was the cause of the breakup."

Charmaine stood up quickly, as if something had just popped into her head.

"Thank you, Kit and Renee, for listening to me, but I think I want to be alone for a little while."

"Are you sure? Maybe you should call your friend over."

"She is upset with me, and I don't have her new number."

“Jessica has it. I will get for you. You know where we are if you want to come back,” Renee offered.

Charmaine left the apartment still in tears.

“What the hell is wrong with you, kicking that girl when she is already down?!” Kit yelled at Renee.

“I was not trying to be mean. I feel for her, but at the same time, I still say, ‘Don’t be stupid.’”

“You need help, Renee! I am going to bed. I hope that’s the last visitor for the night. I think Jessica is right — we *are* in need of a ladies’ night. I hope she goes home and calls her friend, Desire, because I know I would definitely need my friend if that happened to me,” Kit said.

Charmaine was in her apartment doing just that but hung up before Desire could answer the phone.

Who the hell keeps calling here and hanging up? Damn it! Desire wondered.

“Boys, I need you to go get ready to take baths and go to bed. Mommy has had a long day, and she needs some quiet time.”

Jessica’s ass is busy talking about ladies’ night, and Charmaine will be lucky if I ever speak to her ass again. I am not crazy, Lord knows. I just need some time, Desire was thinking to herself.

Desire’s thoughts were interrupted by a loud knock at the door.

“Hello. Is someone in there?”

Desire yelled back at the door, “Who is that?”

A male voice said, “Who are you? Open this door! This is my cousin’s house.”

“I just rented this apartment. Your cousin no longer lives here!” Desire yelled back.

“My cousin died the other day, and this is his apartment. I was just here with him the day before he died, so I know that his apartment was not rented to anyone. Now, open this door now, whoever you are,” the man yelled at the top of his lungs through the door.

Desire yelled back, “I think you need to get away from my door before I call the police!”

“Good! Call them, so we can straighten this out.”

"Listen, I have my kids in here. Could you please just leave? I do not know your cousin."

The voice said, "His name is — sorry, *was* — Eric Wright."

The yelling stopped, and Desire felt the pain in the person's voice.

"Again, I am sorry for your loss, but I don't know him, and he does not live here."

"Lady, I am going to give you until tomorrow, and I will be back with the police."

"Just leave me alone, please," Desire said.

Desire was preparing for bed when another loud knock came from the door.

"Hello. Is anybody in there? This is the police. Open up."

Desire looked through the peephole to verify that it was actually the police. She took a deep breath before unlocking and then opening the door. She felt knots starting to develop in her stomach.

"Sir, I don't know who called you, but this is my place. My kids' father rented this apartment the other day."

"Sorry, Miss. We are investigating a crime. My name is Officer McNeil, and this is my partner Officer Miyake. Do you know Mr. Eric Wright? He was assaulted and later died of his injuries, and this was his last known address."

"No, I don't know him, but there was some guy here right before you showed up asking for him. But, like I told him, I don't know Eric Wright. We just moved in."

"Do you mind if we take a look around?" Officer Miyake asked.

"I do mind, because it's late, and my children are in bed."

"Alright, then, Miss. Can we come back tomorrow?" Officer McNeil asked.

"I don't understand why you would need to. I told you I don't know him, and I live here now."

"Well do you have a current lease that you can show us to prove you recently acquired the apartment?" Miyake questioned.

Desired stuttered with her answer at first, but then she finally said, "My kids' father actually rented the place. I am sure he has the lease."

"Well, is he here?"

"No, he's not, but I will make sure when he gets home to hang a copy of the lease on the door, so everyone will stop bothering me and my kids," Desire said sarcastically.

"Okay, then, Miss. You have a good night."

Desire politely closed the door in their faces.

Officer Miyake looked at his partner and said, "Drake, something doesn't seem right with her. I will check with the landlord in the morning."

Desire tried getting ready for bed again, but the phone began to ring.

What the hell is going on tonight? she thought.

"Hello! Who is this?" she screamed into the receiver.

"Desire, please don't hang up. It's Charmaine. I need you. Des, please. Are you there?"

Annoyed by the sound of Charmaine's voice, Desire said, "Charmaine, why are you calling me so late? You know the boys are asleep."

The fact that Desire didn't hang up on her was a sign to Charmaine that there was a friend on the other end of the line and not the angry person who was mad at her.

"Desire, he left me and took everything," she sobbed into the phone. "All his things are gone, and he took all my money from my account."

Desire sensed the urgency in her friend's voice, and she knew she couldn't turn her back on her.

"I will give you the address. Come over. I will wait up for you."

When Charmaine got to Desire's apartment, the moment she opened the door and saw her, she just reached out to pull her close and hug her tight.

"Desire, I am so sorry for everything. I never thought he would do something like this. He took my car and everything," Charmaine sobbed.

"Why?" Desire asked.

"I don't know. Everything was going great between us. We didn't even have a fight or anything. This just came out of nowhere."

"Did you report the car stolen?"

"No, not yet. I didn't want to get him in trouble if they stopped him."

"Bitch, *what!?* Are you crazy? What the hell is wrong with you? He stole your money and your car, and you're worried about getting him in trouble? I wish I had a way for the police to track Jay down because I would have the police hot on his trail right now."

"Desire, he may come back."

"And you told me *I* was making a mistake by staying in this place, but right now, you sound real stupid."

"You're right, Desire. Can I use your phone?"

"Now you're talking like you have some sense. But you can call them when you get home. I've had enough police activity here tonight."

"What do you mean?"

"The police were here talking about some guy named 'Eric Wright,' who died or something."

"Is this his apartment?"

Desire gave her a skeptical look.

"No, this is my apartment, Charmaine. I think he may have lived here before me."

"Des, I don't want you to get mad at me again, but did Jay show you any papers in regard to this apartment?"

"No, but he must have had something, because he had the keys and everything."

"Do you think *Jay* knew this 'Eric' person?"

Desire paused before she answered. "I don't think so, because that Eric dude was gay. The night we moved in here, some queen came here looking for him. Enough about me and my apartment. That's not why you're here. How are you feeling now?"

"I will never understand why, but I'm okay for now," Charmaine said. "Thank you for being here for me."

"Did you want to stay the night? We have to go to work in the morning. Do you realize that both of our ex-men left us broke?" Desire asked.

The two ladies shared an awkward laugh and a hug for support.

"I will go home, but thank you so much for listening to me. I love you, girl, and the place is beautiful. Thank God, we both have jobs, or this could be far worse."

"I love you, too, and I will see you tomorrow."

"Grandma, can I talk to you?"

"Tawana, what are you doing here so late?"

"Grandma, I love Sam, but I think he still loves Renee."

"Sam never loved Renee, or he would not be with you."

Momma Tyler patted the bed beside her, giving the signal for Tawana to come sit next to her.

As Tawana sat on the bed, she said, "Grandma, he did love her. I convinced him that she was cheating on him. I told him that she was treating him as less than a man."

"Let me tell you something, little girl. No woman can make a man do something he does not want to do. You may have added gasoline to a fire that was already burning. You possibly corroborated whatever he was already feeling, but you did not make him stop loving my daughter. He stopped loving her way before you. You are my grandbaby, and if I thought that Sam was a bad man, I would not let you be with him. But let me ask you this: why are you doubting him now?"

"Ever since Eric died, all Sam talks about is how he hurt Renee."

"Baby, that could just mean that he is thinking life is too short. He is thinking about his friend and maybe about the things he took for granted in life. That is no reflection on how he feels for you."

Their conversation was interrupted by Jessica as she walked into the room, shocked to see Tawana.

"Tawana, what are you doing here?"

"I came by to talk to Grandma. Is that a problem?"

"That attitude of yours really sucks now. If this is what Sam brings out in you, then you need to stay over there with him. Don't bring that mess up in here."

Momma Tyler wanted to change the course of the conversation, so she said, "Jessica, James came by here earlier. He said he left something in your room."

"Did you let him in?" Jessica asked, sounding really concerned.

"Yes — was I not supposed to?" Momma Tyler asked, out of confusion.

"No, you shouldn't have. James and I are no longer together, and I don't want him back in this house."

Jessica walked out of her mother's room and opened the door of her room.

Tawana and Momma Tyler heard her scream out, "What the hell! That son of a bitch!"

They both went running into the hallway saying, "What happened?"

Jessica was standing in the middle of the room, spinning around slowly, looking at the mess he'd made. All her purses had been taken from the closet and turned inside out. Her mattress had been flipped on its side and cut open. All her drawers were open and the contents had been dumped out onto the floor.

She yelled, "Look at my room! He took all my jewelry and the money I was saving for an apartment."

Tawana asked, "How much was it?"

Still looking at the Michael Kors bag lying on the pile of clothes, she answered, "Almost $4,000."

Her mother said, "Why would you keep that much money in the house?"

"I was planning on leaving. I was going to get a money order and put it down on this apartment in Baldwin. That bastard! He knew the money was there because we were going to move together. Thank God, I never gave him access to my bank account."

Momma Tyler took a step back out of the room; then she turned back around to ask, "When were you planning to leave? And when were you going to tell me?"

Jessica barely glanced at her mother when she said, "Aren't you worried about the wrong thing right now? What about my things? Ma, please don't make this about you. He and I spoke about it before I went to Jamaica. He is a true piece of shit. How could I have ever loved someone like that?"

Her mother looked at her and simply said, "They are just things, and you can get them back. You can't cry over spilt milk."

Tawana stepped out of Jessica's room, leaving Jessica slowly picking up her clothes, one piece at a time.

"Grandma, can I stay here tonight?"

"Of course, you can. This is still your home."

With a sigh of relief, Tawana felt comforted by hearing that.

"I thought you didn't want me here in case Renee comes home."

Momma Tyler shook her head back and forth.

"My daughter doesn't love me anymore, so why not have someone here who loves me?"

Jessica was now standing in her mother's bedroom doorway, listening in on her mother's words.

"Mommy, Renee loves you. She is just upset right now."

Tawana asked, "Do you think she will ever forgive me?"

"Tawana, you may have to wait and see about that. In the meantime, since you are here, you can help me clean my room, while I call the police."

"The *police*, Jessica? Do you really think that's necessary?" Momma Tyler asked.

"Hell, *yes*, mother! That bastard stole my money and my favorite chain. I don't care what happens to his ass."

Jessica dialed the number right in front of her mother to show her that she was very serious.

"Hello, 911. This is Jessica Tyler, and I would like to report a robbery. My ex-boyfriend broke into my house and stole all my jewelry and approximately $4,000 in cash."

The 911 operator asked, "What is your boyfriend's name, and why do you believe he did this?"

"My mother let him in my room, so I *know* he did this. His name is James Frazier."

"Can you come down to the precinct to file a formal complaint?"

"Can I do it in the morning?" Jessica asked.

"If he took that amount of money, he could be gone by then."

"I am just mentally tired, ma'am. I've had a rough day. I will take my chances."

"Okay, Miss. Just bring a picture of him when you come in."

Jessica had to think for a moment before she responded, "I don't have any picture of him. He never liked to take pictures."

"How are we supposed to find him, Miss? Does he have a criminal record?"

"No, not that I know of," Jessica answered.

"Well, come down in the morning, and we will see what we can do."

During this same timeframe, Charmaine was back in her apartment contemplating whether or not she should go through with calling the police.

Charmaine kept questioning herself. *How could he do this to me? Why am I still thinking of his feelings? He damn sure was not thinking about me. He played me and made me think he was in love with me.*

As she looked over at the closet and the empty hangers, she realized he was not coming back, so she dialed the number.

I hope they find you and put you in jail, she said to herself before the 911 operator answered.

"Hello. My name is Charmaine Dupree, and I would like to report my car stolen. I believe my ex-boyfriend stole my car. He also took all my jewelry and all my money in my bank account."

The 911 operator made a comment under her breath that she thought was inaudible, "This must be the night for ex-boyfriends."

"Excuse me?" Charmaine said, feeling disrespected.

"I am sorry, Miss; I just took another call where a woman's ex-boyfriend stole her money and jewelry. What is your boyfriend's name, and why do you think he did this?"

"His name is Michael Frazier. He had my car today, and he was supposed to pick me up from work, and he didn't. When I got home, all his things were gone, and I have not heard from him at all."

"I am going to need you to come down to the station in the morning and fill out a formal complaint. There is nothing we can do tonight. Please bring a picture of your boyfriend when you come in."

"I don't even have a picture of that jackass. He didn't like taking pictures."

The 911 operator giggled to herself at the coincidence of the two callers.

CHAPTER 9

All Hell Breaking Loose

"Good morning. My name is Jessica Tyler, and I am here to file a formal complaint against my ex-boyfriend for stealing my jewelry and my money."

"Please have a seat, and someone should be with you shortly."

"Is there a restroom I can use?" she asked.

"Sure, down the hall, second door on your right."

As Jessica stepped into the restroom, Charmaine walked into the precinct and approached the desk officer.

"Hello. I called last night to report my boyfriend. He stole my car and my money from my bank account. His name is Michael Frazier."

The officer smiled and said, "Just have a seat over there, and someone should be with you in a moment."

Jessica walked out of the restroom and noticed a familiar face in the waiting area.

"Hey, Charmaine. What are you doing here?"

"I was just leaving you a message, letting you know I would be in late." Charmaine looked at Jessica with sad hopelessness in her eyes, saying, "He left me, Jessica. He just up and disappeared and took my car with him. I had to take a cab down here."

"Don't worry about that. I can give you a ride, but what happened, Charmaine?"

"He said he was on his way to pick me up, and he never showed up. I called him, and he said he would meet me at the house to explain, but when I got home, all his things were gone. I'd just bought him a brand-new computer. Everything was fine between us. He took all the money from my bank account. I didn't have much, but it was all I had."

Jessica looked at her with pity in her eyes, "Charmaine, you hadn't known him that long, so why would you give him access to your account?"

Charmaine shrugged her shoulders in disbelief. "All I can say is, it felt right. I trusted him. I believed him when he said he loved me and wanted to spend the rest of his life with me. He wanted me to be the mother of his children."

Jessica let out a loud chuckle. "That sounds like my ex, except when I mentioned having children, he disappeared on me."

It finally dawned on Charmaine that Jessica was at the precinct with her. "Wait a minute," she said. "Why are you here?"

Jessica started laughing again. "That fool used my mother to gain access to my room and stole all my jewelry and about $4,000 in cash."

"Wow, Jess. I am so sorry to hear that."

"I am mad, but not really. If that's what it took to get him out of my life, then let him have it. I just came down here to file a formal complaint. Oh, shit. I left my phone in the bathroom. I'll be right back."

Charmaine was still sitting in the waiting area when Officer Miyake walked in with Desire in hand restraints.

"Oh, my God — Desire! What is going on? Officer, this is my friend. What did she do?"

Desire remained quiet and kept her head down, not even acknowledging Charmaine's presence.

Officer Miyake replied, "She is being charged with trespassing, and she won't talk to us."

"Can I talk to her please, Officer? I can find out what's going on."

"Put her into interrogation room 1," Miyake said. "You can talk to her briefly."

"Desire, what's going on here?"

Desire finally broke her silence, "After I took the boys to school, I went back to the apartment to get some papers I was working on for Bob, at the office. That's when the police showed up with the landlord. They asked him if he'd recently rented the apartment to me or Jay, and he said 'No.' He said the apartment is still under lease with Mr. Eric Wright, who apparently is dead."

"Well, how the hell did Jay get the keys to a dead man's apartment? Didn't you say that this Eric dude was gay? Was Jay?"

Desire rolled her eyes at that comment. "No, Charmaine. Jay was a man's man. I don't know how he knew him or if he knew him. All I know is that when the police asked me how I got the keys, and I told them what happened, they didn't believe me. What am I going to do? What about my boys?"

Trying to ease her mind, Charmaine told her, "I will get the boys. Don't worry about that. You have no idea how to get in touch with Jay? Did you tell them he took your money?"

"I told them everything. They won't listen to me, so I stopped talking to them. Maybe you can explain it to them. Tell them something. Maybe they will believe you. Please, if you could go to the house and get my things. Make sure you get the boys' videos and their toys. That's the only things they have from our old house."

"Are they going to let me in? I'm not trying to get arrested, because that will not be good for any of us."

"I don't know, Charmaine," she said, sounding totally defeated. Desire had a revelation as she said, "Oh Lord, Charmaine, what am I going to do about the job?"

Charmaine thought of something quick and excused herself from the room to make a phone call. As she re-entered the room she said, "Desire, I hope you don't mind, but I told Bob that you were in the hospital and that you'd had a miscarriage. I had to say something so you can keep your job once this is over with."

"What!? Charmaine, you couldn't think of anything else?" Desire said, sounding upset.

"It was the only way I could get you at least a week off of work so that you could clear this up. Is there anything else you need me to do besides get the boys if you can't get out of here?" Charmaine asked.

"Thank you. You've done enough."

Miyake opened the door abruptly, "Okay, ladies, time's up. She'll be processed, and, more than likely, she'll be released on her own recognizance."

Charmaine stood up to exit the small interrogation room. "I will wait for you, Des," she said.

"Thank you, Charmaine. I don't know what I would do without you."

Charmaine went back out to the waiting area to fill Jessica in on the situation with Desire.

Officer Miyake escorted Desire to his desk to get a formal written statement. Just then the desk officer called out, "Which one of you ladies is here to file a claim against Michael Frazier?"

Jessica stood up, saying, "I am filing against James Frazier, not Michael."

Charmaine looked over at Jessica and said, "I am here for Michael."

Both ladies were on their feet, gazing at each other, when Jessica broke the awkward stares by speaking first.

"Charmaine, Michael's last name is 'Frazier' also?"

Desire could hear the confusion from where she was sitting at Officer Miyake's desk. "Officer Miyake, wait one minute, please. Jay's last name is 'Frazier,' also."

"Ms. Williams, are you sure? Is this some type of ploy to get out of the charge against you? Because this would be way too much of a coincidence if it were true."

"Officer Miyake, I have three kids with that man. I would know his last name."

Jessica and Charmaine quickly walked over to Officer Miyake's desk after hearing Desire's proclamation.

Charmaine said, "Des, all the boys have your last name."

"Jay said he liked the way my last name sounded with the boys' first names, so that's why they have my last name," she responded.

Miyake asked, "Do you have a picture of him?"

"No, he never liked taking pictures," Desire answered.

"So, none of you ladies have a picture of this Mr. Michael, James, Jay Frazier character?" Miyake said.

They said — pretty much all at the same time — "He never liked to take pictures."

"Can someone give an accurate description of him, at least?"

Jessica spoke up quickly. "I can describe that bastard down to the mole on his left ball sack."

"Damn, Jessica," Charmaine said. "But she is absolutely correct."

Desire shook her head in agreement.

From behind, Jessica heard her name being called.

"Jessica, what are you doing here?"

She was relieved to see a familiar face when she turned around. "Drake, you were right about him. My ex struck again. He stole my jewelry and $4,000 of my cash. He was living with my secretary Charmaine under the name of Michael, and he stole her car, her jewelry, and all her money. I just found out that he has three kids with Charmaine's best friend, Desire. He put her up in an apartment that belongs to a dead man, by the name of Eric, and stole $3,000 in cash from her, too. Eric turned out to be the gay ex-boyfriend of my sister's best friend, Kit. Can you help her?"

"I will see what I can do, but I am the arresting officer in her case. You mean to tell me that he has been dating all of you, and none of you figured it out until today?"

"He gave everyone a different name, Drake. We really didn't know. Charmaine is my secretary and my friend, but I don't tell females all the details about my man. So no, I never told her his last name. She just recently met and started dating him. Umm, that bastard said he wanted me to be the mother of his firstborn. Why would someone do something like this? It just doesn't make sense."

Drake reached out for her hand as a sign of comfort and support. "This is what I'll do. I will drop the charges against Desire, but she cannot go back to that apartment until we figure this thing out."

"Alright, Drake, but she has her clothes and her sons' belongings in there. Is it possible for me to go pick up her things?"

"I will have someone escort you when you go over there, but do not take or touch anything that does not belong to her," he warned her.

"Drake, I will give you a call later. Thank you so much for everything. I have to drop them off first."

"Make sure you call me," Drake ordered. "Ladies, let's go. This thing is crazy. Maybe that is why Eric was trying to reach me."

Charmaine and Desire said — practically in unison — "You know this 'Eric' person?"

"I don't know him like that. I know that he was Kit's ex-man, and he was friends with Sam, my sister's ex-man."

Desire, totally clueless to all the facts, said, "If he's Kit's ex-boyfriend, then he wasn't gay?"

"They broke up because he admitted that he was gay," Jessica said, filling in the blanks for her.

Charmaine sat in the passenger seat, doing the math in her head. "That piece of shit took a total of $10,000 in cash from us, not including the value of my car."

The thought of that rendered the ladies quiet in the car. As they pulled up to Eric's building, Desire burst into tears because she realized she had no place to live again. "You go upstairs with the officer to get her things, Charmaine. I have to call Renee and tell her about this bullshit."

Jessica stepped out of the car to call Renee, leaving Desire in the back seat, crying her eyes out. *This is so unbelievable. I can't believe this. I think I am still in shock. If someone told me that shit like this happened to them, I would think they were lying. I need a drink.*

"Renee, you are never going to believe this shit!"

"Lord Jesus, what's happened now?"

"You were right about James, Michael, Jay — or whatever that good-for-nothing piece of shit chose to call himself."

Totally confused by Jessica's ramblings, Renee said, "Wait — what the hell are you talking about?"

"You heard me right, Sis. James was my boyfriend, Charmaine's boyfriend, and Desire's babies' daddy."

Renee dropped her phone after hearing that. She picked it up quickly, saying, "What kinda sick shit is that?"

"Yes, girl. We all just left the police station."

"Oh, Lord, for what? Since when did cheating become a crime? Because, if that's the case, I want Sam in jail."

"Mommy let him in, and he stole the money I had saved for my apartment and my jewelry. That bastard tore my room up."

"Let me guess: he stole their money, too."

"He got away with about $10,000 plus my and Charmaine's jewelry. And — I can't forget — he has her car."

Renee started reflecting on how much Charmaine was always bragging about that bum. She said, "Now that I think about it, that's why that bitch-ass negro was always in that building. I never saw them together, though."

Jessica agreed. "That bastard definitely covered all his tracks."

Renee thought about one of Jessica's previous statements, and it dawned on her. "Wait a minute — did you say Desire's kids' father?"

"I sure did. He went as far as denying his own kids. Imagine if I would have gotten pregnant, thinking I was the first," Jessica added.

"Wow, Jess. That fool was running game the whole time."

"Did you know that he knew Eric?"

"How?" Renee questioned.

"I don't know yet, but that's how Desire ended up at the precinct. Drake arrested her for trespassing. James gave her Eric's apartment after he died."

"Maybe that's what Eric was trying to tell you. He kept saying you had a friend in common. Maybe that friend was James all along."

"Well, listen. I have to call you back later because they are on their way back to the car."

"Who?" Renee asked?

"Charmaine and the cop. We're at Eric's apartment picking up Desire's things that she left in there. I feel so bad for her. She is sitting in the car crying hysterically. I can't cry because I am way too mad to cry."

"It might hit you later, and then the waterworks will start. I will tell you now: don't call me crying over that fool when it does hit you, because I'm going to call you 'stupid' and hang up the phone on you," Renee laughed.

"Shut up. I've got Drake to ease my pain," Jessica said, smiling into the phone.

"Alright, later. You do know I am telling Kit all about your drama — right?"

"Tell her — I don't care. We definitely need a ladies' night after this nonsense. Bye." Jessica walked back toward the car, where Desire had already pulled herself together and was just sitting, staring at the building.

"Desire, I just got off the phone with Renee. Do you want me to take you back to the shelter?"

Charmaine interjected before Desire could answer. "She's going to stay with me."

Desire's voice cracked from crying so hard when she said, "Charmaine, I already told you that your space is too tight for me and the boys."

Charmaine held her friend's hand and said, "We can make do. If you really don't feel comfortable with the idea, then just stay a night or two."

The tears started rolling down her face again, and she tried to stop them with her hands. "I know you guys are hurt, but he did this to me, and I have three kids by him. He didn't even think about them. He looked at those boys and told them he loved them and me. How do I explain this to my boys? How do I say Daddy left us again and we have to go back to the shelter? I have no money whatsoever now. He took all I had saved for an apartment when my Golden Rule settlement came through. But because I left the shelter, I don't know if I still qualify for the grant."

Jessica tried to sound as positive and encouraging as she could. "Hey, you still have your job. You have no choice but to start saving again. It is what it is. There's nothing we can do about it now. As for the boys, you will continue to raise them to be a better man than their father ever was or will be. You will figure out a way."

Desire nodded her head in acceptance of Jessica's words.

They arrived back at Charmaine's apartment and continued to discuss their predicament.

"So, Jess, how did you know that cop?" Desire asked.

"He was the bouncer from the club when we had our first ladies' night out."

"He likes you. I can tell by the way he looks at you."

"After what we just went through, I am not jumping into anything with anyone. I really thought I knew him," she said, shaking her head. "Can you imagine what I thought? I just keep thinking, who would do something like that to their own children? He took food out of their mouths and clothes off their backs. He damn near sent their mother to jail, and all without even blinking an eye."

"I guess you were hit worse than the rest of us. We have to try and think. Maybe he said something that may give a clue to where he took his sorry ass," Jessica said.

"I don't have a clue. He never made me think he ever wanted to leave here," Charmaine added.

Desire questioned Jessica, "Well, have you ever been to his place? I mean the place he was staying after he left me and the kids?"

"I went to an address that he gave me, but some woman answered the door and said I had the wrong address. He gave me some excuse back then, and I fell for it."

"We all fell for every lie he told us. Looking back," Desire said, "I — correction, *we* — were so desperate for love that we just accepted everything he said at face value. No questions asked."

Charmaine agreed and added, "He was just so easy to talk to, not to mention easy to look at."

Jessica added, "You know what's crazy. I have been cheated on before, and normally, I would be mad at the other woman, but in this case, I feel like this made me closer to you ladies."

They all shared a moment of eye contact and realized they were bonded. The sound of Charmaine's phone broke the moment they were sharing.

"Yes, sir. I will be able to pick it up, right? Thank you."

Everyone was silent, waiting for her to get off the phone.

"What was that about?" Desire asked the moment Charmaine hung up.

"They found my car at the train station in Valley Stream. The police said he left the keys on the front seat with the door unlocked. They couldn't find a fingerprint because the car was wiped clean. He even left it with a full tank of gas."

Jessica made an attempt at a joke. "Maybe he really liked you."

"That's not funny, Jess. I have to go get my car."

"I am sorry. It was a bad joke, but I will give you a ride, if you want."

"Yes, please."

"Well, you guys go, because I need to pick up the boys soon."

"I'll be back, and then we can discuss the sleeping arrangements. Des, are you going to be okay? I know you are taking this a lot harder than the rest of us."

"I am fine, Charmaine."

The moment they got into the car, Charmaine expressed her fear for her friend. "Jessica, I'm worried about Desire. She's not dealing with this well at all."

Jessica downplayed her fear for Desire.

"She said she was fine. I think she is just in shock. She played the fool for him longer than me and you."

"I think it just hasn't hit me yet. It may hit me later when it all just really sinks in. Right now, I just want to go home and soak in the tub."

They pulled up to the precinct next to her vehicle, and Charmaine noticed that the rims of her car were sparkling. "It looks like he had the car washed," she said and shook her head. "Thank you for everything today, Jessica. If it weren't for you, my best friend would still be in jail."

"She's going to be okay. Now that he is out of all our lives, we can move on and be better for it. I will see you later."

Charmaine went inside the precinct to pick up the keys, and, on her way back home, she was fighting back the tears. Her tears won that battle, and she pulled over and sobbed into her shirt. She knew she couldn't unleash her emotions in front of Desire, so she sat there until she was able to pull herself together before going home.

Over at Kit's apartment, Renee was filling her in on what she'd learned from Jessica. "Kit, you will not believe what happened to my sister today. Can you believe that James was sleeping with all their dumb asses? I swear you can't win for losing when dealing with no-good-ass men. When people say you should never share too much information with your girlfriends about your man, I'm sure they didn't see this coming, because when you don't, he gets to sleep with you and all your friends. I know that's not funny, but what the hell? You gotta laugh to keep from crying."

Kit was blown away by what she'd heard. She let out a loud gasp and held her mouth open for two seconds before she could speak again. "James — your sister's ex-man? Who was he sleeping with?"

Renee giggled as she answered, "Jessica, Charmaine, and Desire. Girl, he has three kids with Desire."

"Get the hell out of here. He was playing all of them? That's fucked up. How is your sister taking it?"

"She seems to be taking it very well. I hope she doesn't break down later or some dumb shit."

"She is stronger than that. I thought she was leaving him anyway for that bouncer dude," Kit said.

"She likes him — I know that much," Renee answered. He could definitely help her get over this a lot faster."

"I wish I had someone to help me get over what's his name," Kit said, smugly.

Renee didn't appreciate Kit's remark. "Don't do that. The man is dead. Give him that much respect, and call him by his name. Did I tell you that the apartment that James gave to Desire was Eric's?"

Kit's mouth fell open again. "What!? How did he know Eric?"

"I don't know. Maybe they met through Sam."

Kit was trying to connect the dots between the men, but it didn't add up. "Sam didn't hang out with James that often, so that can't be it. Well, is Desire back at the shelter?"

"No, she's staying with Charmaine."

"In the studio?" she questioned. She doesn't have room for three kids and two adults in that place."

"Hey, let them work the mess out. I am sure she is happy to be there, rather than in jail."

Kit's mouth fell open for the third time. "Jail! What the hell was going on today?"

"Girl, I don't know what was going on today. It must have been something in the air. I thought you had drama with Eric being gay. Then I thought I had drama, because Sam was fucking my niece in my bed, but this shit takes the cake. Oh, I forgot to tell you that he took almost $10,000 total from the three of them."

"Girl, when are you going to stop dropping bombs on me? Oh, hell, nah. Forget all the rest of the bullshit. When it comes down to the almighty dollar, somebody got to bleed. Have they found his ass yet?"

"The police are looking for him, but none of those fools had a picture of him. Who knows if any of those names he called himself is real?"

"You're right. Not to change the subject, but Sam called. He wanted to tell me about the funeral arrangements for Eric."

"Are you gonna go?" Renee asked.

"I don't think I should."

"Kit, I think you should. I'll come with you."

"Renee, please. Just because he is dead does not mean that I have forgiven him for what he did to me. I am not out of the woods. I have to get checked again to make sure he didn't give me anything long lasting. Shit, your sister and them need to get checked to make sure James — or whatever he called himself — didn't give them anything."

The thought of that lingered for a moment on Renee's mind. "Oh, God! Don't say that! I can't deal with the thought of that. I'm tired. Tomorrow is another day. That was enough drama for one day. Can you imagine what they're going through right now?"

"If I know your sister, she's talking to herself right now."

"That's Jessica. You are so right, Kit."

Both Kit and Renee had hit the nail on the head with their assumption about Jessica. *Lord, how could I have played the fool for another man? Why did I not see this coming? I thank you, Lord, for helping me to see some light before I was completely living in darkness, totally blinded by him. I am so disgusted with myself. Why can't I stop crying, Lord? I know it was your will, but how do I recover from this? I still love him despite what he has done. I am a fool who loves a man with no conscience. Drake appears to be a good man, so pray for the healing of my heart. If Drake is a gift from you, Lord, then help me to let him love me the way James couldn't. Amen.*

Jessica went into the house, and as she walked past her mother's room, Momma Tyler shouted out to her, "Jessica, are you OK?"

She walked straight past her mother's room without even looking in her direction and replied in a low tone, "I am fine, Mother."

Momma Tyler went to her bedroom doorway and looked out into the hall, just as Jessica was closing her room door, and said, "I know you're hurting, baby. So, if you want to talk, I am here for you, my daughter."

Jessica shouted back, from behind the closed door, "Thank you, Mother."

"Mommy, why can't we go home?"

"Listen, baby. Mommy and Daddy can't live together anymore," Desire tried to explain to her boys. "We are going to stay with Aunt Charmaine until we can find a new place."

"We don't want to stay with Charmaine. Take us back to Daddy's apartment. We wanna go back now!"

Desire pleaded with her boys to calm down, but they wouldn't listen. Her youngest son began to cry. She saw the disappointment in her eldest son, Jamal's, eyes, and she wanted to make him understand. "Please, I need you boys to understand that Mommy is doing the best she can."

Jamal stood by the apartment door, repeating, "I wanna go back now, Mommy!"

Desire couldn't take it anymore, and she lashed out, "Shut up now, damn it! We can't go back! Daddy left us, so we either stay here or go back to the shelter!"

Her middle son, Jamel, said, "Daddy said he loves us. He wouldn't leave us."

Desire turned to him with rage in her eyes and said, "Then why wasn't *he* staying in that damn shelter?"

Jamal agreed with his younger brother and came to his defense against his mother. "He said there wasn't enough room for all of us to stay in that room. You are lying on Daddy! You said we should never lie, Mommy! Stop lying!" he yelled.

Desire was fed up at this point. "Get your shit, and go find your father, then. Call him! See if that bastard answers the phone for you. I am here doing my very best for you ungrateful kids, and your father gets all the respect. I wish to God I never had any of you bastards!"

The front door swung open, and Charmaine entered the apartment, vexed about what she was hearing from the hallway. The three boys ran and sat on the couch as if they were terrified of their mother. Charmaine shouted, "What the hell is going on in here? Why are you talking to those kids like that?"

"Mind your own business, Charmaine — they are my kids! I'll talk to them however I feel like it."

"Desire, I know you are upset, but don't take it out on the kids. They are not their father."

Desire gave some thought to what Charmaine had just said to her, and she looked at the faces of her boys, sitting on the couch in tears. "I am so sorry, boys. I am so sorry." She walked over to Charmaine, still standing near the front door, and said, "Can I borrow your car? I need to get some air."

Charmaine handed her the keys and stepped aside to let her out. Desire got into the car and took off without having a specific destination. Before she knew it, she was going down a desolate road in Freeport, near the Projects. She remembered coming to this place as a little girl with her father after her mother had died, to dispose of her mother's ashes. She parked and sat in the car and watched as some guy backed his truck up and lowered his boat into the water. The words of her children kept playing over in her mind. She thought about what she'd said to her boys and began to speak aloud to herself in the car, "*Look what this bastard has me doing to my kids. I have ruined their lives. Lord, forgive me, but I think they will be better off without me. I don't have the strength to fight anymore. I can't live like this. Those boys deserve better than a mother who can't provide for them and a father who abandoned them. I didn't protect my kids from harm. Charmaine, I hope you forgive me.*

Desire's phone rang. She looked at the caller ID and initially thought it best not to answer the call.

On the other end, Charmaine was worried about her friend. *Desire, please answer the phone.* Right before the call went to voicemail, Desire answered.

"Charmaine, I am sorry. I need you to promise me that you will look out for my boys. Make sure you tell them that Mommy did her best and that I love them with all my heart."

Charmaine panicked when she heard her say those words. "Desire, what are you talking about? Don't do this!" she screamed. "Your kids need you! Please, Des, come back. Don't make those boys think they were not wanted by their mother *and* their father. More than that, I have no clue how to raise children. You don't want this. Come back. Where are you?"

"I'm sure you'll do a better job than I have. If you have to send them away, just keep in touch with them. Make sure they're okay and turn out to be good men. I have to go. I love you, girl." She hung up on Charmaine, reclined the seat, closed her eyes, and thought, *I didn't deserve this. I lived my life right, and I made the best decision I knew how. I gave love to someone who was unlovable. Why is it that I get punished for his mistake as a human being? I love my children — that's why I have to do this.*

Charmaine was pacing the hall of her building because she didn't want the boys to hear the phone conversation. She kept dialing Desire's number, but the call was going straight to voicemail. She dialed the only person she thought could help.

"Jessica, this is Charmaine. You have to help me find Desire!"

"Why? What are you talking about?" Jessica asked.

"I think she may try to kill herself! She has my car, and I don't know where she went. Can you call your cop friend to see if he can put out an APB on her?"

Jessica sat up on the edge of her bed after hearing that. "I will try to reach him, but who has the kids?"

"I have them. She said she needed to get some air, so she borrowed my car. She was gone for a while, and when I called her, she was talking really crazy. Please hurry and call him, Jess. If they find my car, she may be nearby, and we can help her."

"OK, OK, Charmaine," she said. "I will call you back."

Jessica was so nervous when she hung up, she briefly forgot Drake's number. She finally got it right after the third try. "Drake, I am so sorry to keep bothering you with all my drama, but Desire has taken Charmaine's car, and we believe she is going to commit suicide."

"Jessica, just calm down and tell me what kind of car she has, and I will go out and look for her," he said.

Jessica was able to breathe a sigh of relief, "Drake, you are a Godsend."

Drake knew he had to act quickly, so he just said, "I will call you when I find her."

Jessica wanted to put Charmaine's mind at ease, if she could, so she called her right back. "Charmaine, he is out looking for her now. I didn't want you to worry. He is going to call me as soon as he finds her."

Charmaine felt much better knowing someone was looking for her. "Jessica, you are my boss and my friend, and if I had known that the jackass was your James, I would've cut him down to the white meat for you. Seriously, bless you and your possibly new man, Drake. What's his last name? Because I don't want a repeat of this situation," she said as she let out a slight giggle.

"I'm glad you still have your sense of humor, because this situation is crazy," Jessica replied.

"Jess, I am telling you — the only way I can deal with all of this is to laugh about it. Don't get me wrong. I've had my crying moments, but I tried to laugh more than cry. I think my tears were mostly for my stuff that he took and not so much over him."

Jessica was shaking her head in agreement on the other end of the line. She said, "I must admit, it hit me when I got home. I knew him for so long and loved him so hard, and to think he would do something like this."

"You know what, Jess? I think if we just stop talking about it, that will stop giving the situation life. He will get his, because as they say, karma is a motherfucker. I also think it's because I'd just met him, and I hadn't invested years of loving him. That makes it much easier for me to deal with it. I know it's late, so try to get some rest, but call me as soon as you hear from Drake."

"I will, but what are you going to tell her kids?"

"I told them that Mommy went to go find Daddy to get some money."

That made Jessica raise her eyebrows. "That was stupid," she said.

"I couldn't think of anything else. I don't know why she would leave me with her kids. Mike and I talked about having children, but he was the only man who made me feel like I even wanted to have a baby. With him, I thought I could do the motherhood thing. I guess I have to rethink my judgment."

"We all do. Hold on — I think that might be Drake on the other line."

As soon as Drake heard Jessica's voice, he didn't wait for the formalities. He said, "Jessica, I will meet you at the hospital. I found her down by the Industrial Park in Freeport. She had taken an overdose."

"Oh, my God, Drake! Is she going to be okay?" she asked, panic stricken.

"Yes, we found her in time. They are working on her now."

Jessica was happy to call Charmaine back and give her the update. "Hey, girl. He found her. She's going to be OK. They took her to the hospital. She'd taken an overdose, but he found her in time. I don't think you should drag those kids to the hospital, but I will go and let you know what's going on."

Charmaine was overjoyed with happiness to hear that Desire had been found and that she was safe. She agreed with Jessica about staying home with the kids, but she knew other arrangements had to be made regarding the care for the boys. She told Jessica, "I can't thank you and Drake enough. Tell her I will be there tomorrow."

"Don't worry about it, Charmaine. Get some rest, and we'll talk soon."

CHAPTER 10

All Said and Done

"Sam, is there a problem? Are you missing my aunt or something?"

"Tawana, I just lost my best friend, and today is his funeral, and you're talking about some bullshit that I just don't want to hear right now. If you can't understand what I have been dealing with, then do me a favor and go stay at your grandmother's for a little while. I need my space so I can deal with the loss of my friend in peace. I don't need this pressure right now, little girl."

Tawana felt disrespected by him calling her a "little girl." She started shouting in his apartment, "Little girl! Was I a little girl when you were fucking me? Was I a little girl when I was sucking your dick? You weren't saying that bullshit when I was lying on my back for you."

Out of total frustration with her lack of sensitivity and her behaving like a spoiled brat during a time when he needed an understanding girlfriend, he snapped back at her, saying, "Maybe you're a better girlfriend when you're on your back."

Tawana became enraged and ran up on him with her fingers pointing in his face saying, "Screw you, Sam! I don't care who died — you'd better not ever talk to me like that again."

Sam didn't engage with her. Instead, he turned and walked away from her to de-escalate the situation. "Listen, maybe this is not the time to be having this type of discussion. I am under a lot of pressure. Are you coming to the funeral with me?"

Tawana was still standing there, ready to do battle, but she decided to let it go for now. So she answered, "I'll meet you there. I need time to myself now."

Sam walked toward the door of the apartment, headed for the funeral. Then he looked back at her and said, "We will talk about whatever you want tomorrow. See you at the funeral," as he closed the door behind him."

The moment the door closed, Tawana walked into the kitchen, opening and closing cabinet doors in search of something to drink. *What the hell am I doing here? Do I really love him? I took him from my aunt, and I don't even want him anymore. I am too young to be sitting in some damn house waiting on some man to come home and talk shit to me. I need to experience life, and he is making me feel old. I know he does not think that he can just talk to me and treat me however the fuck he feels, because I'm young. I may be young, but I am nobody's fool. I ain't going to no fucking funeral. He is going to learn to respect me. I don't care what's going on in his life.*

After searching the cabinets and not finding any alcohol, she grew even more frustrated with her situation and decided to call the one person she knew would have her back. "Grandma, I want to come home."

"What's going on?" Momma Tyler said.

"I need to come home. I am too young to live with a man. Grandma, he yelled at me, and I will not tolerate that from any man."

Never wanting her granddaughter to feel like she had turned her back on her, Momma Tyler said, "You can come, baby. You will always have a home here, but I want you to think about what you're doing. You came in here and told me how much you love that man and that you believe he loves you. You risked your relationship with your aunt for that man, so think long and hard about this decision before you make your next move."

"Grandma, I feel like I do love him, but when he yelled at me, I felt like a child."

Momma Tyler knew then that she had to stop coddling Tawana and give it to her straight. "You are a child in a grown-up relationship. Deal with it. Do you think you can come running home every time you get into an argument? That man lost his best friend, and instead of being a supportive girlfriend, you are acting like a spoiled child. If you want to come home, then do that, but you need to understand that this is not how relationships work. The door is always open to you, sweetheart, but you really need to think about what it is that you really want before you make that move."

Her grandmother's words resonated with her, and she felt silly for behaving the way she had. "Grandma, thank you so much. I hope one day Renee realizes that you are the best mother anyone could ask for. I have to go meet my boyfriend at his friend's funeral. I love you, Grandma."

"I pray that your words reach my daughter's heart. Bye, baby."

Renee, on the other hand, was not concerned with her mother because she was busy trying to get Kit to do the right thing, in her eyes. "Kit, are you sure you don't want to go the funeral?"

"I said all that I had to say to him in the hospital. I'm going to work. Now please stop asking me about that funeral, Renee."

Renee decided to let it go, because it was obvious that Kit had made up her mind. "Alright, then. I have to run upstairs to Charmaine's. I need to give her this package for Jessica. I will see you later."

Renee could hear the boys in Charmaine's apartment from the elevator, before she even made it to the door.

"Hi, Ms. Renee. You must be looking for Aunt Charmaine, but did you see my mommy?" Jamel asked.

"No, I haven't seen your mom. Is she not here with you guys?"

Jamal pushed his brother Jamel back and said, "No, she went for a drive last night to try to find daddy to get some money and hasn't come home yet."

Renee gave him a strange look, and then Charmaine ushered her back into the hallway.

"Hey, Renee. Can I help you?"

"Can you give this to my sister for me? And what the hell is Jamal talking about — 'Desire went looking for their father'?"

Charmaine grabbed Renee by the arm and pulled her toward the elevator so the boys couldn't hear through the door. "I'm not going to work today. Desire is in the hospital; she tried to kill herself yesterday. I told the boys that she went looking for their father because I didn't know what else to tell them. Jessica didn't tell you any of this?"

Completely shocked by the news, Renee was almost at a loss for words. "What happened? How did she? I mean, no — I didn't speak to her again after she left last night. I am so sorry about your friend. Are you keeping the boys while she's in the hospital?"

Charmaine couldn't contain her need to be free of the boys. "Hell, no. I have no business with children. Their grandfather is going to let them spend a couple of nights with him until she gets out. With everything that's going on, I am no good for anybody, including myself. I can't believe she did that, Renee. He was not worth it. How could a mother do something like that to her children? It was a weak move. I don't know if I should feel sorry for her or be mad at her."

"Charmaine, at the end of the day, she is your friend who had a stupid moment and did a stupid thing, but you can't turn your back on her now," Renee said, still feeling sad about the whole situation.

"I'm just saying that I'm torn between emotions right now. Last night, I felt sorry for her, but now I'm mad at her."

Renee felt Charmaine needed a reality check because she wasn't seeing the bigger picture. "Well, go to the hospital, and tell her that, because the bigger picture is, she is still here, so you can tell her that."

"You know what, Renee? I think I needed to hear that. Thanks. Your sister has gone above and beyond as a friend and a boss. I am truly grateful to her."

"Thank you for saying that. I have to go. I am going to a funeral today," Renee said.

"Sorry to hear that. I should be grateful that I'm not planning on going to a funeral. Later, girl." Charmaine went back into the apartment to be bombarded with questions from the boys.

"Where is our mommy?"

"Your mommy is fine. She needed some adult time to herself for a little while. Come on, get your things, Jamel. I am sure your granddad is going to be so happy to see you."

"Did mommy and daddy leave us?" Desire's youngest son, Jacob, asked.

At this point, Charmaine was fed up with all the questions. "Please stop asking me all these damn questions, and just hurry up!" She caught herself and realized that what she'd said was inappropriate. "I'm sorry. I know you guys are worried, but everything is okay, I promise."

Jamal whispered under his breath, "We've heard that before."

Charmaine quickly asked him to repeat himself.

He said, "That's what mommy said when daddy left before we went to the shelter house."

Jamel heard the word "shelter," and anxiety set in on him.

"Are we going back to the shelter house?" he asked, sounding scared.

Charmaine closed her eyes for a brief second and took a deep breath as she thought, *Oh, my God, these kids are driving me crazy! Desire probably tried to kill herself because they won't shut the hell up.* When she opened her eyes, she yelled, "Jamal, Jamel, and Jacob — let's go, and please don't get into my car with all that loud talking and asking a thousand questions!"

I love you boys. Please forgive me.

"Desire, can you hear me? It's Jessica. How are you feeling?"

"Jessica, am I still alive?"

"Oh, thank God. You kept drifting in and out. Yes, you are alive. You're at South Nassau Hospital."

Desire cried out, "Why? Why? I don't want to be here. Where are my kids?"

"Charmaine has them, and they are safe. Why would you do something like this?"

Desire adjusted herself in the bed and turned to face the window of the hospital room before explaining. "I just couldn't take letting those kids down again. I just hit rock bottom, and I couldn't find my way up.

You girls were laughing and making jokes about that situation, and all I saw was my world falling apart. My kids had no father. I was dealing with the fact that I had to go back into that tiny room at the shelter. I am a grown woman taking orders from these young girls — no disrespect to your sister — but I know what I had before I met him, and now I have nothing. He stripped me of everything. He took my pride, my soul, my money, and my heart. He was my everything, and deep down inside, I wanted to believe that he loved me. That's why I couldn't laugh with you girls. I gave him the best part of me. We had a good life at one point, and I just don't know what happened. I wonder if I made him into this person who would leave his three kids and woman to rot in the streets. Did I put too much pressure on him? We have three kids, Jessica. How could he do that to us?"

Jessica looked at Desire with pity and despair for her predicament. "It's okay. You have to calm down. Stop crying, and don't work yourself up. James, Jay — whatever his name was — is gone, and we have to move on. He was a weak man who preyed on strong women with individual weaknesses that he was able to use and manipulate our minds to get what he wanted. I can't sit here and say that I felt nothing for him. I was with him for more than two years. Shit, I wanted to have children with him. None of this makes sense to me, either, but I will never give him the satisfaction of knowing that he drove me to take my life. He wanted to see me fail, so my best revenge is to stay strong and move on. If he ever showed his sorry-ass face again, he would see that he could not break me, and you should be the same way."

Desire dug deep into her pity-party bag, which offended Jessica's sensibilities. "We are two different people," Desire said. "It's easy for you to say that. I was with him almost eight years. I have kids, Jessica."

"Your kids — *what*! You keep talking about your kids, but you tried to kill yourself and leave them as wards of the state. Who was gonna guide those boys not to be like their sorry-ass father? The judge, the corrections officer, or their parole or probation officer? That's the life you were leaving for your kids when you decided to end yours."

Drake intervened to stop her, "Jessica, take it easy on her. She just went through a lot."

His statement angered Jessica even further. "We all went through a lot, Drake!" she yelled. "That is no damn excuse. She needs to wake up and smell the damn roses. I was trying to be nice and sympathetic, but this shit is going on too long."

Charmaine walked into the room just in time but was shocked at what she was hearing as she entered. "Hey, what is going on in here?" she asked.

"Charmaine, you talk to your friend because I don't deal well with people who like to throw pity parties. We all were hurt by that man, and, yes, we were lucky enough not to have gotten pregnant and have children with him, but so what? She needs to cut the shit and stop feeling sorry for herself and look out for her sons, who she claims she loves so much."

Drake felt Jessica had taken it too far with her last statement. "Jessica, let me talk to you outside, please," he pleaded with her.

Jessica followed him into the hall of the hospital, saying, "Drake, I am sorry, but I've had enough. All she kept saying yesterday was that she had kids by him. So, the fuck what? You have kids. Deal with it, and move on."

"You are obviously stronger than her, but you don't have the right to tell her how to handle her pain and grief. It's obvious to me that you have not dealt with your own pain and that you are taking it out on her for not handling it the way you think you would, if you were in her shoes. The fact is, you are not in her shoes, so you don't get to decide how she deals. You may not understand her choices, but you have to accept that it was her choice to deal with it her way."

Jessica felt a flood of emotions making their way to the surface, and she tried hard to fight within herself to keep them down.

Drake saw in her eyes that she was about to melt down. He took her by the hand, pulled her close, and held her tight. She tried to fight his embrace, but her body was overcome by the warmth, and she felt her body go limp in his arms. He held her up while she spoke.

"I am in pain, too!" she cried out. "I loved him, too. I think I may still be in love with him, to an extent, but, damn — he left us. *He left us! He left us! He left me! He left me!* How could he leave me like that? My sister used to always say she felt I could do better. She never liked him. She always said she felt he was sneaky. I would never listen to her because I was older. I knew better than her. She said time and time again that he was probably with some other woman. I never believed that. He never gave me a reason to believe that. He made me believe that I was the only one. The only one! I wonder if it's just us that he did this to? You know what, Drake? I am done crying. I am done with this."

Drake realized that she was putting on a front to be brave in his presence. He wanted to assure her that it was safe for her to be vulnerable around him. "It's OK, Jess. It's OK. You just need to let it out. Let it out. Why do you feel you always have to be the strong, brave one?"

"I am young and successful and can't let people see me weak. Not my family, not my friends, and not my coworkers. I especially never wanted *you* to see me weak. I am sorry for crying and acting crazy. I'm OK now. I will be fine."

"Well, since you're fine, I think you really need to apologize to Desire. Not right now, because I don't think she wants to hear anything else from you right now. I also believe that you still need to work out your own issues about what he has done to you, but I will be here for you. You need to go home and get some rest now. I'll tell them you went home."

She leaned in for one more hug before walking away. "Thank you so much, Drake. I will speak to you later."

When Drake went back into the room, he heard Charmaine asking, "What the hell was that all about?"

He decided not to interrupt their conversation and backed out of the room.

Desire looked over at Charmaine and said, "Please don't come in here judging me. I've had enough of that. Where are my boys?" she asked.

"I took them to your father's. I am not good with kids."

"That's OK. At least they're safe. I don't know what I was thinking. I just thought they would be better without me. That's why Jessica was upset with me. I understand her anger," Desire admitted.

Charmaine walked over and sat in the chair near the bed, saying, "Good, because I'm angry, too."

Desire rolled her eyes, telling Charmaine, "Please don't start."

"I don't know what to say to you. I can barely look at you. I am just really disappointed."

"Charmaine, I understand. When I get out of the hospital, I'll go back to the shelter."

"Desire, don't do that, because you know that's not what I meant. I am disappointed in you. You were getting your life together. You had a decent job, and soon you were going to have your own apartment. Why would you throw all of that away for him?"

"I had nothing left. My money was gone, my pride was gone, my room at the shelter was probably gone, and I allowed Jay to take it all away again, just when I thought I was getting it all back."

"I'm not gonna sit here and lecture you, but don't ever do some stupid mess like that again. You still have your job, and Mike did not stop the mail system. Your letter from that program is still on the way, so you can still get your own apartment. Get yourself together, get out of this hospital, and make life happen. You can stay with me a couple of days before you pick up the boys. You need some adult time alone. We're having a ladies' night, and that's well deserved by all of us. You get your rest. I'm going to work, so that I don't get too far behind. You're still covered. After all, you had a miscarriage," she said, laughing.

"Bye, girl. I love you," Desire said, laughing.

"Yeah, yeah. Bye," Charmaine said, blowing her off. I'm gonna go call Jessica before I head into the office. Love you, too, by the way."

Jessica was back in her car feeling like a weight had been lifted from her after talking with Drake. Before she could pull out of the parking spot, Renee was calling her phone.

"Jessica, it's Renee, I need to talk to you or somebody. I am here at Eric's funeral, and Sam is here. He started telling me how sorry he is and that he still loves me. I don't know what to do."

"Renee, you are somebody who will be quick to call someone else 'stupid,' but do you hear yourself? What about Tawana?"

"He said he loves her, too. He thinks he's confused. Then he kissed me, and all I could do was melt inside. He has me confused now. I thought I would hate him for life, but now, I want him back. I miss our friendship. Do you think it's possible to love two people at the same time?"

Jessica felt the tension rising up through her neck. "Hell, no, it is not possible!" she yelled into the phone. "Men say that nonsense all the time so they can have their cake and eat it, too. When it comes down to it, he always feels a little more for one woman over the other. You only have 100 percent of yourself to give someone. If you are loving two people, then they each are only getting 50 percent of you, and that is not love. Love is 100 percent, period. Renee, don't get caught up. He just played you. He was living with and sleeping with your family. You have to be the bigger person. Matter of fact, you need to be the smarter person. Don't give him the opportunity to have his cake and eat your niece out, too. As bad as that sounds, that's all that he will do or hope to accomplish by telling you that. He'll be sleeping with the both of you, if you fall for that nonsense."

Renee took heed to what Jessica had to say, because it all made sense. "See, that's what I needed to hear. Today was the first day that I realized that I still had feelings for him."

"Well, where was Tawana when this conversation was going on?" Jessica asked.

"I don't know. For some reason, she wasn't with him, but that ain't my business. I don't care about her, anyway."

Jessica thought things over briefly, and, knowing her sister, she had to ask, "Are you sure you're not just trying to get back at her on some level? I mean it hasn't been that long since you found out about them."

Renee had a devilish grin on her face as she gave that some thought. "It could be, or maybe I'm just horny and lonely as hell."

"He could just be depressed over the death of his friend, and seeing you brought up some old feelings, because you guys were friends first, and now, that's a loss, also. Maybe that's why he told you that," Jessica offered as her opinion.

"I don't care what made him say it. At that time, I needed to hear it. More than that, I wanted it to be true. I needed it to be true."

"Wait a minute, Sis. I never asked you what you said to him when he told you that."

"I told him that we could only be friends, and that I would always love him."

Jessica rolled her eyes while listening to Renee's response. "What the hell is wrong with you? Why in the hell did you tell him that?"

Confused by Jessica's outburst, Renee asked, "What was wrong with what I said?"

"How is that you have the answers for everyone else's relationship drama, but you can't see your way clear of your relationship crap? You just let him know that it did not matter that he disrespected you by having an affair with your niece. You boosted his ego and then sent him home to his new girlfriend, the niece who stole him from you. How desperate can you be to think about still wanting him? I thought you were smarter than that. He doesn't deserve your friendship or everlasting love."

"I didn't see it that way, at the time. I thought maybe he would think about what he'd done and what he was missing and then feel like shit for throwing it all away."

Jessica cut Renee's thoughts short by saying, "Instead, right now, you probably feel like a fool, and he is feeling like the man."

Renee responded sarcastically, "Yeah, thanks to you. Goodbye." She hung up without waiting for Jessica to say goodbye. *I should've never called her ass, but I know she's right. Damn it, should I go back into this funeral and tell him that we can't be friends? I'm just gonna leave it alone. He'll figure out that I changed my mind about being his friend. Let me get outta here before he comes out here looking for me.*

Renee didn't realize that, while she was in the car talking to Jessica, Sam had already left the funeral and was heading back to his apartment.

Tawana was in the bedroom, getting dressed to meet Sam at the funeral, when she heard keys in the hallway and the doorknob turn. "Sam, is that you? Why the heck are you back so soon?" Tawana questioned, walking from the bedroom toward the front door, half naked. She stopped short in the middle of the living room because there was a strange man entering the apartment. "Hello. How may I help you?"

"I was looking for Sam. I heard about his friend from another neighbor in the building. I just wanted to give him my condolences."

Tawana stood there, half naked, thinking, *Oh, dear God, this man is fine. Where has he been all my life?*

"I'm sorry. I don't think we've met. My name is Gabe."

"I'm Tawana. Would you like to come in and wait? He should be here shortly."

"I don't want to bother you."

Tawana just wanted an excuse to look at him a little longer, so she said, "It's no bother. Would you like something to drink?"

"I will have some water, if you don't mind."

"I have something better than water," she said as she walked back toward the kitchen.

Her comment made Gabe uncomfortable and nervous. "Excuse me? I just want some water. As a matter of fact, I think I should leave. Please let him know that I stopped by."

Tawana came out of the kitchen holding a glass of peppermint iced-tea that she'd made earlier. "Before you go, just taste this," and she handed him the glass, still half naked. Tawana positioned herself in front of the apartment door as Gabe took a sip of the tea.

"Hmmm, that is really good," Gabe said, looking directly in her face.

"If you like it from a glass, then you would love to lick it from my navel. It really adds an extra sweet flavor to the drink."

Gabe handed her back the glass and said, "Could you please just let me out? I didn't come over here for this. Sam is my boy."

"Sam is also not here. Stop acting like you don't want to. You know you do," she said, while rubbing the bulge that was forming in his pants.

Gabe could no longer resist the urge. "You know what? Fuck it. I'm gonna give you what you want, but you'd better not say nothing."

Gabe had his hand between her legs, caressing her sweet spot, when she whispered, "I love Sam, so I won't cheat on him."

He stopped and looked at her with sheer confusion on his face. "What the hell are you talking about?"

"We can't have vaginal sex, only anal. If I let you put it in my pussy, then that would be cheating."

He aggressively grabbed her hand, spun her around, and bent her over the sofa. "Whatever — bend that ass over, bitch," he said.

Tawana and Gabe were getting it on and didn't even hear Sam walking up behind them. "You little *bitch!* Get out of my house. *Get the fuck out of my house!* Gabe, I should beat your ass!"

Gabe stepped back, with his pants down around his ankles and his penis fully erect, saying, "Yo, man. She begged me to fuck her. I tried to leave. She wouldn't let me out."

Sam opened the front door to the apartment and calmly said, "I ain't fighting over no bitch. Just get the hell out of my house, both of you."

Gabe pulled his pants up and did a run-walk past Sam, who was standing in the doorway.

Sam looked over at Tawana, who was now completely naked, and pointed to the open door.

She began to cry and plead with Sam. She said, "Just let me get dressed."

"You'd better get out of my house right now before I help you get out."

Tawana tried to soften him up with words she thought would calm him down. "Sam, I love you," she said.

He screamed at her, "I don't want to hear that shit! You picked today of all days to do the shit. Eric was right about you. He said only a hoe could do that to her own family. Get out!"

Gabe came to the apartment but stayed in the hallway saying, "Sam, man — don't do that to that girl. She is naked. You can't put her out like that."

Sam quickly turned to face Gabe's direction and shouted, "Then take her to your apartment and finish what you started! I don't care what you do with her." Sam started walking throughout the apartment gathering her things, throwing them out into the hall.

"Sam, don't do that. You bought me those shoes. Why are you doing this?"

"*Why,* bitch? Are you crazy? You fucked my man in my house, on the day I buried my best friend, and you have the nerve to ask me *why*? Matter of fact, come on — you gotta go." Sam grabbed her by the arm and started pulling her toward the door.

Tawana started yelling and screaming. "Stop grabbing on me! Get off of me, Sam!"

Gabe was still standing there saying, "Sam, let her go. You're dragging her, man."

Sam looked at Gabe as if he had bullets in his eyes. "Oh, what? You fell in love after getting some ass, literally? Why are you still in my house, Gabe?"

Gabe backed down immediately. "You know what? You're right. I'm out," he said, as he turned to walk back down the hall toward his apartment.

Sam yelled down the hall behind him, "Good, and take this with you," as he shoved Tawana's naked body out into the hallway and slammed the door shut.

Tawana sat on the floor in the hall, pleading with Sam through the door. "Sam, please open the door. Let me put something on," she begged.

"Your clothes will be in the hall with you in a few minutes. Put something on then, and you'd better get away from my door before I call the police. Payback is really a bitch. A bitch named Tawana!"

"Sam, I am sorry," she said, over and over again.

"Go tell that to Gabe."

Tawana went knocking on Gabe's door, saying, "Gabe, please help me. Let me use your phone."

Gabe yelled back, "I am done with you. Get away from my door."

She stood in the middle of the hallway naked and afraid, covering her breasts, and screaming, "Somebody please help me!"

The woman next door heard the cries in the hall and called out to her, "Girl, what are you doing out here naked in the hallway? Come in here, and put some clothes on."

Tawana ran into the woman's apartment, begging to use the phone. "Grandma, please pick up the phone. Damn it! I have to try Jessica. Shit, why ain't nobody answering their phone?" When she ran out of people to call, she realized there was only one person left to try. "Renee, I know you're mad at me, but please help me. He threw me out naked. I don't have any money."

Renee burst into laughter, saying, "You probably deserved it."

"Please, Renee. I would not have called you if I didn't need help," she begged.

Renee took a long pause before saying, "Why should I help you, little girl?"

Tawana was so desperate for help that she just blurted out, "He caught me with another man in his house. Does that make you feel better? Can you please come get me?"

Renee took the time to gloat and rub it in her face. "*Now* you need me? You screwed my man behind my back, and to really show how disrespectful you are, you did it in my bed. Not to mention the fact that you had the nerve to ask for my opinion about your relationship with him. And so now, little girl, you have the audacity to call me when things go wrong. Go to hell! He should've whipped your ass and then threw you out."

Sobbing on the phone, Tawana had to humble herself and concede the fact that she had put herself in that position. "You are right about everything you said. I accept the fact that I did you wrong, but I am naked in some stranger's apartment asking you for help! Please?"

"I will be there in a few. Keep your panties on," she said, giggling into the receiver. Renee hung up and immediately dialed Kit to relish in the irony. "Hey, Kit, would you believe this stupid little girl got caught humping some other dude in Sam's apartment, and called *me* to pick her up?"

"Renee, should I even ask if you are going to pick her up?"

Renee started laughing. "Yeah, I'm gonna get her. But if for no other reason than to say karma is a motherfucker. I wish I could see him, so I could laugh in his face. To me, they both got what they deserve. You should never hurt someone who is good to you."

Kit felt no sympathy for Tawana's situation at all. "I still say you're a better person than me, because her ass would be naked on the corner, and I would drive right by."

Renee was still laughing at Kit as she entered Sam's building. "You are evil," she laughed. Oh, my goodness, Kit — he really threw all her stuff into the hallway. This is crazy and funny at the same time. I'll take a picture and send it to you. I'll see you later. Let me go in here and see what's up." Renee didn't know which apartment Tawana was in, so she started calling her name out in the hall. "Tawana, where are you?"

Just then the door opened, and Tawana stepped out into the hall wearing a robe. She didn't realize he'd really thrown her clothes into the hall, until she saw her underwear lying in front of this woman's apartment. She bent down, grabbing at her things and saying, "Oh, Renee, thank you for coming."

"Yeah, well, you'd better ask that lady if she has a bag that you can put your clothes in, because they are all the way down the hall and around the corner."

Tawana got in the car, still wearing nothing but a robe, and sat quiet for the first part of the ride.

Renee broke the silence by telling her, "I will drop you off at Mommy's."

"Renee, can you let me explain what happened and why we got together in the first place?"

"I don't need an explanation. I know why you did it. You're a selfish, envious lowlife with no discretion about yourself. Do you know why I'm here? You know what? It doesn't even matter, I just want to get you out of my car. I don't think you are even capable of seeing the big picture."

Renee pulled up in front of her mother's house, and Tawana got out of the car as if it were a taxi or an Uber.

Tawana walked up to the front door, saying, "Grandma, I messed up."

Momma Tyler ignored her statement, looking past Tawana, straight into the car, saying, "Renee, my love, I've missed you. Come inside, so we can talk."

Renee never even looked in her mother's direction. She stayed face forward, with her hands on the steering wheel, and replied, "Mother, I am not here for that. I am just dropping her off, and then I am gone."

"You forgave your niece, but you can't talk to your mother?" she asked.

"I didn't forgive her, and I never will. He threw her out, and she called me. That is the only reason I am here. Tawana, take your bag so I can go. Mother, when I am ready, I'll call you. Tonight is not the night."

Jessica walked up behind her mother and shouted, "Renee, come inside!"

Renee finally turned toward the front door and yelled back, "Jessica, please don't start! You need to stop trying to bring us together!"

"You're really gonna let some man come between you and your family? They are your blood!" Jessica shouted.

Renee had daggers in her eyes pointing straight at Jessica when she said, "Were they thinking about how thick our blood was when they allowed him to dilute it with water? I don't want to hear this mess right now." Renee pulled off, making the tires screech.

Jessica said softly to her mother, "Mommy, just give her some time. I guess one day she will come around." Jessica turned her attention to Tawana, who was standing there in a robe, and said, "Tawana, I don't know what you did, but if it's nearly as bad as what you did to my sister, then good for you. What comes around goes around."

Momma Tyler saw the heartbreak on her granddaughter's face and then tapped Jessica on the shoulder as if to say, "That's enough."

"Jessica, let me talk to her alone for a minute. I hear your phone ringing anyway."

Jessica ran upstairs to try to catch the call before it went to voicemail.

"Hello, this is Drake. Did you get some rest?" he asked.

"I am fine now. Just woke up to more drama. I swear I can't take this place or this life anymore."

"Hey, now — you're starting to sound like Desire. Don't scare me."

"Pump your brakes, brother. Ain't nothing that bad yet. What's your story, Drake? You have been so nice. I mean, with all my drama, you still call to check on me."

"Don't make me out to be some saint. I am far from that. I was not as bad as your friend, but I broke a few hearts. Don't get me wrong — I am a one-woman guy. I was in a relationship for three years, and when I found out she was cheating on me, I hated all women. I was smart enough to know not to jump into another relationship, so I decided to stay away from anything serious."

"So, you just let women get serious about you and then break their hearts?" Jessica asked.

"At first, that's exactly what I did. After that, it got real old listening to women cry and pour their hearts out, so I started messing with women who wanted nothing from me but what I was willing to give them."

"Forgive me for being rude. So you only dealt with stink hookers looking for some dick?" Jessica questioned.

"If you want to call them that, Jess. At the time, it was just easier. There were no strings, no one to answer to, and most of all my sexual needs were being met, and so were theirs."

Jessica shook her head. "That's what it all boils down to with men."

"I said I was not a saint. I kept it real with all of them. I told them up front that I did not want a relationship. They said they were OK with it, and then they caught feeling. The reason I'm telling you all of this is not for you to hate me or judge me, but so that you know who I am and where I'm coming from. I think I really like you. I have never met anyone with all the drama surrounding them who still managed to keep their head up. I know you're hurting after dealing with all his issues, but I just wanted you to know that I want to be here for you when you are ready. I also know that you're in the same place I was in two years ago, so I know it's hard for you to trust anyone right now. I understand, so when you need a friend to go to the movies or go out to eat, I will be here."

"Drake, seriously — you might be waiting a long time."

"I have learned to be a patient man when it comes to the things I want. I've decided I want you, and I believe that you will be worth the wait," he replied.

"You are crazy, but I think I like it."

Drake felt that was his opening to ask for a date, so he took a shot at it. "Can we hang out tomorrow?" he asked.

"I would really enjoy hanging out with you, but Charmaine wants all the girls to come by her house tomorrow. Desire is coming home from the hospital, so she wants to do something nice."

"That would be nice. You ladies deserve a good night. From what I've heard and seen, you ladies have been through the wringer."

Jessica smiled and said, "Can I get an 'Amen'?"

Drake laughed and said, "You can get an 'Amen' and a 'Hallelujah!' Listen, I don't want to pressure you, but if you are interested, then give me a call in a few days. If not, give me a call in about a month. I will need that time to get over the fact that I played myself by telling you how I feel about you. I hope to hear from you soon."

"Goodnight, Mr. Drake, and I do anticipate calling you," she said before hanging up. *If only you knew. I think I've already fallen in love with you.* As Jessica closed her eyes, dreaming of a life with Drake, the sun began to rise, and Desire was forced to open her eyes to face the reality of her life, once again.

"Alright, Des. It's time to start your life over. Let's get out of here," Charmaine said, loudly.

"I'm afraid to face my boys. What do I say to them?"

"Don't worry about them; they're fine. You have a few days to yourself to worry about yourself. Let's just celebrate the fact that we are alive, and with each day, we can put him and his issues behind us. I have a nice day and evening planned for us. You weren't able to come to my last ladies' night, so tonight is dedicated to you," Charmaine said, doing a little dance.

"I don't want to sound ungrateful or like a Debbie Downer, but I don't think I want to be around anyone. I feel so stupid about what I tried to do," Desire said.

"I don't think there is a woman on Earth who didn't feel like she wanted to end the pain of heartbreak with the thought of suicide. If anything, you were stronger than the rest of us, because you didn't just talk about it — you did the damn thing," Charmaine said with a giggle.

"Charmaine, that's not funny or anything to be proud of."

"I know, but you can't beat yourself up about it forever."

The nurse walked in, clearing Desire for release. "OK, Ms. Williams, you are all set to go. Don't forget you must attend group meetings once a week, and, if you need private sessions, you can schedule that with the therapist."

"Alright, Charmaine. I'm ready to go." Before they got into the car, Desire asked, "Who's coming tonight?"

"Why? It doesn't matter who's coming — you will be there," Charmaine told her.

"I just wanted to know."

"What you should be asking is, where can you go get your hair done? You look a hot mess. A fifteen-dollar wash and set — on me."

"I'll take you up on that, but can we go see the boys after?" Desire asked.

Charmaine replied in a stern but fair and understanding voice, "No, you don't need to see them yet. Give yourself a break. Honestly, I don't know how you do it. I love those boys, but they talk too much. They questioned me to death while you were gone."

Desire had her first real laugh since everything had happened. "I am sorry. I taught them that no question is a stupid question, and if they are unsure about an answer, then ask another question."

Charmaine chuckled under her breath, "Well, they damn sure enough took your advice to heart. Maybe if we applied that rule to our relationships, we would be in a much better place."

"Here we go. I don't want to talk about relationships. I want an apple martini," Desire said.

"It's a little early for that, but I can call Jess, so she can bring some tonight. She buys this premixed one from the liquor store that tastes better than something you get from the bar."

Jessica was in the process of disconnecting the call with Charmaine, telling her that she would bring several bottles of the Apple Martini drink to ladies' night, when Tawana came into the room, asking, "Jess, is it possible that I can come with you tonight?"

"I don't think so. It is going to be a lot of tension between you and Renee, and I don't want to deal with that tonight."

"I have made many mistakes in my life, but I am so sorry for what I did to her. I just want a chance to make it up to her," Tawana said.

Jessica got up and walked past her, heading toward the bathroom. "Tonight won't be that night. She has gone through enough, and she needs a break from the drama," Jessica said, in defense of her sister.

"I just want a chance to talk to her and apologize," Tawana said, with a sorrow-filled tone in her voice.

"Well, she is not ready to hear that yet, and you need to be patient. Have you spoken to Sam?"

Tawana exhaled deeply before answering. "He won't talk to me, either. Everyone seems to be mad at me. Grandma is mad at me because she lost her daughter over my relationship with Sam, and now I'm not even with him."

"Tawana, I want to sympathize with you, but I can't. I think my mother saw it like if things worked out between you and Sam, then it was worth it. But now, she's lost the respect of her daughter for no reason."

Tawana was trying to be optimistic about her broken relationship. "I am going to get Sam back. He is just mad right now. But I know he loves me."

"I hate the fact that I'm about to say this, but Sam was a good man. He wasn't good to or for my sister, but he was a good person overall. However, now, because of you, he may become bitter against all women. A bitter man is worse than any bitter woman. They perpetuate the cycle; a bitter man creates a bitter woman, who ruin good men, and the cycle continues."

"I am going to make it right with everyone," Tawana said, still trying to be positive.

"I have to go. You have a lot of growing up to do. Goodbye."

The moment Jessica walked out the room, Tawana reached for the phone to call Sam, but, as usual, he would not answer.

Sam checked his phone and saw he had 50 missed calls from Tawana. He turned to his friend and asked him if he wanted some peppermint sweet tea. Gabe said, "Hell, no! That shit got something in it," he said, laughing hysterically.

"Yo, Gabe, man. You were only supposed to see if she would give it up. What made you hit it for real?"

"That damn tea," he said, still laughing. "All jokes aside, man, I didn't mean for it to go that far. She was coming on strong, plus she does have a phat ass. My other head took over, and after that, it was on. I am sorry, dude."

Sam nodded his head as a gesture of understanding and acceptance of Gabe's apology. "I just wanted to find out if she was really for me, before I asked her to marry me."

"It's a good thing you found out now, before she was able to take half your shit. What was crazy is that she said something about having only anal sex because that's not cheating. She took that shit like a trouper."

Sam burst out laughing, saying, "Or maybe you just have a small joint."

Gabe laughed as he said, "You know that ain't true. You saw that monster standing up strong. But, for real, man, did you really love her?"

The laughter for both men stopped when Sam began to answer the question. "I really thought she was the one. I am hurt, but I dodged one hell of a bullet, so good looking out."

"That was some crazy shit. More brothers should start putting these chicks to the test before they jump that broom. Do you regret leaving Renee?"

Sam answered the question without even a pause. "Nope, that wasn't gonna work in the long run, anyway. She was too aggressive for me. She was a good girl and person, and I do love her, but I was not *in love* with her. It was different with Tawana. I saw a future with her. I pictured what our kids would look like. I hate the fact that she messed everything up. These bitches just can't be trusted."

Over at Charmaine's apartment, she was sharing the same sentiment at the exact moment. "These men just can't be trusted. I don't know how I am ever going to get married," Charmaine said.

Jessica wanted to set the tone for the night from the beginning. "Ladies, let's try not to make this night about men-bashing," she told them.

"That would be hard not to do after what we all just went through, but you are right, Jessica. On another note, my girl Desire is here and alive, and I want to celebrate that with a toast," Charmaine said.

The ladies raised their glasses, but no one could think of a good toast. So, they all sat there with an awkward silence until Desire said, "A toast to Mike, Jay, Sam, Eric, and James. Goodbye and good riddance."

Renee said, "I'll drink to that!"

Jessica said, "We all should drink to that!"

Kit said, "Where are the cards? I'm ready to take somebody's money up in here tonight."

"Whatever, Kit! Put some music on, Charmaine. I want to dance," Renee said, standing there dancing to the music in her head. Renee danced her way over to the kitchen area, where Jessica was seasoning somc chicken.

"Charmaine, I think you need to come check on this chicken, because Jessica can't cook chicken for God to save her life."

Jessica, feeling slightly insulted, said, "I can, too, cook chicken."

Renee laughed and said, "All your chicken comes out white. No matter what she seasons it with, the oven just won't brown her chicken."

"James liked my chicken," she said. "Wow — I can't believe I just said that. I am so sorry."

"We're all gonna be doing stuff like that for a while. Have another drink, and forget that you just said that. Matter of fact, let's make it a drinking game. When any of us feel like you're thinking about your ex, or mentions any of their names tonight, then you have to take a drink," Kit said.

"Then we're all going to be drunk up in here tonight," Charmaine said.

Renee decided it was time to ask a question that no one else had mentioned since the ball dropped. "Could we talk about the pink elephant in the room?"

Desire asked, "What the hell are you talking about?" because she thought the question was going to be about her.

"Well, I want to know how it is that you two work together and seriously did not know? How does that happen?" Renee questioned.

Jessica answered in her own defense, "You remember the personal line that you always complained about? Yeah, well, that's how. He only called me on that line."

Kit turned to Charmaine and asked, "You met him the night we all went out clubbing, right?"

"Yep. Remember, Jessica was busy ducking Drake, so when I left with him, she wasn't around."

Renee turned to face Desire, and in a rude and unsensitive manner, she asked, "How the hell did you end up with three kids by him? He couldn't have just decided to be a dog."

"I don't even know this person that we are talking about. He was the kindest, sweetest man you could ever meet. When we had our first child, he could not wait to have more. Then he just changed. I really don't know what happened to him."

"Well, whatever it was must have been bad to make him do some shit like this," Renee said.

Kit grew tired of the conversation and the direction it was headed in, so she wanted to liven things up. "Y'all are starting to depress me. Let's play cards, put a movie in, or something," she said.

"Speaking of movies, Kit, Eric had a lot of movies. When I went into that apartment to get Desire's things, I couldn't believe all the movies he had. I started to take some of his movies," Charmaine said.

"A few of those were mine," Kit said. "The ones that were on top of the DVD player were mine."

Charmaine said, "Oh, I took those because I thought they were the boys'."

"So put something in until I finish cooking, and then we can play Pokeno or Phase 10," Jessica said.

Desire spoke out of turn and asked, "Not for nothing, but did you girls keep up with your gyn appointments? Because he did give me chlamydia."

Jessica shook her head, angry at herself, "Oh, my God! I did not even think about that. I kept saying I was going to make an appointment and never did. Damn."

Charmaine asked Desire to help her in the kitchen, as they laughed at Jessica's attempt at cooking.

Jessica laughed at herself and said, "Well, I am starting the movie then, damn it."

Charmaine and Desire noticed things were ultra-quiet in the living-room area, so they stepped out of the kitchen to see what was going on.

"Hey, what are y'all watching? Why is everybody so quiet? What the!"

Desire screamed, "Oh, my God! Oh, my God!" All the ladies were in complete shock as they watched and listened.

"Yeah, E. That's it, nigga. Fuck me with that foreskin. Turn over; let me get some of that ass."

Jessica shouted, "Oh, my God! Turn it off! Turn it off now!"

"I can't believe what I just saw!" Renee said.

Charmaine's body collapsed into the sofa in disbelief. "That son of a bitch was bi. He could have given us more than just chlamydia."

Tears began to fall from Jessica's eyes, and Renee tried to comfort her. "Jessica, don't cry," she said.

"You don't understand. How could he?" Jessica asked rhetorically.

Kit said, "That dude has some serious issues. What the hell was going on in his mind? Oh, God, Renee — do you think he killed Eric?"

"Kit, you may be right. Maybe Eric was going to expose him for the nasty piece of shit that he is."

Jessica began to aggressively wipe the tears from her face as she said, "Well, seeing is believing, so now we know. I should call Drake."

Charmaine asked, "For what? What can he do?"

"Think about it: the video has his face on it. At least now we have a picture, so they can go after him."

"Do you really think he stuck around after he took everything from us?" Desire said, as her eyes began to water.

"If he's smart, he's long gone by now," Renee offered.

"I swear I will never let another man tell me he loves me without proving that so-called love 100 percent," Charmaine said, drying her eyes with tissue. I want an HIV test done before he can even kiss me goodnight on the first date."

Jessica said, "I am calling Dr. Carl first thing Monday morning."

The ladies looked around the room at each for support. but their eyes locked on Desire. She was sitting on the chair as if in a trance. Charmaine feared that she was going to that dark place that had led her to try to take her life, so she called her name several times to snap her out of it. "Desire, are you okay?!" she screamed.

Desire responded immediately, "I am fine. I'm just stuck for words. I could never imagine him with a man. Don't worry about me. I am not doing anything to hurt myself again. I wonder what he's doing now?"

Renee had a look of disgust on her face when she answered, "Hopefully, he is somewhere getting his ass beat, like he deserves."

"Who's working the bar?"

Oh, no — he did not just walk up in here and push past me like that!

"I'm so sorry, sexy lady. Can I buy you a drink?

"You just ought to, since you nearly spilled mine all over the floor."

"That won't be a problem, but you have to sit with me a minute. You don't look like the type to frequent this environment."

"I really don't. My girls dragged me out of the house. They claim all I do is work, plus today is my birthday."

"Well, happy birthday, beautiful, and what kind of work do you do?"

"Thank you, and I'm an attorney."

"Well, good for you, and what's your name?"

"You're asking a lot of questions for someone who bought me only one drink. What is your name, and what do you do?" she asked.

"Well, I recently came into some money from an investment deal in New York and decided to move Atlanta to see what life will bring me next. I hope a wife and two kids will be in my near future."

"That sounds really nice, but you didn't answer my question. What is your name?"

"My name is James Michael Frazier, but you can call me 'Jay.'"

www.ingramcontent.com/pod-product-compliance
Lightning Source LLC
Chambersburg PA
CBHW030358310726
48979CB00001B/350

* 9 7 8 1 7 3 3 3 0 3 0 3 3 *